Malee: A Tear In the Ocean

Malee
A Tear
In the Ocean

William V. M. McAllister, III

INTRINSIC BOOKS

NEW YORK • MIAMI • CHICAGO

First published in 2015 by Intrinsic Books
IntrinsicBooks.com

Print: ISBN 978-0-9863365-0-8
Ebook: ISBN 978-0-9863365-1-5

All characters and events in the following pages are fictional.
Any resemblance to any person, living or dead,
is entirely coincidental.

Book design and typography by STUDIO 31
www.studio31.com

Printed in the United States of America

Contents

PART I

Malee

As the plane climbed, Michael lifted his head from the back of the seat and looked out his window. As if needing some reassurance that all was well he stared at the ocean below, blue and glittering in the sunlight. Michael had hoped it would create a much-wanted calm, but weariness swept over him with a surprising suddenness. Anxiety shivered through his body, awakening the quiet worry that he was making a big mistake. He pulled down the window shade, leaned back and closed his eyes. "Breathe," he told himself. "Just breathe."

Michael tried focusing his mind on all that had happened during the last few months. Everything that had led him to talk to Drake and decide to put together a new import business with his old buddy. Even up to the moment when he boarded this flight Michael had never considered Bangkok as a high priority destination. Helen had never wanted to go but then that did not matter now. She was gone. Michael shook off the doubt and forced himself to reaffirm that he was not grasping at the first opportunity that had come his way. He was not the kind of guy who acted rashly. No, he was the guy that could make everything look effortless. Good looking, piercing blue eyes, affable, and with a business sense that drew all manner of loyalty to him, he had done better than well for himself. Recent events, though, gave Michael that moment's doubt, had shaken him although he wouldn't admit that to anyone, anyone except maybe his devoted older brother, Jay. Michael closed his eyes and tried to relax into the journey he had before him.

Nowhere to go for twenty hours, his mind began to play through unfocused thoughts. He considered the plan he had drawn up with Drake over the course of the past few months. It was solid. He was sure of that. Burying himself in work, he had spent the entirety of the last four weeks in meetings drafting the sections of the agreement for which he would be responsible, including the back-end of the new venture with Neiman Marcus, or Bloomingdales if Neimans did not work out. He had emailed Drake the finished proposal along with his itinerary to Thailand—a direct first-class flight on Thai Airways.

And here he was, on his way to a country where he didn't know a word of the language. Michael only knew a little about the culture, mostly about the historic importance of the city as a cultural and financial center for South East Asia, and he had heard tales of the sex industry like everyone else. He had to admit that he was a little hesitant but more excited than not about the adventure that awaited. Drake, never a shy friend and certainly one who did not like the confines of long term female relationships, had told him some of his exploits there. Totally foreign to Michael, having been with only one other woman apart from Helen, he grinned, wondering if the stories of bargirls with "happy endings" were true.

As the plane leveled out, Michael's wandering mind took him back to Helen, his wife of so many years. How could she have just up and gone? Simple gestures suggested that she left while still caring for him very much. When he got home on the day she left there were two grocery bags of fresh fruit and vegetables, and one small recognizable brown paper bag nearly overflowing with four persimmons and a dozen passion fruits. He particularly liked these two fruits, and the only store that sold them was a forty-minute drive a way—a sweet footnote in a book whose pages had just been slammed shut on him. The fact that Helen had only emptied her bank account of the

$378,201.53 she had in there when, in a divorce, she could have had so much more, made it all the harder on Michael that she was simply *gone*. This couldn't set in. He could still feel her at times. That was perhaps the worst part of it all, a pull toward an unfamiliar void where, before, it had been tender and caring. She was out there, somewhere, even still.

She hadn't left a note. He had thought things were still good between them, not perfect but good, and thought she felt the same. The only issue between them was that he wanted children and she, for reasons he could never fully understand, did not. Or at least "not yet," she kept saying, even though her clock was ticking louder each year. He wondered if she was having an affair, if that is why she left so suddenly, if she would decide to have children with *another man*. He shuddered, unable to imagine her with anyone else. But for the last few months when he couldn't fathom a life without her he would start imagining her with this guru guy, Bob, the leader of the cult that brainwashed so many wealthy women on the East Coast. Helen was perhaps his most willing, his newest, but certainly his most wealthy convert. Michael had to shut out the poisonous thoughts.

Desperate to come back to the present, Michael asked the stewardess for some orange juice. He readjusted himself in his seat. His long legs feeling cramped even in first class. With the drone of the plane as a steady background, he found himself slipping back to the smell of her hair, the way that she would rest her hand on his back as they slept, the way she would tease him while parading for him in her favorite La Perla Lingerie, brushing of a finger across the back of his neck accompanied by a single sultry kiss just behind the back of his left ear. Even after so many years Helen could easily get a rise out of him, and she always played the eager partner. He was falling into the memory when the thought of her with that pseudo-hippy charlatan popped to his mind. It was maddening, impossible. *It just couldn't be him,* Michael fumed, trying to turn his thoughts elsewhere. Secretly he was devastated by the weight of her absence. That and the sudden, forced career change. Two heavy blows in a row.

The FBI had stormed the offices shortly after Helen had left him, taking his longtime business partner, Ridley, away in handcuffs. Smirking, Michael replayed in his mind a recent lunch. He had met Jay at The Nest, Jay having arrived early and hailing Michael in his usual outgoing way. Michael remembered giving Jay a restrained half-hug, belying the fact that he loved his older brother dearly.

"So," Jay said, "big doings."

"Yeah, big."

"You catch the evening news?"

"No."

"Nice segment on Ridley. Being escorted, if that's the right word, out of Federal Court. Smartly dressed. Nice tie. But," Jay paused, knowingly, "he held his arms out in front of him with a raincoat draped over them. Curious," he said with a laugh, "with no rain in the forecast. But it's good to be prepared, just in case, I guess. I will say that he didn't look that happy about the, how shall I say? Forecast." Trying to get his brother to smile, Jay poured Michael wine from the bottle he had ordered and gave him a nudge.

Michael dipped his index finger into the wine and swirled the finger around the rim of his glass making it hum. He exhaled deeply and let his hand slide down the stem.

"What?" Jay asked.

"Funny," Michael replied through the kind of laugh that suggests it isn't funny. He studied the wine glass as he turned the stem with his thumb and finger. "I remember, oh, ten years ago or so, I read this book on US naval history. Told from many perspectives—you know, from the admiral down to ordinary seaman. There was this one account by a seaman on a cruiser during a major Second World War naval battle. It was in heavy seas—big swells. So big that when his ship rose up a swell, he could see their destroyer escort. And when it dipped into the trough, the destroyer disappeared from view. Up the swell—destroyer. Down the trough—no destroyer. He heard an explosion. Up the swell—no destroyer. Gone. Ten, fifteen seconds at the most," Michael said. "Gone. Just like that. Like it had never existed. You go along thinking everything is fine. And then suddenly it's over. Gone. Like that destroyer."

At the next table, close enough that conversations were quasi-public, a single diner put down his newspaper as the waitress arrived with his lunch. The gentleman looked their way and smiled casually before turning to his meal. Jay and Michael nodded a hello, both noticing that there was a photo of Ridley above the fold of the paper.

"There's the destroyer himself," Jay noted.

"It seems one can't get away from the S.O.B," Michael said.

"You in the clear?" Jay aksed.

"Yeah. Totally. I think only one other person knew what he was up to. Reggie Blank, a malleable guy if ever there was one. He'll turn state's evidence. He's malleable that way, too. And guess what? I got all my money out. *All of it*," Michael emphasized, "with no claw-back on the horizon. That is very big. Otherwise, whose money would it ultimately become? It could have gotten very messy with all of the investors, and it certainly will be for Ridley and the adjustors. I already put ten million into tax-free bonds. Just to ensure that I have a cushion even if everything else tanks."

The man at the next table gesticulated too broadly while talking to the waitress and knocked over his glass of wine. Some spilled on the newspaper and half of Ridley's face went red. But most splattered on the floor and a few drops splashed Michael's trousers.

"Oh, excuse me!" the man said. "I'm so sorry."

The waitress dashed off to get cloths to wipe up the mess.

"Forget it," Michael said waving it off. He dipped his napkin into his water and cleaned the spots on his pants. He looked at Ridley's partially new complexion. "Say, you mind if I complete that painting?"

"Be my guest," the man said with a relieved laugh.

Michael carefully poured some of his wine onto the other half of Ridley's face.

"Quelle artiste," Jay observed. "So many talents. And a wealthy man, to boot."

"I'll survive."

"A man of leisure."

"Sure. Sit back and do nothing. You know I can't do that."

"So?"

"Been thinking about it. Guess there's no hurry."

Jay was unconvinced.

"Michael, you okay?"

Michael nodded.

"I mean you already got hit by a right cross. And now this left hook."

"I'm still standing."

"If you ever feel like taking a knee, you let me know."

"Appreciate that." Hoping to turn the conversation away from the last few months' frustrations, Michael asked, "How 'bout you? That commission come through for you?"

"Don't know yet. Probably a couple of weeks. If I get it, it'd be a dream come true. I'd be full time on it for a year or more. It's a perfect gig." Jay was beaming.

Michael couldn't help himself, feeding on the infectious excitement in his brother, "Well, I've got a new iron in the fire, too. My friend Drake's been calling. He wants me to partner up in a big franchise deal in Asia."

"I've never met Drake," Jay said, taken aback.

"He's never in the States. Hates it here. Go west young man. Far west. Then you'll meet him."

It all had come back to Michael like a waking dream and after being engrossed in his thoughts for over two hours he slowly pulled himself back to the cabin on the plane. Almost eighteen hours left to go on this flight to some exotic location halfway around the world. Michael sighed a dispirited sigh—he had been turning the Montblanc pen around in his hand, the one that Ridley had given him after the conclusion of the biggest deal in their company's history. He stopped and looked at the token from his now indicted partner; it was a sober reminder of the lies Ridley had told him. So much betrayal. Michael was done with it all, the pen now taking on unintended symbolic meaning. He tried handing this pen to the Thai stewardess who had been so attentive to him during the first hour of the flight.

"This is for you."

"Sir," she said earnestly, "I cannot take such an expensive gift, well, not any gift. It's against company policy. I am sorry. It is very kind of you."

Really noticing her for the first time, with what must be her very long hair pulled back into a tight bun, the natural glow of her olive-complexion skin, her light brown eyes—unusual for a Thai he later noted—he could not resist. "Look, how about this," he surreptitiously said motioning her to come a little closer. A glimmer of familiar mischievous mirth, the kind that had been absent from him for a while, crossed his lips, "I am going to drop this pen on the floor. You pick it up and ask me if I lost a pen. I will say no loudly enough for others to hear. Then ask the gentleman behind me. When he says no you just pocket it. Okay? I want you to have it. I am asking you to do this for me. Your taking it will be doing me a favor, honest."

The stewardess smiled a nearly unnoticeable grin at the earnestness but also the playfulness behind Michael's request. Her eyes brightened, as she looked him full on, and unabashedly. It went off without a hitch. As Michael watch the trademark snowcap-lid of Ridley's gifted pen slide into the breast pocket of her tight white button-up shirt, as she gracefully and subtly pulled back her official blue stewardess blazer, maybe just a little farther than she needed to, he felt something that he had not felt since Helen had left: desire.

Michael headed out of customs and directly into the car Drake had ordered for him. When they finally arrived at the hotel—somehow making it through the worst congestion that Michael had ever seen—it was immediately clear that it was an upscale place, luxurious even, especially when compared to the standards of some of what Michael had seen on the way in. An intense feeling that he sensed, even through the tinted windows of the town car, as he passed from the airport to the center of town hit him as he stood in front of what would be his home until the deal was signed: this was a city of contrasts. That and the jetlag had already taken hold, and any bed was starting to sound sumptuous.

A message from Drake awaited him at the hotel front desk.

> *Sorry, but I am delayed. I'll join you in a couple of days. Meantime, check out Julie's. 10th St. on the other side.*

Michael smiled at the note surmising what Julie's might be, knowing Drake as well as he did. He tipped the bellhop 200 Baht, and headed to his room. Michael did not bother to unpack. Shoes off, he lay down and was asleep before he could even register that he was now twelve time zones away, where morning felt like night.

At seven o'clock that evening Michael woke up ready to start the day. *Easy to do in a city that never sleeps.* He looked out the hotel window, seeing Bangkok's nighttime persona lit up for the first time.

He showered and headed out to pass the time, quickly deciding to find out just what it was that Drake wanted him to see—imagining that it would be entertaining and a diversion at the very least. It was raining lightly, and it was warmer than he had expected. Cars, bikes and motorcycles crowded the main roads forcing one to navigate the packed side streets and their nearly impassible sidewalks. *Evidently they were both public and private property*, Michael noted as he opted for the sidewalks weaving his way around food vendors, nearly wall-to-wall stalls, and hurrying people. Stopped by a bottleneck of people he noticed five men sitting around an up-side-down crate playing a card game under the shelter of a Tabac awning. The game blocked the sidewalk entirely. No one seemed to care much about the obstruction, they just forced past, but Michael found himself lingering. The guy winning the game was smiling and providing a steady-stream commentary while the others seemed to concentrate more intently on their own hands. Michael kept looking at the group as he moved to the street, catching his toe as he did so. Stumbling slightly but managing to stay upright, he realized it was just as well that the sidewalk was blocked. On the sidewalks of Bangkok he quickly discovered, one walked looking down to negotiate the slabs that had heaved as well as to avoid outright holes that were ankle-breakers for the unwary. The streets were only slightly better, this in a country where temperatures never dropped below freezing. Michael began questioning his long-held view of the old Western mantra that cycles between the freeze of winter and thaw of summer is what made the sidewalks heave.

Sukhumvit Road cut through the heart of an old section of Bangkok—older in all ways except for the brand new Sky Train that whisked would-be pedestrians in elevated comfort above the sidewalk congestion. For the majority who remained pedestrians, there were a few overpasses where one could cross Sukhumvit Road. *Perhaps "Road" was too limiting a designation,* Michael thought seeing that it was four lanes of wall-to-wall cars with a concrete divide that dissuaded any at-grade crossing attempts.

Michael was forced back on to the crowded sidewalk where he steadily encountered bold stares from women in tight short skirts. All were attractive, many beautiful. Many would have been so even if they had not overdosed on makeup, perhaps even better had they not. He was surprised how athletic a couple of them looked, the two bolder than just stares. The first one body-gestured and called out, "Me love you. Me love you number one." The second approached him, running her hand down his arm and whispering, "Me come you. Have good time. You no forget." As he slipped his arm away, she went firm and pulled back. "Nice man. You, special price." He tugged himself free and walked quickly away.

To avoid another confrontation with a similar group, he crossed over at 14th Street. Here instead of solicitations there were occasional beggars pleading with passer-byes from the metal stairs. On the flat traverse, a clearly destitute woman, cradling her baby, sat leaning against the concrete wall. The woman, unkempt, was clothed in a dress one step up from a rag. Her baby was not as well clothed. She held out her plastic cup with lowered eyes, but her baby looked out at the passing masses through weary eyes, both infected with conjunctivitis. It could not beseech even if it had known how. They sat there silently, her cup less that one-quarter full, mostly with 1-Baht coins, a few 5-Baht bills and one 20-Baht note. The sheer need Michael witnessed in this vulnerable pair made him open his wallet, handing her five 100-Baht notes. She bowed and bowed and bowed, trying to kiss his feet, but he stepped back, hoping to avoid seeing the rivulets that were forming in her once distant eyes. He continued on for a few steps, stopped, returned and took out a 500-Baht note and four 1000-Baht notes and handed them to her. She folded her hands in prayer. Tears were now streaming down her face. He responded with a nod, the only outward acknowledgment he could muster in recognition of her and her genuine reaction to such unexpected succor—and too, of his troubling reflections. Later, when he returned to his hotel, Michael used a different overpass, too guilty to ever use her overpass again—the divide was too large between them, and it would have wrenched at his heart to see her and her child again.

13th, 12th, 11th, one with no sign, then 9th. He reversed direction. *Still no 10th*, he wondered. He turned up the unmarked street. It ended at a run-down wooden building. A sign read *Sukota School for Girl* boasting a lack-of-maintenance exclusivity as the third "S" had worn off. The building was dark. It was beginning to feel like a wild goose chase in a city where he did not know the language and dared not ask the locals for fear of finding himself fleeced, or worse. *Back to Sukhumvit with the bold stares and smiles*, he said to himself, resigned to enduring more catcalls. He continued down the sidewalk, and one of the sinewy girls he had seen earlier made a soft grab for his arm. He avoided it. She feigned hurt and continued catcalling at him as he retreated. After the street with no name, it was 9th again. Getting frustrated he came to an alley wondering why he was on this nighttime mission anyway, *This is a city with a million things to see and do. Great food, or so I have been told, nightlife that is beyond mention. Why is Drake sending me here? What am I doing, thinking about heading down dark streets alone at night?* Thoughts started flitting thought his mind about Drake and his exploits, his own desire that he had felt on the plane, his missing of Helen, what kind of place Julie's must be, and what Drake had had in mind for Michael. He chuckled to himself for even beginning this trek, lightening what was becoming a dark mood. Hitting another street with no sign Michael looked up and down what was barely an alley. *This couldn't be 10th. It isn't even a street!* He thought to himself. Rather it was an unlit dirt path, more potholed than level,

Mugger's Lane, he thought and finally turned back to find his way to the hotel.

With his head time-zone-spinning, he decided to sit for a while at one of the outdoor cafes to clear his mind. A tight-skirted girl approached and stood in front of him. Not a bold move compared to what he had already witnessed, but bold for her. She had the look of a young, inexperienced girl, maybe what Drake would call, "an eighteen plus one." Her demeanor was wholesome—she had yet to acquire that Baht-guessti-mate-calculation-gaze beneath her invitational smile. Her features were fine, especially her nose, her skin whiter than some of the others he had seen that night. He gestured for her to sit. Within a few seconds, she took out a pocket mirror to freshen her eye make-up.

"Better?" she asked.

"More better with none at all," he offered.

She stopped mid-mascara, gave his comment a perplexed smile, but it had hit home, and sadness crept in. He offered her a drink—vodka tonic, the same for himself.

She took a sip. "Me like you."

"You a student?"

"How you know?"

He shrugged.

Someone bumped into one of the two empty chairs at their table and knocked it over, nearly taking the table with it. It was put upright with what appeared to Michael as exagger-ated apologies, but Michael graciously brushed it off, continu-ing his conversation.

"But not," he gestured with his hand, "around here?"

"No. Me die they know."

"How many before me?"

There was no response.

"Too many to count?"

She flashed a quick no, shaking her head slightly.

"So?" He waited for an answer.

No response came.

"That's all right," he said, feeling a little ashamed at having tried to force her to answer. Clearly she was inexperienced.

"Two," she blurted out almost as a confession, looking away.

He glanced at one on the street who had just snagged her prey.

A boy came up with roses and held out one for Michael to buy for "his lady." He dismissed it with a slow hand.

"What do you study?"

"Hotel."

"Then a good job?"

"Then maybe okay job."

She had sipped her drink dry.

"You ever drink this before?"

"No. Me like. Me think good."

He ordered two more—a mistake. Even he was feeling something from the second.

"Me sister, him want come Bangkok. I tell no. Him think me waitress."

"Younger sister?"

"Same."

"Twins?"

"What 'twins'?"

"Same birthday."

She nodded. "Live same day. What you think? Him come Bangkok? Now him no money. Work no good."

"I don't know."

"You good man. You say me."

"She speak English?"

She nodded, her face brightening. "Him speak good English. Same me."

"Better she does not come."

Suddenly she forced her eyes wide open and giggled. "You head. Go round. You funny man."

"You come with me."

"We go long time?"

"Yes, long time."

"How much you pay long time?"

"We'll talk. Later."

She went anyway, not having settled on a price, she stumbling, him moving steadily towards what she assumed was his hotel.

He had her sit in the lobby of the closest hotel he could find while he went to the front desk and spent two minutes with the receptionist. Bhat quietly exchanged. Michael had everything settled, and this "eighteen plus one" and Michael were on their way upstairs.

Once in the room, she steadied herself against the wall.

"Me wash first?"

"No. Bed." He pointed to the king-size bed with over-stuffed pillows and white downy comforter.

"Me wash."

He pointed to the bed again. "No. Bed."

Puzzled, she took off her shoes and skirt. He led her to the bed and sat her down. He pulled back the covers, lifted her legs and swung them onto the bed. She lay down. He sat next to her, his hands pressing down, not too hard, on her shoulders. Looking her straight in the eyes, "Now listen." He shook her to attention. "Listen, tomorrow morning, ten o'clock, someone will knock on the door. You understand? Then afterwards you go. Understand?"

"Me no understand."

"Ten o'clock, someone knock on door," he knocked on the headboard and then motioned to the door. "After, you go. Understand?"

She was a little more awake. "Him you friend? Him pay me?"

"No worry. But after, you go. You must go. Understand?"

"Me understand."

He got up.

"Where you go?"

"You sleep first."

Her eyes were drooping, and she was snuggling into the pillows as he closed the room door on his way out.

Back in his room, he tried to finish the book he had started, but he couldn't concentrate. There was too much to think about. Too much that he had already seen in a few hours on the streets of Bangkok. Too many thoughts of home that still flooded his mind, even in this exotic landscape—people had told him that he was sentimental. Maybe he was. He lay down and forced Helen's face from his mind, and suddenly finding himself smiling, thinking instead of the girl he had left at another hotel somewhere in this huge city, *at least she would have a good breakfast.* He still had a lot of daylight in him and drawn by the allure of the city, Michael found himself setting out again for Julie's on Sukhumvit Road.

Back on the main drag, deciding to take a different route in the hopes of actually finding Drake's hideaway, Michael was accosted by a middle-aged woman standing in the door-way of a foot massage parlor. She beckoned him inside where four leather chairs were arranged barbershop style.

"300 Baht," the owner said from behind the cash register. "Number one foot massage. One hour."

He hesitated.

"Only 300 Baht. Make feet happy."

What did he have to lose? When in Rome or some such cli-ché, he mused and sat down in one of the chairs. His attendant, Yin, was young and tall for a Thai, even in her flat san-dals, which slapped the floor as she casually walked, nearly at a shuffle, over to his chair. Her face was plain and pleasant, and she was slender with small breasts. She wore loose-fit-ting short-shorts and an oversized T-shirt with the words Dallas Cowboys emblazoned in blue on the front, both of which unexpectedly accentuated the few curves that she did have. She deftly straddled her stool, with its accompanying empty basin and "toolbox" of lotions and brushes. Another girl brought over a large pitcher of water from a charcoal stove. Yin removed Michael's shoes and socks, rolled up his cuffs way up, and filled the basin with the warm water. She washed his feet, giving them the most thorough washing of his life. Working on his feet and lower legs up to the knees it took the full hour. Her massage ranged from soothing to invigorating to crunching. At one point he found himself wincing, nearly pushing himself to the back of the chair and away from her hold, simultaneously holding up his hand signaling for her to be more gentle. She spoke little with her co-workers, and the responses to her comments were mostly one or two words. She looked up at him only twice during the hour, without much to express what she thought about her client. Michael surmised that to her he was just two feet attached to two lower legs attached to some Bhat-carrying foreigner.

The exhaustion from his flight seemed to melt out of him as Yin worked his bones and muscles. As far as he was concerned Yin could have gone on for another hour. The matron was right. His feet were happy. She accepted the 300 Baht with a slight bow, then, boldly asked, "You interested in full body massage now? It upstairs." She nodded toward a doorway. "600 Baht. Very nice. Two hour." Out of curiosity, more than anything, Michael followed her up the staircase. He had to turn his shoulders sideways to get up the flight that had clearly been made for someone other than a man carrying Michael's well-formed Western frame. Getting to the second-floor landing, Michael was hit with a dank and musty smell, an overwhelming odor that was mixed with the lingering haze of cheap perfume—the kind you would never buy. The whole floor was dark, save four cubicles divided by bedsheets that were no longer white, all hanging from a wire that was tied to plumbing in the ceiling. One sheet was missing its clips and hung ajar. Each makeshift-quadrant contained a bed with a clean towel, a plastic night table, and a low-wattage bulb that hung dangling, naked, overhead from a dubious looking cord.

Michael gestured for them to descend. As they were heading down the stairs, the matron, in a last effort keep Michael's interest, said, "Only 800 Baht if girl come to your room. Number one massage. You stay close by?" He didn't say, but she knew. His hotel was a block away. He would think about it. He tipped Yin 100 Baht and headed out back to the main road.

The next day Michael returned and paid the owner 800 Baht. Yin, clearly a pro, stuffed her soaps and oils into a small sack. The other girls were all smiles and clapped as she accompanied him. He gestured for her to walk alongside him, but she nodded for him to proceed with her following behind. Security made her sign in and leave her ID card, a very different scenario at this upscale hotel from the place the night before with the poor "eighteen plus one", not that he left her at a low-end dive, but this place really was the top. He had to hand it to Drake. He had certainly set him up in style.

Yin kept behind him like a shadow as they got onto the elevator, but upon entering his room Yin removed her sandals and surveyed the interior in what Michael assumed was her normal mode: relaxed and self-possessed. She declined his offer for a drink from the frig and stood there unabashed, shifting from one leg to the other as he undressed to his underpants in front of her.

"You like hard? Soft?" she asked.

"Start with hard."

The massage began with Michael prostrate on the bed, only his boxers protecting any of his modesty. She straddled him, sitting on his glutes with her same baggy short-shorts covering everything from his lower back to his upper thighs.

The first few minutes were soothing, and then 'hard' started. Yin was strong. While he was still on his stomach, she bent his leg back at the knee and then raised the whole leg toward his back. It felt like she was going to tear his quads loose, and he had to take deep breaths, just to get through the procedure. Then she used her lotion on his back, pressing in slowly and deeply and rocking back and forth with her body. As the conclusion of working on his posterior she walked up and down baby-steps on either side of his backbone. *It's good that she is not any heavier*, he thought, half-laughing as the air was squeezed out of his lungs.

It was all like this until she turned him over and started with his hands. With them, it was different. She bent, stretched, and kneaded them, all very soothing. She pulled each finger with a quick snap. She saw that he liked this, and she did each hand three times. Moving down his arms she bent them closed at the elbow and then raised his whole arm up over his shoulder—except this time it was his triceps that were ready to pop. Satisfied that he was fully stretched, Yin moved to working on his chest, straddling him with most of her weight on her knees, the balance on his upper thighs. Heat was pouring from her loins. She appeared oblivious to the obvious. He was not. A desire that had been quietly awakened was now starting to simmer. He concentrated to control himself as she leaned forward working on his face, stretching the skin in dreamy softness, and then using the same soothing touch down to the top of his boxers.

The massage lasted more than an hour when, without any notice Yin got up and repaired to the bathroom, leaving Michael relaxed and feeling more like himself than he had in months. He was surprised when he heard the shower turn on, and a few minutes later, Yin emerged clad in the hotel terrycloth bathrobe. She had another bathrobe draped over her arm. Glancing at it, she nodded to him—a simple gesture with no comment. He wasn't quite sure why he complied, but, without protest, he did. After he had showered, the room held two bathrobes of awkwardness, but the quiet tension lasted less than half a minute. Yin peeled back the bed sheet, climbed in, then pulled the sheet back up, and a few seconds later her bathrobe dropped to the floor.

"No. No. That's okay." Michael said. "For massage. Just massage. Tip. How much you get?"

"Up to you."

He handed her 1000 Bhat instead of 800.

She was happy.

"I will see you again?"

"Okay," she said.

He saw her three more times. Each time when they left the shop together, the girls downstairs smiled and clapped. Each time it was massage only, but who knows what they thought.

Drake's angular face could turn from a smile to anger quickly. The difference between them was only seen in the landscape of the sharp lines. But then, he was a Mount Everest of irreverence and that, coupled with an easy laugh, rendered him immediately likable. Michael had known Drake long enough that he considered Drake to be an old friend, and often called him one. For Drake that expression was starting to hit too close to home. He carried fifteen more years than Michael. As a rejoinder, according to Drake, they were *longstanding friends*, though to a casual observer they might have looked more like antagonistic brothers replete with all of the ribbing that each doled out to the other on all manner of topics. Their friendship thrived on the many darts and barbs mutually thrown. In reality this joking was a sign of deep respect between the two—Drake bringing something invaluable to his friendships, something that Michael admired. If you sought a temporary escape from the harsh winter of reality to satisfy a dream that could only flourish in your cozy den of wishful thinking, Drake would unleash an avalanche your way that would at least make you reflect on, if not bury you in, the plain facts. It was a cascading torrent that disabused you of your fantasy. Sometimes, he was a heavy snow pack to have piled up around you, but as it turned out for Michael, he proved to be a badly needed one on more than one occasion. Drake was, for Michael, one of the only people he would take seriously, especially when a comment was offered uninvited. This fact was not lost on Drake or on Michael, and was not taken lightly by either of the pair.

Drake was lithe, strong and lean in a way that would make anyone wary of fighting him. Once he had to fight his way out of a bar against three rowdy guys, and he came out of it okay. Drake often chalked up his sometime-temper to having to compensate for his blond hair, which he disliked. Even worse in Asia, it made him stand out when anonymity was his decided preference, yet he never considered dyeing it. It didn't matter much anymore since it was beginning to recede, something any other man would have found disturbing, but Drake, not having vanity as one of his weaknesses, was fine, even happy watching it go.

Drake had an easy way about him but was impatient with women. Even so he received calls, pictures and emails from long forgotten girlfriends in far away places asking when he was going to next be *in country*. Michael had observed him gracious with women but knew that Drake always had one thing in mind. His demeanor indicated that he had little interest in a long, drawn out *pas de deux*. There were one or two exceptions and Michael had often mused that these two must have been mighty good in bed for Drake to hold on to them, even while he was engaging with other women. "If you don't break at least one heart after an affair, you've failed," Drake once observed without emotion. And then added, "and probably failed to protect yourself, which is worse."

Michael warmly greeted Drake in the lobby. His "three days late" had ended up being seven.

"Lots of business," he said. "Had to go to Hong Kong as well."

"For someone terrified of flying, how do you manage to stay in the air so much?"

"That's what airport bars are for," he said through a grin.

Despite the fact that Drake was traveling light as usual, the bellhop who had first attended to Michael fawned over the opportunity to assist Drake, an overture that Drake dismissed with a couple of words in Thai.

"What? You two got something going together, or what?" Drake motioned to the bellhop with his thumb.

"Fuck you," Michael retorted, noticing that the bellhop was still lingering.

Drake laughed. "No, not me. I'm asking about you two."

"Last comment still stands," Michael said, chuckling.

Both headed onto the elevator and then to Michael's room.

"Christ, what's all this stuff?" Drake asked shaking his head, "You brought all this?"

There were two suitcases and an army duffel bag in the corner of the room.

"You think I'm ever going to help you carry this shit? So when's the steamer trunk coming?"

"Tomorrow."

Drake plopped down on a chair. "So, how was Julie's?"

"I couldn't find it."

"No. No, tell me you're joking. Come on, really? Oh, Christ Almighty."

Michael laughed through his nose. "Jet lag. You buy that?"

"What I bought was a basket case with too much baggage."

That afternoon Michael and Drake went through the preliminary negotiations with the Jim Thompson people to discuss the deal that had brought Michael to Thailand in the first place. Michael was glad that he had already been in Bangkok a week. His jet lag was all but gone and he felt strong about his presentation outlining the distribution proposal, referring to Neiman Marcus only as a very upscale chain. He felt like they had nailed it as Drake ran through the rough numbers. Neither of them raised the issues of the franchise fees with an upward sliding scale, pricing specs for different types of clothing, contract minimums, exchange rate provisions, delivery guarantees and penalties—in other words, none of the nitty-gritty details. The three Thai businessmen sitting across the table didn't raise any of these issues either. This meeting was clearly called for setting the groundwork in the hopes of each getting the best deal, and both sides knew it.

After the meeting Drake and Michael walked back to the hotel, leaving the three Thai contacts to talk among themselves.

"They're counting on American impatience," Drake said. He continued, "They figure they'll just wait us out."

"They need us more than we need them," Michael said. "I know the numbers that work. They're just guessing at them."

"Another reason they'll wait," Drake added. "But we won't be the ones to propose numbers first. Eventually, they will."

"And if they guess wrong, we either have a very good deal or no deal. Unless they cave."

Both were pleased with the day's outcome and to celebrate Drake decided that he would *really* introduce Michael to his own version of Bangkok. Whisking Michael off to Nana, a large complex of bars filled with girls of many "persuasions" available to accompany you back to your hotel. They landed at the Hollywood Bar. There the dancers only wore bikini bottoms and each wore a red plastic tag around one of their ankles, each with a different number. It seemed a kind of minimalist uniform, making the girls' wares obvious, displaying precisely what it was each girl had to offer—physically. Michael found himself trying not to stare.

They ordered a round of beers. "Don't drink too fast. We'll stick around 'til ten o'clock. You'll see."

Drake filled Michael in on the ins-and-outs of bargirls and the etiquette of the bar, Full bikini dancers got 6500 Baht a month, topless 7000 and nude 8000. Hostesses 7000. A girl pushing thirty had difficulty picking up a customer with the conveyor belt rolling out a new crop of eighteen-year-olds every year. So the older ones would do tricks instead of turning tricks. A few could even manage to make 8000, tips not included. "In the bars, they get union wages without the unions. It's when they negotiate with a customer that they become entrepreneurs. It's all economics, and everyone knows the exchange rate."

Drake invited two of the dancers up for drinks. For Michael, conversation was via smiles and laughs. Drake conversed and bought them second rounds: whiskey both times. "They could drink these 'whiskeys' all night and still not get drunk. Easy to hold your liquor when there's no whiskey in it. We get the real stuff, cheap quality of course. Which is why I only order beer. They can't water it down."

A few minutes before ten, their waitress brought them two more beers and another round of whiskey. At ten o'clock sharp the dancers left the stage, the waitresses disappeared, the lights turned bright and recorded circus music started to blare. A bar girl who looked to have pushed past thirty walked up onto center stage. The old hands cheered. A stagehand brought up a small, clear-plastic bucket of Ping-Pong balls. Michael handed Drake a 1000 Baht note.

"Something the matter?"

"No. I'm calling it a night," Michael said as he tried to stand and answer simultaneously, hiding his disbelief that the rumors he had heard were *actually* true.

"You might miss a catch."

Michael, finally upright, stood to his full height and squeezed past knees on his way out.

"I guess I'll see you tomorrow."

"Like I said, *it is all economics*," Drake called after him.

Michael left and re-entered the street's loud hush—a quieter din than the bar, but one still arising from a wider range of economic circumstances. He found an empty table at a bar abutting the sidewalk and ordered a rum and Coke. Michael didn't care much for rum, or Coke-A-Cola for that matter, but somehow, tonight with the sultry heat of the city, it sounded like it would hit the spot. The waiter returned with a small glass with rum and ice and opened the Coke bottle. As the waiter was filling the glass, and with Michael off in some other hemisphere, a young woman seated herself at Michael's table. She was attractive with everything on just tight and just right. When Michael refocused he was surprised to discover her there.

"You buy me drink?"

"What would you like?"

"Same you."

He slid his drink to her, the top of the straw still sporting the nub of the paper wrapper that the whole straw had come in.

"You no want?"

"Later."

She downed the drink with a couple of pulls on the straw. He bought her another. He studied her face. She was pretty. She was wearing an expensive-looking earring on one ear, nothing on the other. He gestured to the naked one.

She frowned. "Me lose tonight. No know where." She pulled on the empty lobe. "Good earring. Gold. Man buy. Angry self."

He shrugged sympathy at her loss and paid the tab.

"I stay you tonight? Make you happy?"

"Maybe another time."

"You girl leave you?"

"No."

"Why you sad?"

"Not."

"You no sad?"

"I no sad."

"Handsome man. Me pretty girl. I come with you. We no sad, even if you sad."

Drake had already clued Michael in on the issue of "time". The girls always tried for *long time* first. More time, more money. Long time was around four hours. Short time was up to two hours. One hour if the man was just as happy to see the girl go. There was one other category: all night. This was usually only 1000 or 1500 Baht more than long time because it meant a break from hustling, the possibility of something long term, like a week or two developing, and sleeping in a nice bed, having room service meals. There were always extra drinks if the girl wanted them. All-nighters were infrequent requests.

"How much?"

"3000 Baht. Long time."

He shrugged.

"Only 2000 short time."

"Long time?" Michael said, realizing he was playing along with her just a bit for fun.

"Okay, you nice man. For you, 2500. You nice. I no forget you. You special. I special you."

"I'm tired."

"I wake you up," she brightened.

"Maybe another time."

She pouted, but quickly rebounded, "Where you stay?"

"Hotel."

"What hotel. I come tomorrow. You say time."

"Better I find you."

With a sweep of the hand, she gestured to the packed street. "How?"

"I'm good at finding." And with that Michael had made it clear that he was not interested. She finished the second drink quickly and excused herself, leaving Michael to his reverie.

On the way back to his hotel, Michael was looking down, alert to the uneven pavement to which he would never grow accustomed, even though he was beginning to manage with less effort while still maintaining a healthy respect for its characteristic moguls. Then suddenly, there it was, resting against the wheel of an orange-juice pushcart.

She was not where he had left her. She'd probably already hooked up. But he kept looking—another bar, another side street, and then another street. She was nowhere to be seen. He continued on his mission anyway. He wasn't sure why. Maybe it was to make up for dismissing her and making her feel bad? Maybe it was just who he was—someone who just felt things. Someone who knew that to her it meant more than she could earn easily. Turning down another street, Michael realized the setting was unfamiliar to him. As he turned to retrace his steps, he saw her through an open doorway. She was leaning against a bar rail with two other girls, a threesome of miniskirts. He took a few steps inside the bar and gave a slight wave to get her attention. She gave him a blank stare of non-recognition. So much for *"I no forget you,"* Michael thought. But when he lifted up the earring and dangled it, she squinted a smile, clapped, hands high up, and ran, tiny step, up to him. He placed the earring in her open palm. She gave him two pretend kisses and reattached the earring. She offered again to be a duo. He held up his hand no and took his leave. "I like you," she called out, loud enough that he heard it. He did not even know her name.

With the three beers at Hollywood, the search for the girl with the missing earring and the unfamiliarity with his surroundings, Michael found himself totally disoriented. He had no idea which way to turn, and as panic crept in he realized he could not remember the name of his hotel. He racked his brain. *No, this was not possible, lost in Bangkok a couple of blocks from your hotel with no way to ask directions.* The hair on the back of his head tingled. His indecisiveness about which way to turn was interpreted by some of the girls standing nearby as his trying to make up his mind which one of them to select. Their smiles became more alluring, their gestures less subtle, in some cases brazen. One girl sidled up to him, "Me go your hotel. Me stay with you. Long time."

He started walking. He stopped abruptly, mouth agape. His passport was in the safety deposit box at the hotel. One had to present a passport or other Identity Card to check into a hotel. Anxiety was setting in. Breathing was halting. He needed to make it stop and make a plan. He decided to get his mind clear and ordered a coffee at an outdoor bar. Slowly breathing easier, he started going through the alphabet, hoping one of the letters would trigger the name. He went through it a second time. He buried his head in his hands, blocking out the light.

"I sorry you sad." A street girl seemed to materialize, seated beside him. "You sad?" she asked.

"No."

"You look sad. I sit with you."

He buried his head again.

"I thirsty."

"Get what you want," he said with a wave of his hand.

"What?"

He looked up, a little exasperated, "Drink whatever you want."

She said something to the waiter in Thai and ordered something, the same for Michael, whatever it was.

Suddenly he jerked his head up from his hands. "Hey, you know the hotels here?"

"What?"

"The hotels. Here. You know the names?"

"I know all hotel. Where you stay? I tell you if good."

"No. Just tell me the names. The hotels here." He gestured with his hand.

"I no understand."

"That's okay. Just tell me the names. All the names."

She went through the names. After five, she paused to think, and his spirits sagged. When she came to his, the seventh, he recognized it instantly.

He shook his head and laughed. "I like you."

"I come with you?" She perked up.

"No, that's okay. How many drinks you like?"

She pouted. "Two," she said softly.

He slid his over to her. "And thank you very much." He gave her 200 Baht in case she wanted three.

He found his way back to the Landmark Hotel, then again venturing out from there, being careful to note every street he turned onto. He was surprised at himself, that even after a week it was still easy for him to get turned around. He did not think of himself as particularly naïve, nor a *green* traveler, but here he continued to get disoriented by the streets, the constant activity, by the overt signs of a morality that seemed so foreign to his own. Michael headed back onto one of the major roads looking for diversions. Wanting to clear his mind, he thought he would do a little shopping, think about business, see what else was out there that might be worth bringing to the States. He found it impossible to window shop without being accosted by girls, particularly the lean yet very muscular looking ones. He brushed past a couple of prostitutes who made their interests known as he entered a tourist store that offered high-quality merchandise. There was a large display of stingray wallets and purses that had caught his eye so he made his way over to take a look. He had seen these for sale in the States and had remembered that they all had said Made in

Thailand. Now here they were at twenty percent of the price Stateside. He selected a wallet and then decided that both the wallets and the purses would make excellent presents back home. He negotiated a lower unit price for two, then slightly lower still for three. He ended with eight (five wallets and three purses)—the point at which the owner said he could give no further volume discount. The unit price had dropped a further twenty five percent off of the stateside prices—*a good lesson for dealing with the Jim Thompson people*, he thought.

Walking back to the Landmark, he mused about his purchases and to whom he would give them when he got back home. Helen popped immediately to mind. "Old habits," he thought to himself. This was just the type of present she would appreciate. After years of shopping for her he knew that she would have loved it. He tried to imagine what she would say when she opened it, that genuine smile, maybe even a kiss. One of the purses was distinctly more attractive than the other two. He would give that one to Helen if he ever saw her again.

The next night Drake took him to another topless place. The girls had the standard red plastic tags on their ankles, again each with a different number. Drake thought that Michael looked a *little* more comfortable in this space than the night before, so he went for it. "All right, I'm waiting for you to pick," he insisted, between sips of beer. "And don't invite one over and buy her a drink unless you are going to negotiate. They will lose face that way. And *never* make a Thai lose face. It's a big deal here. In the right circumstances, it can even be dangerous. How about it?"

Michael became reflective, thinking about the girls on the street from the night before, the ones he had toyed with a bit and those who had pawed at him, and then blurted out, "Hey, how about the two girls at the Hollywood Bar?"

"That was different," said Drake. "We were...that is, *I* was waiting for the show to begin. Like everyone else. Everyone knows it's completely different. Then it's just drinks, and that's fine."

"How many cultural nuances does one have to learn to not get killed?"

"Just one more. Never say anything derogatory about the King. That is taboo. Besides, he is a good King and highly respected. The Queen as well."

"Thank you. It's very nice to know that you don't want me to get killed," a smirk crossed his lips and then he found himself chuckling.

"I don't want you to get killed. I want you to get laid."

After the girls had finished dancing, Drake told the waitress he wanted to see Number 28. She came to their table for a drink. She knew him, and they laughed as they chatted in Thai. After the next round, Michael told the waitress he wanted to see Number 17.

Her name was Klung. She was slender but otherwise the least attractive of the girls, by a lot. She spoke some English.

"You serious?" Drake asked.

"Yes."

"They have first-class medicine in Bangkok now."

"I don't follow."

"Good eye doctors."

"You're so helpful."

"You got charity balls."

Drake stepped into the negotiations. He knew where the advantage lay. Long time was 1500, not the usual 3000. Klung collected the bar fine from Michael and went to change.

"Let's make it 2000," Michael said.

"What? You crazy? You sound like a rate buster."

"What about that thing you said about losing face?"

"What, with her face?"

Michael dropped the subject.

Klung showered quickly, then wrapped herself with a towel. Michael showered longer and then took even longer drying. Klung was in the bed covered by the sheet. Her blouse, skirt, bra and panties were folded neatly on a chair. Michael sat on the bed, facing her. They remained like that for some seconds.

"You no like me?" Her hand pawed him.

"No, that's not it. I want to give you 2000, not 1500, and you can go if you want."

Klung burst into tears. "You no like me?"

"No. No, don't. Yes, I like you," he said in the version of Thai he had picked up. He lay down beside her. She hugged him tightly and assumed this was the start. It was not. Gradually, her tears dried, but not the tightness of her hold. They sat together on the bed, talking as best they could, for nearly an hour.

In her sometimes English, he pieced together her story. She looked straight at him when she told him about growing up poor in Ubon, learning that it was an agricultural region in northeastern Thailand. She averted her eyes when telling him about becoming a bar girl and then almost never getting picked by a customer. She pulled the sheet up uncovering her left thigh to show him a scar. "Last time, bad man do." She could not explain how this happened in a way he could understand. He touched the scar.

"Hurt?"

"No hurt now. Make leg ugly."

"No. Leg is okay."

"Me need customer. Or bar says go. Then no money. Other bar no want." Her eyes went downcast, then back up to him, pleading.

"You hungry?" he asked.

"No eat all day."

"Only breakfast for me."

He ordered room service for them both. Despite the late-ness of the hour, that was no problem. Thirty minutes later, a white-clothed dolly was wheeled in with cold cuts, veggies, and a variety of fruits—some of which he had never seen before—pastries, soda, and a pot of coffee. Michael declined her offer to feed him, and watched as Klung ate like someone who had not eaten in a long time. She smiled at being able to show him how to eat the unfamiliar fruit. The pale green one with thick skin was crunchy and only a step up from tasteless. The deep purple one with many small seeds was sugar-sweet. One of them had to be peeled first to extract a tan juicy ball. This was Klung's favorite, and he encouraged her to eat them all except the one he tried.

Afterwards, she glanced toward the bed with raised eyebrows.

"That's okay," he said. "It's all right to go now."

He gave her a 2000 Baht tip in addition to the 2000 for long time. She stared in disbelief. He nodded. She looked about ready to cry. He held up his hand motioning for her to stop. She hugged him. He dismissed the tip with a nod. She turned at the door. "You see me more?"

"Well, I don't know," his voice trailing off noncommittally.

After she had left, Michael sat down by the remaining food, some of which was still untouched. He picked up a piece of the purple fruit, put it to his mouth, hesitated, and then put it down. He knew he would not see her again. He no longer felt hungry.

Drake's breakfast was orange juice, bacon and eggs, white toast with butter, coffee and Lipitor.

"So, how was Miss Thailand?

Michael gave a dismissive shrug.

Drake looked at him suspiciously. "Oh, no! No, don't tell me. Oh, Christ! Okay, now it makes sense. What did you tip her?"

"It's not important."

"You son of a bitch. You're going to make the rest of us go broke. Just because you can't distinguish between water and money gives you no right to drown the rest of us."

"You? You keep telling me you get it for free anyway." He laughed. "All it costs you is airfare."

"Economy Class."

"Whatever."

Drake finished the last half of his coffee in one gulp. He sat back and studied Michael for a second.

"So how do things stand with you and Helen?"

"I still haven't heard from her."

"You alright with that?"

"Is there a choice?"

Drake shrugged. "What's step two?"

He pursed his lips. "Well, it's not…"

A couple of tables away the plates slipped off a waiter's tray. They both turned, watching the frantic cleanup and profuse apologies to the man whose white slacks were splattered the first few inches up.

"That'll cost that poor slob a month's wages," Drake said with a laugh. "Anyway, you were about to say?"

"Let's not talk about this now," Michael said hoping to dismiss the line of needling questions, "I haven't decided."

The next day Drake was going off to Singapore for three days to attend to one of his other businesses. Plus he was meeting up with a former girlfriend who had written him out of the blue, one whom Drake hadn't seen in more than two years. He read Michael Gina's letter. It was explicit about what appealed to her vis-à-vis Drake, both the anatomy and the uses to which it was put. She had enclosed a photo as well. It was certainly designed to encourage another visit sooner rather than later.

"Would you go back for that?" Drake asked.

"Well, you would."

"That wasn't my question."

"She's not my type."

"So, who *is* your type?"

"Well…"

"You are in bad shape."

"Actually, the women here are attractive."

"Oh, you've noticed? That's encouraging."

"Actually, very attractive."

"You're welcome."

"I suppose I should thank you."

"Just pick an attractive one next time. That'll be thanks enough. Oh, and, by the way, tomorrow we'll call and tell them we have to reschedule the meeting.

"Give them something more to think about?"

Drake raised his eyebrows. "We'll go to Cowboy tonight. Can't leave you with a lonely night."

"Look, maybe I'll just sleep in tonight. You know, time zones. I'm still catching up".

"No way, Hopalong Cassidy. Better saddle up, we're taking a ride to Cowboy. Go get your nap. I'll pick you up at nine."

Cowboy was a short walk from the hotel, and even in the continual misting rain the sidewalk was packed with street vendors, smiling and available girls, more aggressive prostitutes, foreigners looking to score, and an assortment of beggars here and there. No one except a few tourists ever paid any attention to the rain, not even the vendors grilling chicken on open-air braziers with coals that hissed their annoyance.

Michael and Drake passed the Mercedes Benz showroom that was closed for the night. It was hard not to notice that the whole place was packed with three million Baht cars, all nearly glowing on the brightly lit showroom floor. The view of these beautiful machines was partially blocked by the prostitutes lined up outside the floor to ceiling pane glass windows. Unlike the cars, not all of the girls were sparkling new, and some, fresh to the scene, carried an unease that had yet to wear off. The others, clearly used, and hopefully certified by the State, engaged passers-by with stares and smiles. The brightness of the showroom allowed these girls to better broadcast their figurative wares that were clearly reflected. One wore lipstick that looked like it was borrowed from the metallic red Mercedes sedan behind her. Another girl standing just to the side of a black Mercedes Coupe called out, "Me take you on high-speed ride. Back seat job." She smiled at her command of English. Others beckoned each guy who passed, but not the younger ones who only smiled and fidgeted a little. A few of the ones who clearly had more miles on them looked like they worked out regularly at the gym and were much bolder than the others. One grabbed Michael's arm by way of offering herself.

"You like that one, the one who just grabbed you?" Drake asked.

"Pretty face, but I don't know. Something's wrong."

"Lady-boy."

Michael looked back. That proved to be a mistake. She, or whatever, interpreted this as a "come on" and Michael had to shake her loose a second time.

"She likes you. You lucky boy with Lady-boy."

Michael threw Drake a jab to the arm with a little zing to it. They continued on.

"Yeah," Michael said, "the shoulders, the build, the legs, it's all obvious once you said it."

"Everything's obvious to you once I've said it."

Cowboy was another enclave for men interested in *willing* and *available* young women. It was wall-to-wall brightly lit dance bars. With an amusing sense of sincerity, young respectably dressed female hawkers invited, and sometimes implored passers-by to enter. The classier bars had a curtained entrance where you walked through the opening in the middle. The others had stings of closely spaced beads that the hawkers swept open for entrance. Drake and Michael walked the

length of Cowboy, Drake looking for a place to land. At the
end of the street, there were two classy-looking bars where the
hawkers ignored them.

"They only cater to Japanese. They won't even let you in."

"What?"

"Japanese have fat wallets and with their little dicks, they
don't want competition."

All of this made Michael feel like he was in his early
twenties again, wet behind the ears and getting schooled by
his older friend about life. It was disconcerting just how much
of the world he had not seen or experienced, despite his years
traveling with Helen and then all over the world for work. He
shook off the sensation as they retraced their steps.

Drake chose Sunshine Delight. A dozen or so girls who all
looked to be in their twenties were on the stage, twirling and
gyrating around chrome poles. They were topless but not bot-
tomless. Each had the same kind of red disk with a white
number attached to her bikini. Some were into the music and
looked for eye contact. Some looked bored and were going
slow motion. The bar was half empty. A hostess came up to
seat them. Drake pointed to two open seats on the third of
six rows, each row elevated above the one in front. The hostess
took their drink orders.

The dancers rotated on and off the stage like a hockey
front line—the only difference was that the rotation was every
two to three minutes in hockey; here it was every fifteen.
Michael was commenting on the relative attractiveness of the
dancers as one just off her shift came over to their table. Her
English was sufficient to say her name, age, and where she
was from. Beyond that, she understood numbers and not a
whole lot more. Drake chatted with her in his Thai, translating
for Michael the most salient information that he understood.
Drake did not order a drink for her. He said one word to her,
it sounded like "yang," meaning, as Drake explained it, "not

right now. I'll let you know if I'm interested later." Michael marveled at the economy of the Thai language.

"Don't buy them a drink if you're not going to negotiate. Remember what I said about losing face. That's bad. Listen, you got to take one or we're going to be here all night. 'Cause I'll catch hell from the girls here if I let you leave solo." Drake took a long drink of his beer. "You like our hostess? Perky. Speaks English, too."

"She's available?"

Drake smiled, "Is that a serious question?"

"Price any different?"

"It's what you negotiate. Offer her 1500 for short time, 2000 long. Go for it."

Michael, feeling schooled by Drake, decided to reassert himself and beckoned her over. They quickly settled on 2000, plus the standard bar fine of 600 for taking a girl out of circulation. Her name was Wan. She collected the drink tab and the 600 and went to change.

"You gonna choose one?"

"No. I'm going to try another bar," Drake paused, "where I think the girls are nude. Used to be nude here… when the police owned it. Nude is illegal."

"What about the girls you know here? Losing face?"

"There's no such thing as collectively losing face. It's an individual thing. And in case you didn't notice, I didn't invite anyone over."

Wan wore a sleeveless top and a non-suggestive skirt. She carried with her a small purse and large tote that matched in their lavender and pink chrysanthemum pattern. The other hostesses were all smiles with her and gave her cheek kisses. Wan was shorter than the other hostesses and wore pumps with four-inch heels. Michael had quickly figured out that the Thai, especially women, were sensitive to the height differential between them and 'firangs.' A firang was the designation for any white person, especially a rich American. At a four-inch elevation, and with Thai sidewalks making those in New York City seem level, the heels were exceptionally wide. Despite this, it seemed to Michael a minor miracle that she could walk gracefully, let alone upright, in those stilts.

On the street, Wan wanted a whisky.

"You like the stuff?" Michael asked.

"Oh yes, I do."

He bought her a shot from a vendor. It was low grade, but she threw it back like it was water. She had a second. At the corner, there was a pool hall unlike any that Michael had ever seen: the two corner sides were open-air and the two others were for equipment and a bar.

"Can we play a few games?" she asked with eager casualness.

"Sure, I guess," Michael said, a little surprised. "You any good?"

"I love to play pool."

She was fairly good relative to Michael, who was relatively bad. She won two of the five games. Two of Michael's wins stemmed from the rule they set that you did not have to call your shot. She was so happy when she won that, in retrospect, Michael wished he had let her win three or four.

On the walk to the hotel, they passed many hookers who gave Michael a beckoning smile, but then let it fade as soon as they discerned that Wan was with him. There was only one exception. It happened on the packed sidewalk, when this one girl inched up to Michael almost without his knowing.

"Next time, okay? I wait here for you."

"No, thanks," and he very gently nudged her off.

Wan was impressed by his room. She held up her arms to feel the air conditioning.

She made a beeline for the TV and turned it to a Thai

soap opera. The only interest to Michael was the stark whiteness of the performers.

"I see how it end, okay? It end very sad."

"You've seen it before?"

"No."

"How do you know how it ends?"

"All end sad."

"Be my guest," Michael said, a little amused.

She did not understand the expression, but that did not
bother her as she went right back to watching.

Michael shrugged and picked up the newspaper that he
had yet to finish reading. Now that she was in his room he was
not sure how eager he was to get started. Despite the fact that
she had all the characteristics of a Thai beauty—dainty but
not fragile, light coloring with dark sable-like hair—he was
feeling a little apprehensive.

As the soap was winding down, Wan got Michael's attention by pointing to the bathroom. She said nothing. It made
Michael laugh out loud being ordered around by such a petite
woman. Her bold smile in making the motion, however, suddenly got him going. Emboldened by the rush of desire, he
followed her orders and offered to shower first.

When he emerged in the hotel-issue, terrycloth bathrobe,
Wan was nowhere to be seen. Her purse and carrying bag were
no longer in evidence. Michael's antennae went on full alert.
A quick scan of the room came up empty. He took one deep
breath but was suddenly startled as she leaped onto his back
piggyback style laughing with delight. He spun around so fast
that she slid off, easily landing on her feet. One of the sofa
cushions was on the floor, the second askew, was on top of the
third, but still on the couch.

"Under those?" he asked amazed.

"Fooled you, didn't I!" She exclaimed.

"You sure did." He laughed. "At first, I thought you'd left."

"I no leave you."

She tossed one of the cushions from the sofa onto the floor and sat on it. Michael stood in front of her, over her. She rolled back slowly; feet spread in the air. Her white panties were front and center. They were snug and followed her contours.

"Looking at something?" she asked.

He nodded.

"Like what you see?"

The question called for no reply.

She sprang to her feet. "Then you have to catch me."

Michael made a grab for her, but she was too quick. They were on opposite sides of the king-size bed, eyeing each other warily, playfully. Michael climbed onto the center of the bed, ready to spring in any direction. Wan stepped back with a big grin. He lunged but missed, the softness of the bed dissipating his energy. Then it was a race around the room. Wan darted and ducked, scampered over the bed faster than he could. Her diminutive size made it all the more difficult to catch her. He latched on to an arm, but with surprising strength she pulled it free. Her elusiveness was releasing more and more of the animal in him. In the end, his endurance outlasted hers, and she was in his arms. They were both sweating.

"You need new shower," she teased.

"We shower together this time." He scooped her up and marched into the bathroom with her arms clinging to his neck.

There was plenty of lather and laughter as she washed him. She dried him off in a knowing way, lingering while applying ever more firm pressure as she moved down his frame. He left the lights in the room on full.

"Light too bright," she said.

"For a beautiful woman, light never too bright."

"Me shy." She started to turn a few down, but his hand arrested her intent.

"Me shy, too."

All the lights stayed on.

Nitroglycerin is tricky stuff. With care, it is relatively easy to handle. Except under one condition: when stored in an unheated building where the temperature falls below freezing, the nitro freezes too. As the weather warms, the nitro warms. When it warms to one degree above its freezing point, well then, be careful. In the shed where it is stored, if you close the door with a thud, no one will ever find you, or the shed for that matter.

Wan went nitro. Michael had never experienced a woman so eager, not that he had a ton of experience outside of Helen, but sex with Helen was the farthest thing from his mind at the moment. Shed splinters were flying all around. It was the wildest ride he'd ever been on. It was amazing how much nitro was packed into her body. She attacked but was smart enough, or experienced enough, to know that a gentle attack would drive him the furthest off the chart. Amidst all the intensity, he had a moment of an inside laugh when the thought of the word *cowboy* flashed through his mind as she was riding. The way she went from a walk to a gallop and back to a walk was unbearably wonderful. Then it was his turn to take charge, and it was obvious that she was not faking anything. Their coupling had a marvelous unhurried intensity to it.

They were both spent and soaked afterwards. After a respite and a quick shower, they had another go. This time, she moved like a panther with tease, and then a little willingness, then backing-off with tease again. If her intent was to drive him crazy again, she more than succeeded.

They showered again. They barely dried off before Wan nudged him into bed and snuggled up against him. He was happy just to be with her.

"What you thinking?" Wan asked.

"Why do you ask?"

"You look thinking."

He didn't say anything, of course, but he *had* begun thinking of Helen, now that the fireworks with Wan had died down. Their sex life had been fine. In fact, he loved having sex with her. She was a loving and a skillful participant, but Wan had brought sex into a whole different territory, one that he had never known existed.

"I was thinking it's great being in bed with you," he said quickly, trying to cover the moment's silence. Then, changed the subject, "How long have been working at Sunshine Delight?"

"Three month."

"Ever gone out with a man before?"

"One time?"

"What was it like?"

"Him get drunk. I sit with him."

"That was it?"

She nodded.

"Tell me about growing up."

Michael just lay there listening, learning that she had grown up dirt poor in the northeastern province, that she was the fifth child, and that her family was so poor that they could not feed another mouth, which, as it happened, was hers. Very early on she was sent to live with her grandmother and grandfather in a village that was a one-day walk from her home. Her grandmother was strict, and when Wan turned four, her grandmother gave her chores from morning to night, with the exception of Sundays. Her only toys were a bicycle tire rim, which she learned how to keep rolling over rough terrain, and a doll, that was more an object of escape and comfort than it was a plaything. Wan loved her grandfather who was very kind. He was also very smart and could repair anything with makeshift tools and materials. At the insistence of her grandfather, Wan was relieved from enough chores so that she could attend the village school, such as it was. She became the best student in English and arithmetic. Her determination and performance did not escape notice in the village.

At fifteen, an older man, mid-fifties and the richest in the village, expressed an interest in marriage. Wan said no, but her grandmother insisted she marry him because they, too, with increasing age, were having a difficult time with an extra mouth.

One night, she packed up her few things, a little food, and ran away. She had no sandals, and her feet were bloody by the time she reached her family's village. She had not seen any of them in more than a decade. They barely recognized her at first. Two of her brothers had died, and her parents were worn and aged. She told them of her determination to go to Bangkok and somehow they manage to find the money for sandals and a bus ticket.

Penniless in Bangkok, she was left with the same option that any girl from the country in a similar situation faced. Wan was young and attractive but the bars would not hire her because she was under eighteen. She was forced to the street.

Drake had already impressed upon Michael that family was *king* in Thailand, and that daughters were responsible for the well being of their aging parents. "Family, it's a steel trap," Drake said. "For a Thai daughter to live in the city and not send any money to parents, oh, bad, bad daughter. That's where I come in." He laughed. "But Mama, she always knows. Papa, he likes to believe some bullshit story."

Wan started to tell Michael about being so young and alone in this huge city. "Pretty street girl wear nice clothes taken first. Me taken last. Man he rough. When he know I virgin, he give me 500 Baht more. I cry all night. Me want to kill self. I buy pretty clothes. Other girls tell me how make money. But I no like street. Eighteen I get bar job. Now life better, but no good. I send money to Mama and Papa. No money for self. I study English. English good for good job. You think?"

Michael nodded.

She spent the night with him. She was not accustomed to the air conditioning and used Michael for warmth. He gave her double what they had agreed to that night, and for each night after the first. She was frisky, mischievous and playful without fail, and he loved being with her. They took many of their meals via room service. She watched soaps while he read, and he helped her with English every day.

One day, he took her to see the Big Buddha Temple. He carried a pack with him. When they were ready to return, he asked to wait two minutes before she followed. At the bottom of the stairs, she found that new shoes had replaced her worn-out pumps. They were four-inch heels naturally.

That night, afterward, she lay snuggled up next to him for warmth.

"I want to ask you something."

She nodded.

Even though Michael had been practicing safe sex, he asked, "What about AIDS?"

Wan explained that the bar girls went for a VD examination every week and had an AIDS test every month. They had to have their health card stamped. Wan showed him hers. "No stamp, no work. Even police bar."

"What does this say?" he asked pointing to upper right corner.

"Birthday."

"So how old are you."

"Eighteen." She held up a finger. "Plus one day."

"Come on."

"Nineteen."

He raised his brows, doing the quick math.

"Yes, it say nineteen."

"You were only asked out one other time?"

"Men look at stage. Think we no go. No number, they no ask."

Michael described another hostess.

"Cindy?"

"The one who greets you?"

"Cindy."

"She's very nice."

"What about me?"

"You number one."

"Good. Cindy no go out."

"Really?"

"She university student. Hostess summer for money."

"You're not just saying that?"

"No."

"You were talking with another hostess before we left."

"Somo. My best friend. She like you."

"Not my type."

"Still like you."

Waiting for the right time to schedule a meet with the Jim Thompson people left Michael with a ton of unexpected free time. He found that he had watched BBC news enough times to already detest its introductory music, and had finished the books he had brought. He was thankful that Asia Books was nearby despite the fact that the books were expensive—three times the USA price—but he bought two and plowed through them quickly. The bottom line was that, with him and Drake determined to have the Thai's make the first move regarding the details, he had more free time on his hands than he wanted or was accustomed to having.

He and Drake had coffee together every afternoon at a small place a block from Michael's hotel.

"So how are things with Miss Wan?"

"She's a pistol. And a very nice person."

"So how many dips a day?"

"Three. Most days."

"Impressive. I thought that might be a real stretch for you."

"I am younger than you, you know. Don't make judgments by slipping into projection—to use psychological terminology."

Drake laughed. "Ah, a shot fired back. You are coming around. That's encouraging. Three times, eh?"

"Most days."

"Four?"

"Not yet. Anyway."

"Two—she likes you. Three—she wants you to stay with her. Four—she admires you."

"And five?"

"She's scared shitless."

"Six?"

"You're scared you're going to disappoint her. Someday."

"I won't ask any more numbers."

"I would have told you when you got to mine."

"Some people don't consider zero as a number," Michael countered with a smile.

Drake laughed. "You're starting to sound like me. I want credit as your teacher."

Michael was happy to have Wan around, and she was content, shopping for fruits and vegetables and pre-cooked dishes for them to eat in the room when they didn't take room service or watch TV. She was always ready for another romp. Three times a day was just fine with her. She was a continuous bundle of exploratory energy, and was happy to stay with Michael. It was all a kind of blissful hiatus from the stress of the previous months for Michael.

Michael and Drake met with senior representatives of the Jim Thompson Silk Company at Thompson's Bangkok headquarters. After three hours of cautious negotiations, the Thai's finally went first in proposing specific terms that were naturally too lean on all key points. By prearrangement, Michael remained stern and quiet while Drake asked them about the details in Thai, on the assumption that their translation into English must have been flawed. Three hours of discussions ensued, all of it gracious, resulting in little movement toward agreement, other than delivery guarantees and penalties for late deliveries. It was agreed, however that each side would reconsider all the points and concerns raised by the other side on the other issues. Michael demurred on setting a date for the next meeting until after he and Drake had developed a counter-proposal.

Drake, unbeknownst to Michael, had made plane reservations to the resort island of Samui in the Gulf of Siam for the entire following week. He told the Jim Thompson representatives that he and Michael had business to attend to in another country, and when Michael found out, he posited the idea to Drake of taking Wan along.

"When you go to the restaurant, you don't bring your own food."

"Well, what about this Dawn you said you were taking?"

"She's utensils. Have to treat her to a vacation now and then."

That night, he told Wan he was leaving on a trip. He did not say where, just that it was business. He gave her an extra 10,000 Baht.

"Me want see you more."

"I hope so."

"You come bar. You come soon?"

"I'll try."

"Me wait you. Me love you." She said this last thing in a way that resonated truth, a desparate truth that Michael felt in his gut.

The plane touched down on the short runway. An open-air mini-bus took them to a set of buildings well disguised as anything but a terminal. Drake shook his head as Michael's two suitcases and duffel bag were loaded into the trunk of a taxi. The three of them piled into the packed car, Michael, Drake, and Dawn, who was cherubic and oval faced. She smiled a lot, it seemed like most of the time, and even when she was not smiling her face was. She no longer sported the trim figure she once had, but she was still slender by American standards. She spoke English slowly, painfully, and not well. Another smile accompanied by a short laugh told you that she was stuck again in an English construction, searching for a word or a phrase. There were a lot of short nearly nervous giggles as Drake pushed her to speak English.

At first, Dawn seemed a bit simple, but she was hardly that. She was an astute observer and missed little. She even picked up some nuances in a language she barely understood. Dawn was early thirties and given that Drake's preference was for the *legal age of consent*, his attachment to her was all the more surprising. Drake confided to Michael that Dawn was insatiable in bed. Nevertheless, Drake often found it necessary to leave her alone for a few hours in the Bangkok apartment he had rented for her to attend to other business—the monkey kind. Michael was sure she knew. As for her predilections and goings-on during Drake's long trips to other countries, trips of sometimes several months, the presumption by Drake was that Dawn was chaste. "I ought to hire a dick just to make sure. But I'm just a cheap prick," he once told Michael dismissively.

Koh Samui was a yet undiscovered tourist island. It was mostly overgrown and verdant, and only had one paved section of road through its main town. There was a Buddha Temple further north of the center, but the town itself was comprised of two outdoor bars, one dance bar, three restaurants, one lady's clothing store, an art gallery, a gas station, a transportation rental store, a handful of taxis, local housing, and a government administration building. Adjacent to the main road, there were a dozen beach resorts, all well kept and adequate to accommodate the light tourist traffic.

The sea there was a beautiful azure, with its warm water and gently sloped sandy-bed. It was idyllic, and nothing like Michael had ever experienced.

Drake rented two bungalows at the Bann Mann Resort. Drake's was fifty feet from the water, had a king-size bed, a real closet, and a full bath. Michael's was the next one back and had twin beds separated by a night table, one chair, no closet and a shower without a bathtub. The early evening ritual began the first night—sitting on the veranda of Drake's bungalow, listening to the slosh of the waves, eating smoked almonds and cashews, drinking vodka with something, and talking about Thai culture, politics, history, or science. Dawn smiled and took little of it in, but always seemed content with a second round of whatever it was they were drinking. Once in a while, Drake translated some snippet of the conversation, and she would nod.

"Goddamned American women," Drake said, commenting about the sexual differences between Asian and Western women. "They only shower afterwards. Never before. Thai's are so much more civilized."

That first night at around eight o'clock they all went to the fully outdoor bar called O'Neill's. Five bargirls were sitting around at two tables waiting for customers that is, all but one, Joy, who was waiting for her Englishman to show up. One of the bargirls sat on Michael's lap and hugged him. Dawn, who was on her third vodka of the evening, found this amusing and giggled. The bargirl was pleasant, acting as if she was just kidding, which of course she was not, and Michael gently edged her off and laughed along with the joke.

"Dawn will find you the right girl," Drake said. "She's great at interviewing. Takes it seriously."

Joy stood up ceremonially. All eyes went to her. "Today's my birthday," she announced, "I am twenty-two." Everyone clapped, and the bartender brought out something approximating a cake, cut it into eight slices, and Joy handed each of the girls a party favor: a pink condom. Michael bought Joy and the other four girls a drink. All ordered whiskey—undoubtedly the diluted kind. That made a big hit with the girls, as that drink alone would cover their minimum for the night, at least as far as O'Neill's was concerned. It made an even bigger hit when Michael ordered them all a second drink before they had finished the first. Michael and Drake contented themselves with a beer each.

As they were laughing and flirting over these two rounds, a young woman emerged from the dilapidated shack that O'Neill's offered up as a restroom. She wore a blue blouse and a sheer, flowing skirt that came down four inches below her knees. She had long, shimmering black hair that flowed down to her lower back. She had a wholesomeness that emanated from her that none of the other girls came close to. Even slightly unsteady she walked with natural grace. It was an intoxicating motion that took Michael's breath away. As she approached, she looked uncommonly pale, and at first Michael thought she had OD'ed on whitening cream. *Anything to make your skin whiter was good in Thailand,* Michael thought, remembering that the ads on the TV soaps that Wan watched more often that not featured products that promised to make your skin lighter. *Not so unlike in the U.S,* he mused, *when a foreigner watching TV there would assume that all Americans were obsessed with cars, beer, and their medical ailments.* This girl's whiteness, however, stemmed from another cause. She had just thrown up.

"This my sister, Malee," Joy said. "She come today mine birthday. I make her drink. She no like drink. She get sick. I sorry I make her drink." There was some vomit stuck on the left side of Malee's hair. Michael beckoned her to an empty seat next to him, summoned the bartender and, with a towel and water, cleaned it off. Malee was embarrassed, but she was feeling too ill to show it much. She started to feel through the rest of her hair. Michael made a reassuring hand sign. She gave him a weak smile of thanks.

"Would you like a little water?" Michael asked.

She nodded shyly in the affirmative, just once.

After a few minutes of sitting there, next to Michael, she was feeling well enough to take a sip.

Dawn pulled her chair up next to Malee and engaged her in a pleasant prattle as Malee recovered, but Drake gave Michael a significant stare. Soon, the two girls were having a time of it, all smiles, giggles, and heads turning in feigned embarrassment. Eventually Dawn came over to Michael. "Her girl for you. Her very nice," Dawn said to Michael, then whispered to him when Drake was not looking, "not like others."

Connect Four, a kind of vertical tick-tack-toe game, was set up on one of the tables. As Malee's complexion had assumed its natural milky-almond color, a sure sign that she was feeling better, Malee gestured, silently asking if she would like to play. Michael pulled his chair up closer, and they began a friendly bout while sitting side by side. Michael was unfamiliar with the game but understood the gist of it immediately. He thought he would go easy on her. She won. He paid more attention. She won the next three games. The others found this exceedingly funny and raised their glasses to her. Michael, the gracious and increasingly smitten opponent, did too.

As Dawn began to feel confident with her handiwork, she got up from watching Malee and Michael, and rejoined Drake at another table, vacating a spot next to Malee. An overweight German who had shown up a few minutes earlier took an interest in the game and invited himself to the empty chair. He was smoking like a chimney. At the end of the next round, Malee gestured to Michael to change places with her. "Me no like smoke," she whispered. Their bodies touched as she passed behind him. As gentle as the contact was, it reaffirmed the firmness of her breasts. Despite the rapidly repeating thoughts about Malee's obvious *charms* that were cycling through his mind, Michael toughened up, focused, and won both of the next two games. Malee clapped.

Another German showed up to the bar, took an interest in the game, and pulled a chair up next to Malee, pushing into an already tight spot. He pulled in too close for Malee's comfort, and she edged her chair closer to Michael. Squeezed closer together, her leg brushed against Michael's. Instinctively she pulled her leg away from contact, but she caught his eye, immediately looking a little abashed, and turned her attention back to the game. The recently arrived German, intent on studying the play of the game, or, more likely intent on Malee, leaned in closer. The German's foul breath wafted over to Michael. Malee shifted away from the odor, inadvertently forcing Michael's left leg make full contact with her thigh. Michael pressed back, slightly. It was delicious contact, her heat flowing through her diaphanous skirt. He felt her press back, now, into his leg, stronger, too. Her leg agitated up and down in a rapid motion, as might be the case if one were nervous, for example, about how to counter an opponent's latest move. He couldn't focus. As her leg bounced next to his he felt her muscles through the skirt, and with each bounce he found it harder and harder to concentrate. She turned momentarily, looking up from the game. A wide innocent grin crossed her face, making her eyes smile too. A spark inside him ignited his desire. And though he exposed no outward sign of it, he was starting to feel a kind of gravitational pull that he had not felt since he first met Helen. But this was all together different— more immediate, more intense.

He lost that round, while Malee smiled a victorious smile.

"No, no," the smoker said in his version of English, "you must have to here instead. You don't see right." Michael liked the smoke and the advice in equal measure.

By nine o'clock, Joy's Englishman arrived—forties, complete with a bad haircut, a ruddy complexion and looking slightly emaciated. She greeted him with a quick kiss.

Michael learned later that the Englishman was paying her 12,000 Baht for the week.

The other four bargirls had not scored yet, and Michael bought them another round. He was now their image of the ideal firang: clean and trim and rich and easy with the money. One of them said he had beautiful eyes and gravitated to him, standing just to his side. The other bar girls laughed encouragement. She asked with her hip rubbing his arm if he were interested. Michael was politely unresponsive, and she retreated to her stool, feigning just harmless playfulness.

While all were still engaged watching the rounds of Connect Four, two blond, blue-eyed young Swedes entered the bar. The bar girls were agog and quickly clustered around Adonis and his twin brother. Yes, the two young men were happy to spot them a drink. They fished through their pockets and, between the two, were able to scrounge up enough for the four girls and themselves. The girls were friendly enough until the drinks were gone, but then their interest drifted away as they resumed their lookout for richer fare.

"Would you like something else to drink?" Michael asked Malee.

"No, no." She rubbed her tummy.

"Some tea, I mean."

"Okay, tea. Okay."

"I'll get you some."

Michael had to push past the bad-breathed German to extricate himself, and pressed hard enough to make it clear that Bad-breath needed to shift his chair further away from Malee.

Malee took the tea in small sips, testing her stomach. In sitting back down, Michael sprawled his torso toward the Chimney to block him from advancing closer to Malee while she re-initiated leg contact, modestly, letting Michael increase the pressure. Midway through the next game, feeling a little claustrophobic from the continued press by the two Germans, Michael stopped and turned to Malee asking, "Why don't we go for a walk?"

She averted her eyes. "Me talk sister first."

Joy excused herself from her date while she and Malee conferred in hushed tones off in a corner. Then Joy went over to Dawn, and they talked. Finally, Joy came back to Michael. "Me sister very good. Her no work like me. Dawn say you good man. My sister look good man."

Michael nodded. He gestured for Malee to stand up. She hesitated for a split second before arising. He dropped a bill on the table more than sufficient for the tab and led her out of O'Neill's.

They walked closely, their fingers occasionally touching as their arms swayed. There was an exchanged of electricity each time there was contact. They happened upon the only art gallery in Samui as they walked further up the street. Each chose their favorite painting; it was the same one, a vase of flowers in watercolor only half finished with the rest still in a penciled outline. "Me like. Tell things come. Good things. They come. Pretty colors come. Me think good painting," Malee shyly expressed her preference and optimism.

As they left the gallery Michael looked at Malee and turned her to him, "I'm staying close by, down by the water. Let's go sit and listen to the ocean."

They stopped back at O'Neill's on their way to his bungalow. Drake and Dawn were still there as were the two Germans, the latter in the thick of Connect Four, their consolation prize—the Chimney looked like he was besting Bad-breath. Adonis and his twin were gone as were Joy and her date. None of the four bargirls had scored. One of them toasted to Michael. He waited while Malee fetched a small cotton sack. As they were readying to leave, Dawn gave him a smiling wink. Drake sidled up to him, "You owe Dawn big time," he whispered.

The path to the bungalows was rutted and dimly lit by path lights, half of which were broken. He carried her sack and took her hand to guide her.

At the beach, they removed their shoes—his Docksiders and her plain flat sandals. He rolled up his pant legs. She held her skirt well above her knees. They sloshed in the ripples along the shoreline, walking toward where the lights of the next resort shined. On the way back, they held hands.

"I no see big water nighttime."

"Never?"

"No."

"Where do you live?"

"Bangkok."

"You came far. How did you travel here?"

"Me no understand."

"Boat?"

"Train. Then boat."

"Long trip."

She nodded.

"You like big water nighttime?"

"I like sound. I like, um…" she scooped up some wet sand.

"Sand," he said.

"San. And I like san and…" she demonstrated by holding one foot out of the water.

"You like sand between the toes?"

She repeated "san between the toes" several times. "What fish live big water?"

"Little fish."

"No eat me?"

"No eat you. No eat me," he said pointing to each of them in turn. "Little fish. We eat them."

"Better that way."

"Yes, I think so," he laughed.

They returned to the beach. Lights from their resort danced on the rippling tide.

"I want look at big water. Light so pretty." They sat on the sand and apart from some distant laughter now and again the only sound was the surf rolling in and over the beach. He watched her gazing out over the water.

"Where do you stay?"

"Sleep Joy bed."

"Two of you in the bed?"

"No now. Now Joy man in bed. I sleep chair big room."

"That's okay?"

"Mai dee."

"What?"

"No good," she translated. She made a circular turn of her head holding her neck. "Morning, no good here. Very um, I no know word."

He put his hands on her neck. "Neck."

"Nik no good morning." She resumed looking at the water.

"Sore neck." He demonstrated by rubbing his neck and grimacing.

She repeated, "sore nik."

"Yes. Are you cold?"

"Little cold."

"Wait here." He returned a minute later with a blanket and a towel. He dried off her feet with the towel, then sat next to her, draping the blanket over both of their shoulders. He scooped up sand and sifted it through his fingers onto her toes and asked about her life.

Michael listened intently as she told her story—broken English phrases spoken in unguarded earnestness made the telling that much more endearing, Michael thinking to himself that *English was a marvelous language. You can butcher it and still be understood.* He made out that Malee lived in Bangkok and worked as a seamstress, piecemeal work, really. Six ten-hour days per week for 4500 Baht a month left her with an aching back, strained eyes, and puncture wounds. She lived with a female roommate in a dingy one-room flat without air conditioning and one bathroom for the whole floor. If she skimped on meals, she could save enough for a bus and boat trip to Samui to visit her sister once a year. She never had money to help out her parents as Joy did, and this made her feel like a bad daughter. Put succinctly, she had a poverty level job with no opportunity for advancement and no way to meet a future husband. Such was one of the paths for uneducated, pretty young women trying to escape the grinding poverty of the farm fields, leaving home only to find poverty in the city. Malee was like so many others. It hurt Michael to think about this, about how lovely she was and how limited her choices seemed to be. Lost in his reverie and the sound of her voice, her feet were already buried above the ankles by the time they left beach. He held her hands while helping to steady her as she unburied herself. Never letting go, he escorted her to his cabin.

The bungalow was just the one room and a shower with a curtain serving as the bathroom door. The window drapes closed for privacy or mostly closed anyway. The air conditioner had two settings: low and noisy. The shower had hot water as long as you ran it no faster than a trickle. He put her sack down next to one of his suitcases. They sat on one of the beds side-by-side, close but not touching. With Malee, it was different. He felt like a grade-school boy on his first date, already besotted not knowing what to say. He assumed she would raise the issue of price, but she said nothing. He smiled nervously at her. She reciprocated and then looked down.

He let his fingers drift over the top of her nearest hand. She looked at him again and smiled. His feelings toward her were already so strong, finding himself amazed at how gently and quickly she had enchanted him.

Then the transition—he moved his hand, resting it on her thigh, mid-way up, a respectable distance, his thumb sliding back and forth. She placed her hand over his; it was a light touch, not intended to stop him, but rather to join him. They sat like this for a couple of minutes. With his other hand he ran his fingers over her forehead and let it descend ever so slowly over the top of her nose, over her lips, down the chin and neck and into the valley. She did not resist or stiffen. He cupped a hand over one of the firm hillocks.

"I wash first," she said.

"Wait."

The room was configured wrong for sleeping together. Even at this late hour, Michael found two maids who made the necessary adjustments, moving the night table against a different wall, finding a new plug for the lamp. They pushed the two twin beds together and turned them ninety degrees so that the separation was perpendicular to the way they would sleep. They then installed a form fitted bottom sheet over what now was a king-size bed, and tucked in a king-size top sheet and light cotton blanket. All the while, Malee watched the bustling activity while sitting in the one chair seemingly, or so Michael thought, without embarrassment or unease—her calmness only increasing her desirability.

As the maids were leaving and the room returned to a peaceful quiet, Malee arose, looked at Michael, lifted up her hair to the top of her head and gestured. He found her a shower cap, watched her as she closed the curtain, and then heard the shower turned on full, quickly turned down until it was just above a trickle. She showered for ten minutes and re-emerged with the towel wrapped around her the way every woman wraps a towel after bathing. Michael's shower was three minutes at the most. He wrapped his towel at the waist. She had folded back the blanket and the top sheet.

They sat on the bed. He caressed her shoulders and cheeks with his fingertips. With her eyes, she followed his fingers when on her shoulders and looked straight at him when they toyed with her cheeks.

"Your tummy okay?"

She did not comprehend.

He rubbed her stomach in a circular motion, questioningly.

"Good," she said.

"You are so very… I don't know what… special. I'm not even sure I'm here."

She did not understand the words, but she understood what he had said.

"You no fat like other firang. Pretty nose. Good nose. Nose strong, man good fortune. Dawn like you nose, too. Her say me."

They both laughed. And they sat, looking into each other's eyes. Michael felt an ache, not the kind that the word usually connotes. It was the pang of anticipated wonderment, and he wanted it, to hold it, to let it linger as he savored it, even though to linger was unbearable. She must have understood that too, or maybe she even felt the same, because she invited him with her eyes. He put his hand to where she had folded her towel. It rested there as if unwilling to open the present, not wanting to end this delicious moment. She gave the towel a little tug, and it fell away.

Michael had always found a woman more sexually appealing wearing suggestive, alluring clothing in a state of partial undress rather than naked—for him, promises of things to come trumped things that already had. He had never spoken of this mindset to his friends who all seemed to share the opposite viewpoint. For the first time in his life, Michael was aligned with his friends.

He turned the night table light on. Malee shielded the light with a hand in front of her eyes. "No light. Me shy." Michael turned the light off. Facing the headboard of the newly configured bed, Malee said a short prayer to Buddha—a ritual Michael soon learned she performed each time before they made love. Finished, she lay back on the bed as smoothly as if she were moving through water. Her breasts lost none of their uplift. She was shaved except for a thin line of black hair in the middle. Michael was breathing through his mouth. He kissed her lips. Her mouth opened to the exploration of tongues. She gently pushed him back and turned her head away.

"Suck my milk," she whispered.

Under his lips, her breasts grew firmer and firmer and then hard, and the little temples on the two hills rose to full height, and she came with little yelps. Each yelp sounded like a failed attempt to suppress sound. Finally, she lifted his head off. She wanted to shower again. He wanted her to stay. She showered, much quicker this time. As he waited, he removed a little box from the pocket of his folded pants on the chair next to his side of the bed. He studied the picture on it—a silhouetted couple in a standing embrace. Below it was written, "Paquet de 4 Capotes."

She climbed back into bed. She was not a blushing virgin, Michael quickly discovered as her little whimpers gave way to moans. She signaled what she wanted more of with the palm of her hand on his upper arm, moving faster and faster until he reached her preferred tempo. Sounds lifted from their lips and encircled them as they climaxed together. It was the most complete and right sound he had ever heard. Though Malee knew nothing of the Richter scale, she must have realized that something within Michael had just slipped like a tectonic plate. The first time she was surprised by its magnitude. Then amused by the number and intensity of aftershocks and the prolonged body-wide shivering as if he were freezing, a shivering she had never experienced before.

They were drenched in sweat. She wanted to shower again, but this time he would not let go. After things had calmed, she laughed softly.

"What?"

"You come. You come big."

"That good or bad?"

"Good."

"I too big?"

"No."

"Thai men big?"

"Me say no."

"Good or no good?"

"Small but very hard."

"So…good?"

"So, okay. But you better."

"So you've been with Thai men?"

"One."

"Tell me about him."

"Husband."

"You're married?"

"Me divorce."

"I see," he said with a relief that he did not expect.

They slept with his arms and legs wrapped around her. God knows how she slept entrapped that way, but she did. At first Michael did not fall asleep. Instead he watched the slow heave of her chest. He studied his sleeping beauty. Her skin was so smooth and her face in such repose that he could not help wondering who it was who was entrapped.

Then, as he drifted toward sleep, he recalled that once as a boy, while hiking in steep country near their summer home in the Pacific Northwest, he had slipped on loose rock and had fallen off a ledge. He was in free fall, for how long he didn't know, falling to his death, but it was with an overwhelming regret, not fear. How strange, not to be afraid while plunging to one's death. And then, the upper bough of a fir slowed his fall a little, and each bough below it a little more until finally he was not falling. He was cradled in a bough. He wasn't sure if he was alive. Maybe this was how death felt. But then he realized that he was breathing, and surprisingly that he was *not in pain. If he was seriously hurt, he thought, he could not feel it. Maybe this meant that he was badly hurt because he had read about soldiers who sometimes did not know that they were wounded, even badly wounded, until later.* He felt around. No. His jacket was torn beyond recovery. Skin scratched everywhere. Small bleeding wounds on each leg. His shoulder was sore. That was all. He never told anyone about this except Jay, many years later, thinking then that maybe he did not tell anyone else because he could not figure how he could describe this sensation to someone who had not experienced it—*they listen to your words and think they understand, but they don't. They can't.*

At first, he thought that the same thing was true about what he felt with Malee, that deep twinge that began that first night. But still, in a way, he *was* trying to describe it, maybe because a few lucky people would know what he meant.

Michael and Malee missed the ten-thirty cut-off for breakfast, but the waitresses paid no mind. They joined Drake and Dawn, who were finishing a second coffee. The dining area was a covered veranda with overhead fans on low, creating a lovely breeze. A quarter of the dining area was still in sunlight. Their table was at the far end of the shade. Breakfast was pretty much what you ordered. The orange juice looked suspect, a Thai version of Hi-C or worse. But it was real and fresh squeezed, and Michael had four glasses.

Drake leaned over. "The sound-proof ones are over there," he nodded at a set of smaller bungalows further back. It was

not the last time when the girls' limited English proved helpful.

"Right," Michael said with a laugh. "How come you're up
so early?"

"Swimming. She'll only go in before the sun's up. And
she still carries a fucking umbrella. We did our sleeping in
the water." He laughed. "I mean, watching her try to escape
from me holding her umbrella. Bloody thing got soaked. She
ruined it. Anyway, afterwards she didn't mind. I told her we
were like fish."

"So what's the plan for today?"

"She wants to buy shoes. No fucking way I'm going shopping for shoes. I gave her some money and told her to take
Malee. That okay?"

"Sure."

"That way Dawn can learn how her handiwork is working
out," he said with a wink.

"Malee has too much class for that."

Drake wanted to check out some old haunts in town. So when
the girls when hunting for shoes, Michael and Drake walked
to the outskirts where Drake found the shop from which he
had rented motorcycles the last time he was on Samui. It was
still in business. In the afternoon, they swam. The girls had
returned from shopping, but they did not join in.

That evening, Drake had arranged for dinner on the beach
with table and chairs surrounded by a hexagon of kerosene
lanterns. The land breeze was gentle, and there was nothing
flying around that wanted to bite you. Twenty feet from the
table was an assortment of food on a large well lit-up table.
Fish and shellfish from the day's catch were laid out on ice,
along with fruit and vegetables of all description. There was
also a large bowl of salad greens. You picked out what you
wanted, and the attendant went off to cook the things that
needed cooking.

When the main course arrived, Malee removed the skin and deboned Michael's fish. Then she insisted on feeding him. Dawn did likewise for Drake. Neither girl would begin her meal until both Michael and Drake were satisfied. Malee and Dawn demurred on dessert. Dawn pointed to her waist and laughed. A third bottle of wine was opened. Dawn was far enough along that she spilled half her drink. Malee was only drinking water.

Drake leaned back in his chair. "Does it get any better than this?"

The next night, they arrived at O'Neill's around eight o'clock. Malee rushed to meet Joy. They spoke so fast that Drake could not follow. "What're they saying?" he asked Dawn.

She giggled. "They talk Michael." She finished the rest in Thai.

"So?" Michael asked Drake.

"Malee said you're a big prick."

"Useless to ask you anything."

"No. I just don't give straight answers. That's all."

By ten o'clock that night, the four of them repaired to their respective bungalows, and Joy headed off with her Englishman.

Michael and Malee sat on the bed. Michael stroked her hair. She gazed into his eyes, not boldly, and not in a way that made him uncomfortable. No, she looked at him in a way that any man would wish a woman would gaze at him. He undressed her slowly, and he neatly folded each article of clothing, setting them on the chair, then they took the customary shower. He would have liked to shower with her, but the shower was, at best, sized for one person. In bed, Michael turned the light on again. Malee protested politely. "No," he said, "from now on, the light stays on. So I can admire you all the time."

They took things slowly. He could not help touching her, gently. Her breathing gradually deepened. They made love. It was of a kind that he had never experienced before. As they crescendoed together, her body became rigid, her skin temperature went to sizzle, her breathing froze for maybe fifteen seconds, and then she just exploded into an out-of-control orgasm so physical that he had to hold on as he came with her. Her abdomen contracted again and again and again. He held her tight, and he just wanted to hold her tighter still and become as one together. Afterwards, she went completely limp. Her breathing was shallow, silent panting, and her eyes were half-closed.

Her eyes opened more fully, "Me go pee-pee."

"No, stay here with me."

"No. Me go. Me go. Me come back."

With her thighs squeezed together, she ran as fast as she could to the bathroom. He heard the toilet flush and then the shower turn on.

She returned towel wrapped and climb into bed and snuggled next to him.

"You showered again?"

"Me all wet."

"You were wet so you decided to get wetter?"

"Me no understand."

"Oh, nothing. I love you showered, unshowered, reshowered, deshowered, preshowered, postshowered, subshowered."

"Me big no understand."

"I love you." It just came out. He was so enraptured, so happy to be with her that the words just gushed out of him.

"Lak Michael."

"Lak?"

"I love."

"I just want to hold you."

"Me like hold."

Michael and Malee left early for O'Neill's the next day. On the way they passed an old crippled army veteran. He was sitting on the sidewalk, in the shade, leaning against a building. Both of his legs were missing below the knee, what else might have been missing was not discernable. He wore a tattered army shirt with a medal on the left side. In one hand, he held a shiny army mug. There were a few small denomination coins at the bottom. He did not press the mug out toward Michael, nor say anything. Michael halted and dropped some money into cup, the kind that makes no clinking sound. The old man put down the cup and bowed once. Michael nodded, and they walked on.

Malee slipped her arm through his. "Khun Michael good man." Drake told him later that the prefix "Khun" was the most polite way to address someone.

"No. More sad than good," Michael responded.

She did not ask him what he meant, but instead tugged him closer to her and smiled up at him. From that moment on, she always addressed him as Khun Michael, and, after he learned the meaning, he addressed her as Khun Malee.

The two couples waited for Joy to get to the bar around her customary eight o'clock arrival time. She showed up in a good mood. Her Englishman, now departed, had given her 15,000 Baht. She and Malee chatted for five minutes before an American who had just showed up quickly took a hankering to Joy. His paunch spelled money and Joy exuded vivaciousness and enthusiasm, the kind that would interest a pot-bellied American sitting alone at a bar in Samui. She had bold, friendly eyes, with no pretense there. Plus she spoke better English that any of the other girls, having learned it from her many one or two-week engagements.

Joy's allure was not of the usual kind. She sported dark skin; impossible to avoid living on a beach resort island. Her face was less than an ideal shape—too round from the eyes up and too long from the nose down—and it was also pocked with mostly old, but two new, pimples. But, that didn't matter to the men that Joy was attracting. She had a to-die-for figure and clothes that broadcast that asset, or, as Drake put it, "Fuck-me-clothes." She was always the first to be picked, and after three rounds of drinks, gratis the American, she and he left together.

The next night, Joy took Michael aside as soon as she arrived. "Me tell you. Sister lose job if no return to Bangkok tomorrow. She no know how tell you."

"I understand. I will take care of things. I will take care of Malee."

"Me know you good man."

Over the course of a few days, Malee and Michael developed a post-lunch routine when the heat of the day suggested one might be better served indoors. Michael gave her English lessons, and she was an attentive pupil—if not a little amused that a firang would want to teach her English—and she was a quick learner. At the outset, her favorite expressions were: "what's up?" (a typical American slang term that she loved), "you've got to be kidding" (she said Joy could use that one), "here's looking at you" (despite that fact that it had little utility for a tea drinker), and "rain check". There were benefits to these lessons. A Thai woman speaking decent English had job opportunities open to her, opportunities that would otherwise be non-existent. And they conversed a little better, allowing for more banter, playfulness, and heightened intensity during sex.

While sometimes feigning shyness, Malee was always willing, even during her period, the only difference being that then she insisted on laying out towels underneath which she later cleaned in cold water. Michael loved her willingness and her graciousness—graciousness to such a level that only the French had found the word: gentillesse.

The Thai, by and large, were a gracious people; it permeated their culture. But even by Thai standards Malee stood out as unique. *If only they could export their graciousness to America,* Michael thought, *what a finer country we would be.*

It would be a mistake, however, to equate this graciousness with any national sense of weakness or inferiority. To the contrary, when Drake and Michael were in Bangkok they were held up from crossing a street as a Thai regiment passed in perfect lockstep on its way to celebrate the opening of a new government building. Michael sensed right away that these soldiers, properly lead, were as good as the best soldiers of any other army; and Thai generals and officers had a reputation of competence. How else could Thailand have remained independent with a Giant Dragon not so far from their northern border?

Malee had been asking to visit the big Buddha Temple after the first few days of being with Michael. It was situated on a bay about ten kilometers from town, and finally they decided to go. Before going he took her to the one clothing store in town where he let her pick out a new blouse and skirt along with matching shoes—she wanted to look her best on the visit. The skirt was long, the same as she had worn when he had first met her, but the fabric was so sheer that it rode her contours with each step. Watching the skirt play with her legs, Michael tripped over an uneven elevation in the sidewalk. She led him to a motorbike taxi stand with the intent that the three of them would ride together. Michael hailed a regular taxi. "That too expensive," she said. Michael viewed it as cheap life insurance and insisted. She negotiated the cab fare, the wait, and the ride back. It was a five-minute negotiation.

The back seat had so little leg room that even she had to splay her legs against the back of the front seat. The skirt dropped against her inner thighs and undulated in the wind coming through the open windows. She put her hands over her skirt to quiet it down. He lifted her hands off, and she laughed softly. The driver glanced at them through his rear view mirror, giving a kind of knowing glance that Michael caught before the driver looked again to the road. Michael did not take in much of the scenery on the drive out. He was already happy with big Buddha.

At the sacred complex, Malee and Michael had to ascend a long, wide staircase barefoot. He placed his shoes next to one of the seemingly hundreds of pairs already there. Malee put her new shoes next to his. As Thai shoes never came in his size, he was wary about leaving them unattended, but there was no option. She read his thoughts. "No one take. Ever."

The temple's dome was gilded in gold leaf, and for a contribution of some small, but seemingly, standard amount you could buy a square of gold leaf to further adorn it. This despite the fact that there were so many gold leaf wafers that they were piled on top of one another three or four deep. With girllike enthusiasm Malee took Michael's hand and led him to all the attractions. First there were the urns overlooking one side of the bay. Malee told him how much money they should put in each one and what type of good tidings each would bring— health, children, wealth, long life, and so on. He gave her the money for the offerings, pleasing her immensely. She bowed in prayer after each deposit. She half-skipped with him, shuffling in tow to the candles. They each lit one, touched them together, melted wax to hold up the bottoms, gave a prayer and left an offering. She insisted that he make a prayer of his own. "What did you pray for?" he asked. "I will tell you. I prayed for you."

"I same. I pray you."

Then it was off to the big bell where for 20 Baht you could hit it with a wooden hammer for special luck, the exact nature of which was unclear to Michael. They took turns. She went first. Then he gave it a gentle tap. "You hit harder. Harder better." He hit it again. "No. Much harder." He gave it a real clonk, loud enough to turn the heads of everyone in sight. Malee cupped her hands over her nose and mouth to suppress her laugh. "Very, very good luck," she said, giggling.

They went to see the Elder monk. He was bald, dressed in an orange robe, draped monk-style, had deep wrinkles and one of the kindest faces Michael have ever seen. He was sitting beneath a ten-foot statue of the Buddha with dozens of lit candles all around him. They knelt feet back, before the Elder. Malee metamorphosed into a young girl, virginal, more smoothly beautiful than ever as she listened intently to the Elder's soothing voice. Everything inside Michael quieted, and he felt that he was in the presence of serenity. The monk looked alternately at her and at him speaking words of prayer. Michael could half-understand without understanding a word. It was a long blessing, and she nodded many times, each time holding her hands together in reverence and then bowing. Each time Michael looked at her he was given his own blessing. The Elder's invocation was long enough that Michael's knees were killing him. When they arose, she whispered 200 Baht. Michael did not hand the offering directly to the Monk. Instead, he put the two bills in the urn that stood next to the holy man. The Elder bowed with benevolence, never looking at the amount.

The temple itself was closed for repairs so Michael and Malee walked toward the far end, overlooking the bay from the far side. Across the mud flat there was a profusion of flowers in a random rainbow of color. Michael decided that the temple grounds were more like a park setting than hallowed ground. It all would have been picturesque except for the stench from a large pile of something rotting below the railing. They did not linger. Their shoes were where they had left them, the cab had waited, and Michael was completely absorbed with Malee on the ride back.

Spending every day together, Michael and Malee started getting into a routine of intimate familiarity. When Malee washed her hair every other day, Michael would comb it straight, careful to remove snarls. Malee sat very still as he let the comb slide through her hair on its journey to the small of her back. On each pass, he left a swath of furrows as in a plowed field, only to be rearranged on the next pass while she purred. Sometimes he used his fingers, like oversized tines, letting then slip down the black waterfall to rest on the indent in the small of her back. Then he went back to the comb, sometimes combing her hair until it was nearly dry, the only comment by either was an occasional "more hard" or "more soft" from her.

One such time, she spoke of possibly cutting her hair shorter.

"Never!" Michael interrupted her thought, "I wish it were even longer."

"One time more long."

She opened up her carrying bag and retrieved a picture. It showed her sitting on her knees in front of a large Buddha at a temple in Bangkok. She was wearing a short sleeve shirt and a very long skirt. Her hair was draped over one shoulder and nearly touched the floor.

"Show me how long that was," Michael said eagerly.

She stood and put her hand a foot below its present length.

"I would have loved to have seen that."

"Me sixteen." She handed him the picture.

"What?"

"For Khun Michael."

"No, I couldn't. You have copies?"

She shook her head no.

"Then really, no, I can't."

She put the picture in his hand. "For Khun Michael. I grow hair long for you."

Then she retrieved a second picture of herself in a clinging, blue satin, floor-length dress with her hair coiffed up. Though the picture was primarily of her, the surrounding landscape showed itself to be a rural setting with other people in the background.

"Me model once."

"Where?"

"Ubon. Men come with cameras. Pick pretty girls. Five. I one.

"You still have the dress?"

"No, men keep dress. But pay many Baht."

"You model only one time?"

She nodded affirmatively.

"How old?"

"Seventeen. Mama very proud."

"This is Ubon?" he asked looking at the dingy background in the picture.

She nodded and handed him the picture.

"No copies?"

She shook her head no again.

"I can't take it."

"I want you have. Make me happy."

That night, after they had made love, Malee nuzzled her face against his chest and then looked up at him, "Me want make my milk bigger for you."

"No! What are you talking about? Never. You're perfect the way you are."

"Firang like big milk."

"Not this firang."

She put a hand on one of his pecs. "You bigger than me," she laughed.

"No, I am not. And you are perfect. The only firangs who want big here," he put his hand on her breast, "have big bellies," which he gestured, "and drink beer and smoke."

"Oh, I no like that. Smoke make me sick. Big belly ugly.

Now no big milk for me."

"Okay."

"Lak Khun Michael."

"Lak Khun Malee."

"You eyes. Many color. Me like look." She snuggled in closer to study them. She reached up and touched his eyelash. "And here, so long. What you call it?"

"Eyelashes."

"Eyelasses."

"Shhhzzz," he corrected.

"Eyelasses," she whispered.

"No, no, *eyelaSHIZ*," he said, emphasizing the end of the word again.

"Eyelashes."

"Yes."

"Yes, eyelashes perfect."

"Why are you looking like that?"

"All girl want you eyelashes." She pet his hair. "Hair silk. Me like do this."

"I like yours better."

"No. No better. Long but no silk."

"I get lost in your hair."

"Me no understand."

"Hard to explain."

"Hard to…

"To tell."

"Oh."

She shifted so that her hair draped over his face, hiding it. He savored the fragrance.

"Me think understand."

The next day, Michael and Drake were having afternoon tea on the veranda of Drake's Bungalow, something that had become a kind of ritual for these two friends while in Samui.

Michael swirled his near-empty teacup, studying the pattern of the circling tealeaves.

"What?" Drake asked.

"Oh, nothing."

"An expression that always means the opposite."

"Well, Malee, of course. And, well, Helen."

"You and Helen have one thing in common. You both carry a lot of baggage, but while your baggage is upstairs in your room, hers is upstairs in her head. I never said anything about it, but I never understood why you didn't leave her instead."

"I loved her. Guess maybe makes you wonder what was I thinking."

"You weren't."

"You know, it's funny. I still do love her. Before all this happened with, you know, Malee, even right after Helen left, I felt in some way we were still connected, in an absurd way, hyper-tenuous, but still an inexplicable connection. Now, I've messed myself up. I don't know. Right now, I don't have a clue about anything."

"You never have a clue when if comes to women. You are the most clueless *smart* person I've ever met."

"So what are your thoughts, oh wise one?"

"Helen is going to do you a big favor by never coming back."

"I don't know about that."

"Well then God help you if the choice is not obvious. Set Malee up in Bangkok, and then run our business from here. Which, by the way, would make a lot of sense. Carbon copy of Dawn."

"But, well, there would always be at least, you know, with Helen, sort of like, I mean there would always be some half tones. You know what I mean?"

Drake dropped his napkin on his empty plate and pushed it toward the center. "No, I don't know. I'm tone deaf."

The next day, Drake set up an outing to the tropical rain forest in the center of the island. It was a sixty-kilometer trip. Drake went to the motorcycle rental shop.

"What? Are you crazy? I've never driven one before."

"They're not hard. You'll get the hang of it."

"No way. That's completely out."

Drake threw his hands up in frustration.

"I'll hire a taxi and follow you," Michael said.

"Now you're the one who's crazy. Cause half the trip's on a dirt path."

"Then I'll hire two motorbikes with drivers, too."

"What do you mean, '*too*'?"

"The taxi until the road ends. Then the motor bikes for the rest."

"You're making this into a goddamned safari. What are the motorbike drivers going to do?"

"Follow us until we get out of the taxi."

"And the taxi?"

"He'll wait until we come back."

"You are nuts."

"No way I'm taking Malee on a motorbike on an unpaved road."

"She does it all the time. She doesn't mind!"

"But I do."

"Christ! I can't take you anywhere."

"Yeah, you can. I want to go."

"This is going to cost you a fortune."

"I don't care."

"Of course you don't. You have that luxury. But I have a reputation to protect. Next thing I know, you'll hire a police escort. And besides, you know, the damned taxi won't even keep up."

"I'll tell him to drive fast."

"I need to get a couple of drinks in you."

"Oh, that would make a motorcycle a lot safer!"

"All right. But you owe me."

"If your goddamned motorcycle breaks down, I'll let you ride in the taxi. Shotgun. So now we're even."

The arrangements were made. The three drivers Michael hired were puzzled and amused, and then started talking amongst themselves. "Just another crazy firang," Michael was sure they were saying.

"It's a fucking embarrassment having you with me. Here, throw these in your trunk."

"What are they?"

"Just throw them in."

"How were you going to carry them without a taxi."

"Around your neck."

Even at full throttle, the taxi was having trouble keeping up. Dawn turned and waved with her ubiquitous smile. Drake hit a pothole, and she almost fell off. Instinctively, Drake reached back, saved her and brought the bike to an abrupt halt.

"See what you did," he called back.

"Just keep moving."

At the end of the road, Michael and Malee switched to the motorbikes. Michael paid the taxi drive one quarter of the agreed upon fee. He protested.

"Tell him he'll get the whole thing when we get back."

Drake took one of satchels and Michael hung the other over his shoulder. Drake went first. It was a bumpy ride, at times jarring, and following Drake made it a dusty one as well. After twenty minutes, they came to a barrier with a universal "No Motorized Vehicles Allowed" sign. They walked up the path a few hundred meters to where it forked.

"You take the right path. There's a nice waterfall up there," Drake said. "We'll take the left. We'll meet back here in, say, three hours."

Michael looked at him quizzically.

"The three hours is for you."

Michael looked inside the sack. There were two bottles of water, food for lunch, a hand-scythe, a bar of soap, and a sealed envelope.

"What's in the envelope?"

"When you figure out the rest, open the envelope. Not before."

The path was part of a nature preserve. It was well maintained, and walking was easy, even for Malee in her sandals. The lush green above made it a cool and pleasant walk. Michael and Malee came to a scenic waterfall in fifteen minutes. They had seen no one else on the trail.

The force of the waterfall created a light mist, and where the mist wafted there was a meadow of waist high grass. It was like the pictures of paradise that Michael had seen on postcards. It was hard to believe that it was real and that he was sharing it with Malee. Enjoying the majesty of the site Michael and Malee sat silently by the water's edge, putting their feet into the natural pool. They didn't leave them in for long before they decided it was time for lunch. Sharing the food that Drake had packed as well as one of the two bottles, Michael sat pondering Malee, thinking about how well and how naturally she fit this landscape. He playfully unbuttoned the top two on her blouse. She put her hand over the third and looked around nervously.

"I afraid people."

"No one's here."

The argument was unconvincing.

They put on their footwear and went to explore the surrounding area. There was a small cave a short rise from the stream. It was big enough to walk in without stooping and small enough to see where it ended. It was private, and the floor was hard. Michael took the scythe out of the sack and looked out at the tall grasses. Then he opened the envelope. It contained two condoms.

Michael was not adept with a scythe, but Malee knew how to use it, so they took turns. Soon they had a thick bed of grasses laid out in the cave. Malee was still nervous, but she did not resist his unbuttoning her blouse this time.

"I must wash," she said. He could hardly decline himself if she washed, so he decided to go too. After she had undressed, he draped his shirt over her shoulders. Fortunately it had long tails, but she still looked nervously from side to side as she descended to the stream.

To say that the water was bracing would be an understatement and so they finished up as quickly as possible—it would have been even quicker had Michael not let the soap slip out of his hands once, having to chase after it as it swirled away from the pair. In the cave, he held her feet until they warmed. She refused to dry off in the sun, so they both shivered, but with bodies together they soon warmed.

The smell of the cut foliage created a sense of nature in Michael, but as a mattress, the grasses were a failure. He let her ride on top. Every time Malee heard a sound she froze and held her breath. "It's just an animal. Or some tree in the breeze," he said, which did nothing to reassure her. It was turning out to be a classic version of coitus interruptus. On top of that, no matter how he shifted his weight, there was always some little outcropping that caught him in the back just wrong. She pounded up and down, and when she came, he came. Never were pleasure and pain more perfectly married. Afterwards, to his astonishment, she washed again in the stream. Michael declined and never opened the second condom.

When they returned to the fork in the trail, Drake and Dawn were waiting for them.

"So?" Drake asked.

"I figured it out first."

"I figured you would. The waterfall is my favorite spot."

"So why didn't you go together."

"Noise bothers me," he said.

Michael just shook his head. "Can we get off that topic?"

"Besides, the way we went, there are some nice cottages just up over the rise. You know…bed, hot water, and all."

Michael looked into Drake's sack. There was no scythe. "You son-of-a-bitch."

He shrugged. "You made love under the stars."

"What stars?"

"Just because you can't see them doesn't mean they're not there."

It only rained one day during their two weeks in Samui, but it was a steady, heavy rain without any wind. It started in the early morning and continued through the night. A sprint from one bungalow to the other one was a wet affair, as was the sprint to the dining veranda for lunch. It was an indoor day. Drake and Michael had agreed upon a signal that a chair in front of their door meant "Do Not Disturb" and when not otherwise engaged, they spent the balance of the day hammering out the final details of a counter-proposal for the Jim Thompson team.

"They're going to shit when they read this," Michael said.

"The Thai never shit in negotiations. You never know what they're thinking."

"But bet they're wondering what's taking us so long."

"Because we're unimpressed with their offer. I figure every week is worth about one more percentage point for us."

"We hold out until we get our eighteen percent and they…"

"Don't want to go above twelve percent I figure," Drake finished Michael's thought.

"Six weeks."

"That sounds about right."

Michael stretched. "So, what about tonight?"

"We can go to Wild Horses for drinks. You know, the place we pass on the way to O'Neill's. Strictly minor league compared to Bangkok, but I've got to get out of this bungalow for a couple of hours."

"What about the rain?"

"What rain?"

"You know, that wet stuff that keeps falling down."

"Don't pay any attention to it."

For Dawn, the rain was a *big* deal, and she no longer had an umbrella. She borrowed a wide-brim hat from the establishment but looked none-too-happy even so. Michael and Malee followed along to Wild Horses with weather-dampened enthusiasm. Coincidently, Joy was at the self-styled saloon with a new German. As the two couples walked in and spied a beaming Joy, they headed over to see her and her date. Michael noticed that Wild Horses was not topless. Most of the dancing girls were showing some paunch. Their performances were right in line with their looks. In any event, the girls' professional interest was directed at the single guys.

The bar table was too small for six. Joy had another one brought over so that Malee, Michael, Drake and Dawn could join her and her date who had been drinking cheap scotch. It was clear that Joy was happy for the company, the German being one of those types who preferred living higher off the hog when he thought someone else was picking up the tab. As they settled in, making a nice cozy group, the German happily switched to Johnny Walker Black, and all partook, that is all except Malee, who had her usual tea.

The six of them were seated so close to one of speakers that it was impossible to hold a conversation without yelling. Drake asked the waitress to have the speaker closest to them turned down. When, five minutes later, nothing happened, Drake yanked out all the speaker's cables. No one seemed to notice. The German spoke a little English, but, to Michael's surprise, Joy could rattle away in German about as well as she could in English. Drake confined his comments to the basics, which girl a specific customer would hook up with and kept score on his predictions. He was a 400 batter.

When the waitress brought the bill, there was an awkward moment as she was uncertain to which man it belonged. Drake paid it no attention, and the German suddenly found something of interest that required him to turn his head away. Michael took the bill and handed it to the German.

"So kind of you, mein Herr."

The German looked distressed. "Maybe ve shplit, yah?"

"Yah," Drake said, "it's about time for us to split." The four of them stood up, nodded to Joy, and left.

"Thanks again," Michael said looking over his shoulder at the German. He hoped he had not taken the money out of Joy's pocketbook, but it gave him such pleasure to see the look on the German's face.

The walk back in the driving rain was no more pleasant than the walk over. The only difference was that Drake, a little wobbly on the way back, slipped and fell. He rejected any help offered in getting up.

"Damn rain!" he said, in anger trying to mask his embarrassment.

"What rain?" Michael said ironically, unable to resist.

The following night was clear and calm, the ripples of the incoming tide barely audible. Malee was asleep, the slight heave of her chest the only movement. The moonlight gave definition to her face. Michael propped himself up on an elbow. He looked down at her for maybe thirty minutes until his stare woke her. Without a stir, she opened her eyes.

"What?" she asked gently, her arm reaching out, touching him.

"Nothing," Michael rejoined, happy that she was awake now.

She smiled. Down below, he felt himself spring into action.

"You go sleep," she said.

"I like to look at you."

"How long you look?"

"Long time."

"You want love now?" She touched his face.

"You go back to sleep."

"I no sleep before you."

"Why not?"

"You happy first."

"I am happy."

"You happy sleep first."

"All right." He rolled away from her and once on his side, lay his head down on the pillow. She left her hand on his back, a familiar comfort that he had not realized he still missed.

It was hard to believe that their two weeks in Samui had already passed. So little had happened, yet so much had occurred— meeting Malee, the trip to the Buddha, the waterfall, not to mention that they dined on the beach every evening except for the one rainy day. It was time to go and as a kind of farewell dinner, Drake arranged for a feast on the beach surpassing all the others they had shared together. The attendants were liveried, while the catch of the day included five different kinds of fish as well as an assortment of shellfish, the likes of which you can only find when living so close to the water. There were unusual vegetables and unfamiliar fruits that appeared for the first time, and the wine was a couple of notches above the bottles they had already shared. At the outset of the meal the staff, now quite familiar with the guests, presented Malee and Dawn each with a necklace of white flowers. Michael thought the fragrance resembled that of gardenias. They chatted and enjoyed an excellent meal, great company and what felt like a perfect night.

Later, they made it a perfect night in bed. Michael left the lights on low. For many minutes, they only touched—the slow motion gentleness, the light touch belying the depth of feeling it communicated. Her gentle caress brought him to a state of bliss. In the low light, her face glowed and her serenity infused him, and he had an overpowering desire to give all of himself, all of his being, to her. He felt the same desire from her. No matter how physically close they were to each other, they were not close enough. Their subsequent climax was a climax of love.

After Malee had fallen asleep, Michael remained awake and reflected again on all that had passed in these two short weeks. He had to laugh to himself that his first thought was of their English lessons. And there had been plenty of English lessons. Malee proved an adept pupil, even coming close to the "th" sound. Some of her new favorite expressions were, "Nice to meet you," "You look great in that," and the dreaded, "Let's go shopping." As a variation on the first of these expressions, Michael taught Malee the proper english phrase, "Delighted to meet you," delivered with appropriate haughtiness. She burst into laughter each time and tried to mimic it, but as she had no inate haughtiness, her attempts were as funny to Michael as his were to her.

"The pen of my aunt is on the table."

"When to use?"

"Never."

She was puzzled. He had kissed her, and the lesson ended.

His mind drifted from the English lessons to the evening rendezvous with Joy. They always arrived a little before eight o'clock. Otherwise there was the chance they would miss her for that evening. When Malee hit her with, "You look great in that!" Joy did a double take before smiling at Michael. Like-wise, when Joy introduced the American she had snared for a week, Malee responded with, "Nice to meet you."

There had been plenty of time for reading during these

languid days. Michael finished a history of Thailand, as well as *A Bright Shining Lie* that Drake lent him as a "must read." There were several dozen books in the bookcase next to the bar, books discarded by previous guests. Michael perused them. He rarely read fiction anymore, but one title piqued his curiosity, *Take the Sorrow* by a certain T. S. Whitmond. Michael did not read it, but thumbed it, and landed on the dedication page that contained but a single phrase, "A Dispassionate Memory of a Passionate Time." He puzzled why that phrase resonated so deeply as he put the book back on the shelf.

Malee busied herself with Thai potboilers, or at least the covers looked like paperbacks that were sold in American drug stores, and the two spent hours reading in the serenity of each other's quiet company.

Fortunately for Drake, shopping had been curtailed by the fact that there was only one women's clothing store on Sumai; even Dawn became bored with the offerings. Malee, less interested in the commodity of newness, was happy to go along to the shops, but never pressed Michael. Despite the limited options and Malee's frugality, there were two times when Malee accepted gifts: once when they visited the Buddha Temple; the other, over her protests, when he bought her a bikini—her first.

They had gone swimming once—on the day that it rained. "This is 'rain check', right?" she asked. Michael shrugged and hid his laugh. Malee had never been in the ocean and was not surprisingly apprehensive. The gradient was slight and even at 50 meters off shore it was only waist deep with no swells. With Michael holding her hand, having convinced her to go at least that far out, he found a waterlogged tennis ball, and they played catch. The rain was heavy—a waterfall of small drops—but then for a brief spell it changed. The volume of water falling was probably the same, but the individual drops had decided to band together and then fall as fewer, heavy drops. Michael interrupted their game of catch and watched as Malee was bombarded by these tiny missiles, each one announcing its identity for an instant as it propelled its tail of water into the air. It was an easy metaphor.

Before their last night in Samui, Michael had already made up his mind and asked Malee to come to Bangkok with him. She eagerly agreed—it would be her first flight ever. Michael was so in love with Malee that the thought of leaving her behind never really occurred to him. He had a responsibility to Malee, as he was the cause of her losing her job, no matter how terrible it was. Though he was fully aware of this important reality, it did not enter into his decision to ask her to come with him. He would have asked her to come to Bangkok with him even if she still had that job to go back to.

Drake silently approved of Michael's good judgment as it demonstrated Drake's effectiveness as his teacher. Malee was different from Wan in that Michael could now set Malee up for as long as he wanted, and, according to Drake, he could still enjoy the offerings around Bangkok—a very "Drake" thing to consider. Dawn was simply delighted and all smiles; her matchmaking skills had been validated.

Through Michael, Malee had entered a fairytale land where the trappings of wealth must have dazzled her. Though she was not materialistic by nature, an enchanted dinner on the beach that cost more than she made in a month, had to seem like a dream. Then there was the promise Michael had made to Joy about taking care of Malee. Joy had not even ventured to inquire what the amount and duration "taking care of" encompassed. Malee could not turn down the chance to be with someone so good to her, someone she had come to care for. Of course she said yes.

Drake and Michael's flight was full. The only opening for the same day was a single seat on a flight that left six hours earlier than theirs. Michael explained the situation to Malee, bought her a ticket and gave her the key to his hotel room.

When Drake and Michael left Bangkok for Samui, Drake checked out and left his stuff in Michael's room. Technically, they would split the room cost, but Michael never made any mention of it. The collective worth of the items in the room was more than Malee's annual income as a seamstress. It never even occurred to Michael to question her honesty. When he mentioned this to Drake, his only response was, "I'm not worried."

Their plane was delayed, and they arrived eight hours after Malee. Everything in the room was exactly as they had left it. Malee was watching a Thai TV-movie. She had not even gone out to eat because she wanted to be there when they arrived.

More powerfully than when Michael had first arrived, Bangkok, especially at night, reaffirmed itself as the heart of Thailand. The air was polluted with cars that moved slower than the feet of passing crowds, and when he stepped back on the commercial drag it was familiar—all vendors, crowds, and sex. The street merchants had usurped the sidewalks long ago. Many spots were complete with awning-covered stalls, hawking you name what. There were books, clothing labeled "pure silk" which of course they were not, pirated movies, porno DVD's, wood carvings of everything selling for under 500 Baht or even under 100—sometimes in front of an elegant store with wood carved antiquities starting at 200,000 Baht. You could buy everything from counterfeit watches to stingray wallets and purses, fresh fruits and vegetables to fresh-squeezed orange juice on ice. Sunglasses, T-shirts with messages that only an idiot would wear, and charcoal braziers steaming with delectable dishes for peddlers and customers alike were all available day and night. Storefronts ranged from massage parlors to open-end bars, from junk shops to high-class boutiques. Hookers and lady-boys abounded—from those seated at open-air bars to those leaning against storefronts. It made no difference the storefront behind them, whether classy or second-rate.

There were always tourists haggling for something or other, driving the price down and getting fleeced in the end anyway. There were guys looking for hookers, guys with hookers walking back to their hotels, small groups of young guys being loud and trying to find the best bar, beggars, and a group of three middle-aged Western women looking as out of place as polar bears would have been. Half of the time Michael and Malee had to walk single file to thread their way through the crowd, him leading the way and holding her hand as they wended to and from their hotel.

And then there was the Royalty. On two occasions in the past, Drake had seen how the Royalty lived up close and personal—which was otherwise hidden behind walls, literally and figuratively, without fanfare or public knowledge. On one of the two occasions, Drake was invited to an event at one of the first Prince's estates. Among other things, Drake counted fourteen cars, each garaged. The fourteen were comprised of seven different manufacturers—Rolls, Bentley, Ferrari, Jaguar, Mercedes, BMW, and Cadillac—with a vintage model and the latest model of each. One servant's full-time job was to dust and polish the cars to showroom shine. He was paid 10,000 Baht a month, more than many Thai made for much harder work. There was also a warehouse of wood carved antiquities in such profusion that the warehouse was chaos. "It looked more like firewood than antiquities," Drake commented.

Meals for Michael and Malee were a multi-tiered affair. Breakfast was part of the hotel price, and so was dinner, that is if you did not mind finger-food and drinks for your fare. For lunch Malee mostly wanted to dine at one or another of the street vendors' makeshift cafes. Some streets had five or more eating "establishments" in a row. Almost all offered rice, a multitude of vegetables from which to choose, and chicken or beef, the latter cooked to order on a charcoal grill. The dishes were served piping-hot and eaten at one of the several rickety tables where uncomfortable chairs were set up occupying a whole section of the sidewalk. Malee always ordered for them both. She usually had a Coke and Michael two small bottles of fresh squeezed orange juice. More elaborate dinners were usually reserved for nights with Drake and Dawn.

Twice a week Malee and Michael ate at Robinson—a department store with a restaurant on the top floor. Malee always ordered two extra-large bowls of noodles, one spicy for her and one medium spicy for Michael, both with everything you could possibly want floating on the top or resting at the bottom. The department store part of Robinson was a puzzle—the number of sales girls was at least twice the number of customers, at times approaching three times as many. Their main function seemed to be smiling and cleaning the glass display cases.

On the way to Robinson you passed Asia Books. Michael was particularly drawn to the numerous history books, all marked with high prices. Knowing that he had a stack of excellent books at home on his bedside credenza, he found himself reluctant, hating to be ripped off but he ended up buying a few anyway.

Once, at lunchtime, it was raining so hard, that street eating was most certainly ruled out by both Michael and Malee. "I go bring lunch back."

"What about the rain?"

She picked up his raincoat. "Me wear."

"You're not going out like that?!" She was wearing only her bra and panties. She buttoned up the raincoat. *She had come a long way from the shy girl he had met in Samui.*

"You give 300 Baht. I bring food and Baht."

He gave her the money.

"You sure?"

"No one see."

"I hope no one catches a glimpse."

"What you say?"

"You know what I like."

"I know. And orange juice. Two."

"Make it three."

Malee left, a little pleased with herself.

There was a knock on the door.

"Would you like me to make up the room now?"

"Maybe later. Is that okay? Like three o'clock. Is that too late?"

"No." She handed him a card. It stated in English, "I am your new maid. My name is Prang. Please call 7454 if you need anything." Michael put the card on the dresser, not paying it much mind. Malee was back in fifteen minutes, a little waterlogged, but with a delicious lunch for two and 80 Baht left over.

A few days later Dawn invited Michael and Malee to dinner at her apartment—rent was on Drake, naturally. It was a small one-bedroom apartment, more than comfortable by Thai standards. The floor of the apartment was a minefield of shoes, some of which apparently had lost their mate. *Buying shoes must have been one of her main activities,* Michael thought as he tried to avoid stepping on one of the wayward heels. He was shocked by the sheer volume and variety when Drake commented, "Don't ever get involved with a shoeless one from the village, or this is what you'll end up with." Neither Dawn nor Malee caught the drift of the comment, but Michael looked up, catching Drake's eye as they both nodded knowingly.

Dawn was not much of a cook. Dinner was spaghetti with store-bought sauce, a typical house salad and too much wine. Malee ate little but managed to be gracious about it. She later told Michael that spaghetti made her throw up. For the first time since Michael arrived in Thailand, with Drake toasting everything under the moon just to get more liquor into Michael, he over-imbibed. Drake and Dawn found it exceedingly funny to see Michael tipsy while Malee was more surprised than humored. "Me like you drink much," Dawn said. She was not far behind him. When Drake was not looking, she was a little too familiar with Michael, briefly changing his mood, but as Drake shifted back, all was quickly repaired with laughs and more cheers from Dawn. Malee, if she noticed, said nothing to Michael, although he worried about it later.

After dinner, Drake and Michael repaired to the balcony with cigars and Delamain XO Cognac poured into the proper cognac glasses. "I'm impressed Dawn has the right accouterments for cognac," Michael said slurring his words a little. Drake chuckled. "She thinks these are funny shaped water glasses." He shut the door. "I still can't figure out what she does except buy shoes. I've had her taking English lessons for three years now, and she still can't speak worth a shit. I think she thinks that classes are like some kind of pill. You take them and, bingo, you speak English. Like getting rid of a headache with aspirin. Her English is worse than Malee's! If I didn't know Thai, we couldn't talk. She doesn't have any family, you know. Raised by an uncle and aunt. Both dead now. Her uncle raped her when she was ten. She told me she didn't even know what was happening. Hard to believe, with that kind of inauspicious beginning, she still loves it. I mean I can't keep up with her. I have to cry uncle." Suddenly he laughed at his unintentional pun.

"What does she do with all her time?" Michael asked.

"Beats me." He took a long drag on his cigar. "Waits for me. I'm pretty sure she doesn't have sex apart from me. She waits and buys shoes." They smoked in silence for a few minutes. "I like how quiet it is here. You know, the apartment not facing the street. She even has that little interior garden down there. But her green thumb turned out to be albino." He paused for a bit, waiting for a jab or a response from Michael. Nothing came. "You okay?"

"Yeah."

Drake finished off the little left in his snifter. "How about a refill?"

"God, no. I'm spinning as it is."

"You're a funny drunk, you know that? You know how many times you tripped over her shoes."

"No. How many?"

"Once for each pair."

"Really? All right, I'll take another cognac."

Midway through the refill, Drake waxed philosophically. "If you want to mess with a woman in bed, first you mess with her head. You mess with her mind, *then* it's a straight shot to her pussy." He didn't say anything about what if the "messing" went the other way.

"It would seem Dawn has messed a little with your brain."

"With my dick."

"I don't buy that."

"I wasn't selling it."

"No, you are hiding it."

"Remember that time you hit me with that Goddamned expression, *projection?*"

"Yeah." Michael gave a laugh, too liquor-long, at the remembrance.

"Well, don't project."

"Only if you don't hide."

"You know what you are. You're a fucking romantic. You know that? Literally." Drake leaned forward. "You know what a fucking romantic is? A fucking romantic is someone who is otherwise very, very smart, but who is made very, very dumb by a woman."

Around ten o'clock Drake insisted that they all head out to one of the bars. It was prime time.

"Nana, not Cowboy," Michael whispered to him.

Drake rolled his eyes. "So, am I *not* supposed to figure out why?"

"Just be quiet, will you."

"That's what I kept telling you in Samui." Drake couldn't help but laugh at his own wit.

"Then just shut up."

"Man. You are a mean drunk."

At Nana, Drake chose Heart of Love, an all-nude club. Drake and Michael were the only two guys, maybe in the history of the establishment, who walked in with their own dates—the odd couple squared. Dawn and Malee were as interested in the doings as Drake while Michael was thinking about being back at the hotel with Malee later. Dawn invited one of the dancers over for a drink on her break, and then another. They were the two sexiest from the shift that had just finished. They disappeared for a minute to dress in bra and panties. The four of them were jabbering away in Thai. A second round of drinks arrived. Michael had switched to sparkling water on his first drink. Malee had been on Coke-A-Cola the whole time.

"What the Hell are they talking about?" he asked Drake.

"It's too noisy and they're talking too softly. Only thing I picked up is that the big fat bald guy with the black shirt is a regular, a big tipper, but he wants *everything*."

"Tell them to invite that hostess over."

"Switcheroo time?"

Michael shot him a look. "She'll know English."

"Probably knows how to put some *English* on it, too."

Her name was Mary, and her English had fewer fracture lines than most.

"I can't stay long."

"I'll buy three drinks, one for each of you," Michael said.

"I can stay then." She loosened up after her second drink telling Michael that the quiet man on the top row was a police

Captain. "He has special room. When he want girl, she go right away. Then he go home family." Michael made a "my lips are sealed" sign. She told him details about each of the prettier girls as they rotated on the stage when it was their shift. Michael ordered another round. "Number 27 very nice. She know what to do. You see. She go soon." Sure enough, a few minutes later, she went to the back room to change. "You nice man. Next time, you want 27, you tell me. I get her for you. But 3000, not 2000. Long time 1000 more."

"I'll remember. How about you?" he teased.

"You pay 3000?"

"Sure," he said playing along.

"Then okay." She squeezed his arm. "I wait you."

Back at their hotel room Malee was fine but Michael was still dealing with the whiskeys. "What were you four talking about?" he asked.

"They like you. Handsome man. Good eyes. They say when Khun Michael young man, must be more handsome man. All girls want Khun Michael then. I say you kind man. I think Dawn like you very much. Her say so."

Michael let the topic drop.

Malee had an old cassette player and took out the one cassette she had in her sack. It had been a long time since Michael had seen a cassette player and seeing it amused him, immediately taking his mind off of other things. They lay in bed, clothes on, Michael sobering up, while she played it. Each song was a different singer—Rock and Roll, all in English. One song struck Michael in a way that none of the others did. It had a particular refrain, "Worried, oh so worried, that you let me down," a Shakin' Stevens song that haunted him. At first he thought it was the booze, but the lyric stuck with him, not letting go. When the song finished, he had Malee rewind it. He had her play it a few times.

"Why you like song so much?"

"I don't know. There's something about it. I don't know what. Maybe it's *my* song."

"What you mean, your song?"

"I don't know. Makes me think."

"You have girl before?"

"Yes. But she is gone now."

"How go?"

"Just gone."

"You sad now?" she asked, trying to mask her concern.

"No." Her hugged her tighter and kissed her softly on the lips. "No, I'm very happy. So very happy. To be with you." He began to let his hand float over her body. She purred softly.

"We get ready bed now. She took her toothbrush from her sack. It was so far past its useful life that the bristles were going more sideways than up-and-down. He didn't know why he hadn't noticed it before and fetched a new one from his suitcase and gave it to her.

"Let me see your teeth."

She gave him a fangs-exposed smile. They were white, straight and beautiful.

"Do you use dental floss?"

"I no understand."

"Dental floss."

"I no understand."

He showed her the container he was using. She shrugged. "Here, let me show you." He did his teeth. "Now you do yours. I'll show you." She was apprehensive. "No, this is very important. You have to use this. Your teeth are too pretty. I don't want you to have problems. Here, open up." She tried to mimic what he had done but she was lost. He had to help. He had never flossed someone else's teeth. It was like tying someone else's necktie—what had become instinctive with your own neck, was confusing to the point of impossible when trying to do it for another person while facing him—you had to stand behind him and pretend his neck was yours. Flossing was worse because you could not stand behind the person; you almost had to think of it as a mirrored image. Michael used two strands: one for her teeth and the other for his when he needed to remember how he positioned his fingers between two particular teeth.

Even though their mouths had met many times before, this felt like a new kind of intimacy. He did every tooth. There was blood on the floss. Both of them were alarmed, but for entirely different reasons. He tried to explain this, but it was beyond her English. He insisted that she floss every day. She nodded agreement. After two days, she could do all but a few of the back ones. He did those. After a week, she could do them all, and there was no blood. And better yet, she had become a floss enthusiast. As a precaution, and uncertain what kind of floss was available in Thailand, he had packed two containers in each of his bags. He gave her three of the containers, calculating that this should be about a year's supply.

In bed, it was playful and unhurried, intensity building at its own pace. They pawed and tussled, and rolled. She teased him by mimicking his orgasms. She found this perpetually amusing. He retaliated by mimicking hers, and she turned away in embarrassment, giggling. Her closeness and warmth were intoxicating. Michael opened up a condom to put it on. She placed a hand on his, constraining him. "I want you give me baby."

His mind went blank.

Those simple words, and so much changed. Suddenly time was not the same. It was moving, but its speed was altered. His yearning ache for her was the same, but all reference points were confused. Or they just disappeared. He didn't know which.

Maybe he should have expected that this was coming—

he could be surprisingly naïve at times, he knew that, not a quality he much liked, and one that Drake played on.

He was responding. Yes, he was speaking, but it seemed like "yes" and "no" at the same time. It was like being hit fast and slow by the same punch. Fast was "yes" and slow "no".

Then out of nowhere a bizarre episode played out in Michael's mind, a seemingly unrelated reflection that only took a few seconds to complete. Jay had told him about a college friend who had endured Navy fighter pilot training. This friend told Jay that the most terrifying test he endured was to be harnessed to a seat, dropped into a large cold-water tank, and turned topsy-turvy for fifteen seconds so he had no idea which way was up. Holding his breath he was to remain harnessed for thirty seconds, and only then release himself from the harness. By watching his air bubbles rise he would know which way was up. There were instructors at the side of the tank to rescue him if he began to drown. This test alone produced the largest percentage of washouts by those too terrified to take the test and by those who had to be rescued too often. His friend had passed but not before nearly drowning.

Malee's request was not terrifying—rather the opposite. But there was no light with which to see the bubbles, and even if there had been light, he would have had no idea which direction the bubbles were going.

Time slowly came back to normal speed. "I don't know. I have to think. This is…um, I need time to think." After a pause, the duration of which he had no recollection, she put the condom on him, and they had sex. It was good sex—it was impossible not to have good sex with her—but the previous times it had been better.

Afterwards, Michael remained awake long after Malee had fallen asleep. His thinking was taking him nowhere; it was dead end after dead end. At some point, he must have drifted off because the stroking of her hand across his chest woke him. She could arouse him at will, and did. She started to put a condom on him. She got it backwards at first and had to go the other way.

"Yours?" he asked.

"No, yours."

She sat above him and eased him into her. She was just under forty-six kilos—a feather on top. She moved in slow motion, very slow motion. She continued this way on and on, and on. Now he was on top. Neither spoke or made a sound. His wish to never let it end was almost as strong as his driving urge to consummate. It had been a long night, and now the sun shone red through the gap in the curtain and then brightened to a more intense orange. She came with the brightness of the rising sun.

They missed breakfast, lingered in bed until lunchtime.

Finally, they got up and showered together, enjoying each other as if the night before had not had a hiccup, but after lunch, Michael went for a walk. Malee did not question why. He thought about many things, oddly enough fixating on Genghis Khan as part of the reverie. Michael had read that during his lengthy reign, Genghis Khan impregnated thousands of women. After the conquest of a town or a city, his lieutenants selected a handful of the most beautiful young women, and Genghis has his way with them. Any lieutenant who held back on one of the beauties for his own enjoyment did not live long.

Through studying Y-chromosome data, it was discovered that each male offspring from these conquests carried some of Genghis's genes, and they, the offspring, were themselves prolific. Given the smaller world population at the time, genealogists have calculated that today sixteen million males carry some of his genes. *Talk about immortality*, Michael mused, wondering whether his initial urge to say yes to Malee's request was because he carried Genghis' genes. What would it be with a child? A month every year in Thailand? Two months? A move to Thailand?

Helen drifted back into his thoughts. Then she was front and center. They had talked about children, but it had only been talk. Now she was gone. Or was she? He didn't know. After all they were still married. Was he now happy now that she was gone? The answer was a resonant yes, but still, he hesitated. Was Drake was right? Was he just a fucking romantic? No, with Malee it went deeper.

That night he slept fitfully. Instinctively she snuggled next to him for warmth. The room was always too cold for her. During the day she wore a sweater and did not complain. It was one of his sweaters, black cashmere. He loved to see her in his clothes. He gave her his sweatshirt—her head peaking out from the oversized hood melted him—and an orange silk T-shirt that, if any more sheer, would have been improper to wear in public.

The next day things returned to a kind of normal. There were things left unsaid, as Malee did not bring up the question of a baby again. Michael was happy to let it go. She spent some time each day watching Thai soaps, an activity that she loved, while Michael would read the news or a book, glancing over at Malee often. And each day they would continue her English lessons.

Two, sometimes three times a day, Malee and Michael made use of the sumptuous king-size bed. If at night she still would have preferred the lights low, she no longer protested his turning them all on full blast. One time, after a particularly torrid round, Malee said, "Me go bathroom."

"Why?"

"Good love make pee."

"I have to test, how good," he teased.

"Too good. Please, no can hold."

He pressed on her lower abdomen. "You mean here?"

"Nooo! Pee bed, pee bed. No want." She pressed her legs together, and her face scrunched up. He let her up with a laugh, and she ran for the bathroom.

After Malee returned to bed they held one another. Michael was stroking her hair, and he asked her to tell him more about life in her village. He was perpetually curious about the woman who had captured his heart. Malee didn't say much at first, but then she slowly started telling him about her first marriage. In Ubon, Malee had married at eighteen and had a daughter by the time she was nineteen. During the latter stages of her pregnancy, her husband lost interest in her because of her shape. He started seeing other women including a former girl friend. Malee divorced him over the betrayals, but her mother-in-law had influence with the judge, and Malee's now ex-husband won custody of their newborn child complete with a provision that Malee could only see her daughter with his consent. That consent was never granted, and from the time Malee's daughter was three months old mother and daughter had never been together. That was six years ago.

"Me very sad. Me want to kill self. No see he, no good. Me go crazy. Mother of husband no care. Me go to he home. He mother angry. Make me go away. Call police if me come back. Me saw baby one time in village. Me want hold her. Me cry all night. One week. Me want die. Me baby die me." Michael teared up and began to say something. "No. No talk. Me too sad talk more. Cannot think on she. Me forget or me die. No talk." Tears rolled down her cheeks. He held her very tight.

Michael and Drake had another negotiating round with the Jim Thompson Company. The Company's Thai negotiator had met their proposal half way. Michael shook his head. He was unwilling to compromise on the royalty unless they would accept more favorable franchise terms. The session ended without accord. They set a date for another attempt to reach agreement.

Drake had made reservations at a fancy restaurant, hoping to celebrate major movement in the deal. Despite the delay in the deal they decided to go. They took the Sky Train to the last stop. There were few pedestrians and twenty motorcycle taxis parked near-by. All the drivers wore blue crash helmets. Drake spoke to the driver first in line.

"It's 30 Baht each." He looked at Michael. "There's no tipping."

"Wait, how far is this place?"

"About five kilometers." He smiled. "Why, you want to walk?"

The road was empty, and the drivers hit 90 KPH. Michael's knuckles went white on the lazy S-curves.

The restaurant was opulent. They were seated at the only table one floor up and with an unimpeded view of the stage. Stuffed cushions replaced chairs. Two attractive waitresses were in attendance at all times. Drake had preordered the food, which arrived in a steady stream of courses. As usual, Dawn and Malee fed Drake and Michael each course before they themselves partook in the feast. As they were chatting away enjoying the luxuriant atmosphere, a gong sounded, and the stage lit up. Seven pretty young women dressed in golden costumes with pointed hats flowed out onto the stage. When the five-piece band sitting just offstage began, the women danced in perfect sync, their hands and fingers moving as gracefully as fish in water. Their fingertips meeting in delicate patterns while the rest of their fingers undulated as if boneless. The girls danced for half an hour followed by much applause from the packed restaurant after each routine.

"Can you do that?" Michael asked as he turned to Malee who lit up as she began moving her hands in a similar fashion.

"Where did you learn that?"

"Mother teach him daughters."

Not to embarrass her, Michael did not ask Dawn to demonstrate. It had been a lovely evening and as promised, the motorcycle drivers had waited outside for them. The ride back was even faster, horses smelling the stable.

The deal was still in the waiting game stage. Michael and Drake talked about alternate strategies, but there was not much else to do but wait it out. During this down time, the day of the Jim Thompson clothing sale was to take place. One day and one day only, it was the most famous sale day in Thailand. Jim Thompson silks were top draw, and his company was known to purvey the finest Thai silks. The Thompson brand lived on, but Jim Thompson himself had mysteriously disappeared some years ago, his body never found. Foul play was suspected, especially since the inquiry into his disappearance had generated scant interest by the police.

Each year, if he was in country, Drake took Dawn to this sale event. As a friendly gesture, the Company had given Michael and Drake coupons entitling them to an additional fifty percent off the sale prices. The two couples took a taxi to the outlet store on the outskirts of the city. It was a cavernous warehouse were thousands of women were frantically searching for just the right article or just the right bolt of silk—three yards being enough for a dress for the average Thai woman, four for tourists. A handful of bored and likely disgruntled men were standing around. The prices were so good and the selections so immense, displayed in stacks ten, fifteen, even twenty bolts high, that this was the only time Michael saw Thai graciousness on hold. The manners of the women were a 50-50 cross between English politeness and Spanish rudeness.

"Okay me buy nice silk for Mama to make dress?" Malee asked.

Michael nodded. He followed her around. Malee was efficient and had made her selection within ten minutes. She was
content with the single purchase.

"Mama be happy. Me tell he present from you. Now me
like Joy. Not like brother. He do no thing. Only son. So she
like king. She no job. Makes Mama buy thing for him. Him
have motorbike. I no like brother. Lazy boy."

Dawn was another story. She went into a buying frenzy,
carrying two huge canvas bags, selecting every item that
caught her fancy. Her first bag was already half full. Drake
pulled Michael aside.

"Every minute in this Goddamn zoo is costing me 1000
Baht even *with* this fucking coupon. Do me a favor. Help her
out by wandering with her, deciding what works, which, you
know, pattern or color looks best on her. She'll pay attention to
your opinion. The more you think about it, the more you save
me. I told her we're leaving in an hour. God, I hate this place."

With Michael's help, Dawn filled only one bag. She
pleaded for more time, but Drake half dragged her out once the
hour was up. Michael's tab was 3600 Baht; Drake's was more
like 30,000. "I owe you big time," he whispered to Michael as
they got into a taxi speeding away from more temptation.

Drake and Michael had a private lunch together, and Michael
opened up, "I don't know… you know, about Malee. You'll
never guess."

"She wants a baby."

"How'd you know?"

"Wild guess. Just be thankful you don't have to try to make
your living as a prizefighter because you'd never see it coming."

"I don't know what to do."

"That's an easy question to answer."

"No, I'm serious."

"Wait. You're not thinking of doing something *really* stupid, are you?"

Michael shifted in his chair.

"What? You must be ready for 'the Home.' You mean marry her? You're not going to marry her. You're going to marry a family. A whole Goddamned village if you're unlucky. You going to spend a month or two every year in a village that makes Ubon look like New York City? And guess what you are going to find out?" He couldn't help laughing. "Mama and Papa, they need a new home. And they're too old to work now, too, so somebody's got to support'em. And Joy, she wants to stop hustling. Can't blame her. And brother got sick, and Mama's got cancer. And guess who's got all the money?" He chuckled. "A one-man Social Security System praying that Mama's cancer takes her quick. MichaelCare!" He smiled at his witticism.

"Stop. Damn you. Just stop! It's not exactly what I was thinking."

Drake stared at Michael.

"Come on, will you?" Michael said looking away.

Drake put his hands over his eyes. "No. Nooo! You've got to be joking. Not the States. Christ! I've never seen anyone get so dumb right in front of my eyes."

"Well, it was… it was just a thought. I know it's not practical." Michael kneaded his hands.

Drake got up. "I got to go read a newspaper or something. Find out what the other crazies are doing." He turned before leaving. "By the way, what did Eisenhower say about Asia?"

"He said, 'Never get into a land war in Asia.'"

"Right. And what does Drake say about Asia?"

"I don't know."

"'Leave Asia in Asia.' You're lucky I'm your friend." And with that he was gone.

But the matter did not end there. A couple of days later, Michael raised it again while just the two of them were having coffee. "I can't just leave her. I mean what's she going to do? Try to go back to that terrible factory job. I can't do that. I can't let that happen. You know what? She wants to open a suk. Sell women's clothing. I asked how much she'd need. She said about 80,000 Baht. What do you think?"

"I think you've lost your marbles. You are a savvy business-man when you put together a deal, and we negotiate it. But I get nervous when I see you going brain dead in front of me. You know why most new businesses fail?"

"Sure. Under-capitalized."

And she's going to open a suk for 80,000? It'll either be half a store without merchandise or half the merchandise without a store. Come on, what's the matter with you? And, by the way, what's she going to live on in the meantime?"

"Well, I'll make it 160,000 and explain it's just for living expenses."

"Look, then, if you're going to insist on being a fool, give her 80,000 to live on, not to open some stupid store. Tell her you'll give her the other 80,000 when you see her again. I mean, look, it's only going to take you a few months to put together a deal with either Neimans or Bloomingdales. And then work out the logistics so we can launch right away."

"80's not enough."

"It's more than enough. More than she makes in a year, and you'll be back much sooner than that. Plus… plus… and now listen… it'll guarantee she'll be here waiting for you."

"I want to give her 160,000 now."

"What're you bothering me for then? If you're pussy whipped, you're pussy whipped."

"All right, I'll think about it a little."

"Don't. You'll end up with 320,000."

"You're no help."

"A thankless job. If only you knew how much help I was."

Michael could not sleep. He lay in bed staring at the ceiling. Malee was asleep. The only sound was her breathing and occasional muted sounds from the street. On the outside corners of each eye, tears formed and wet rivulets found their slow path down his cheeks. He made no sound or movement, only tears—steady and many. Malee awoke. She reached out to his face, to the corner of one eye and felt the wetness. She wiped away a tear. She moved closer and wiped a tear from his other eye, then the tears with both hands.

"What Khun Michael?"

He did not answer or move.

"Khun Michael. What?"

He shook his head slowly.

"Tell me, Khun Michael, what wrong?"

He shook his head again. He wiped the tears, too, and their hands touched.

"I no make you happy?"

The tears flowed faster. His nose was stuffy, and he swallowed audibly.

"I leave if I no make you happy."

He squeezed her hands to hold her there. "No. No. You make me too happy."

She propped herself; her face was directly above his. "I no understand."

"You make me *too* happy, and I am leaving in three days."

"I know you leave."

"I have never been so happy in my life. I never want to leave. I know I have to."

"But you come see me again. Yes?"

He nodded affirmatively, "Soon."

"So that okay."

He shook his head. "I don't want to leave. And when I wake in the morning, I know I will hate the day because that means it has taken one more day from me."

"Everything be okay. We be happy for three days, okay?"

"Maybe you do not know how happy I am."

"Maybe I happy same way."

"Are you?"

"Yes, Khun Michael."

He breathed in heaves. They held each other.

"Please you no cry, Khun Michael."

He nodded. But his tears were not listening. He freed himself long enough to grab a handful of tissues to blow his nose.

He must have fallen asleep. He had no idea when. He only knew that when he opened his eyes it was daylight. There was a small bouquet of flowers between him and Malee.

"I get up early. I love Khun Michael."

He turned away. "I'm sorry. I have to stop this."

She placed her hand on his back. "That okay. We have good day today."

"Play the song for me again before we get up. "Worried, oh so worried that you let me down." He played it over and over.

The next day Malee, Drake and Michael were in Michael's room. Drake did not want Dawn involved in the discussion.

"I want to give you some money," Michael said. This money is for you. I am only giving it to *you*. When you spend this money, it must *only* be for you. I am not giving it to your Mama or your Papa or Joy or anyone else. Do you understand?"

Drake translated to make it crystal clear, and Malee nodded.

"I want you to spend some of the money for English lessons. You need to learn English to have a good job."

She nodded again to the translation.

"I will come back in a few months, maybe sooner, and then we can discuss what you asked me for. Okay?"

"What did she ask you for?" A beat. "Come on, what did she you ask you for? Make yourself clear."

Michael did not answer the question. "Just translate what I said, please." A little vexation entered his tone.

"All right. I didn't need to ask the question anyway."

"I am going to give you 160,000 Baht and you wait for me. All right? With the understanding, it is only for you."

She nodded.

"Did she understand what I said about spending the money just on herself?"

"It was not a complex thought," Drake said a little sharply. "I think I should go now."

After Drake had left, Malee burst into tears. Her body shook. She talked through her tears. "Khun Michael, no one be good to me like you. No one be nice to me ever. You good man. Lak Khun Michael."

"Lak Khun Malee."

Later that day, he deposited 160,000 Baht into her bank account. It had 430 Baht before the transaction.

The next morning, Michael and Drake had coffee together. Drake handed him a summary of their joint expenses. It was a lot of cash, but neither said a word, just split it 50-50.

"Thanks again for yesterday," Michael said.

"No problem."

"What do you think?"

Drake shrugged.

"Come on, what do you think?"

Their eyes locked. For the first time since Michael's arrival to Thailand, there was compassion in Drake's eyes. He waved off the question.

"Come on, tell me."

"She loves you. I think she's going to break your heart after you break hers, because you cannot or rather, will not give her what she craves most. And when she comes to understand that, she will still love you but will have to try to leave you. The only glue that can hold you together is your generosity. And I'm not even remotely suggesting that she's a mercenary. She's about as far from that as one can be. Look how she trusted that you would care for her without, as far as I know, ever even raising the subject. But she deserves a better material existence. And you obviously can give that to her. And she may not find anyone who can provide for her. Then she can be your Dawn. And have a comfortable but incomplete life."

Michael sat stunned, speechless. He swallowed audibly. Neither spoke for at least a minute. Finally Michael spoke. His voice was constrained, "You paint a life of heartbreak."

"Comes with being a fucking romantic."

Michael put his fist to his chin, and his head turned a little back and forth. He bit down on the knuckle of his index finger.

"God, you make it so... I don't even know the word."

"Truthful."

"I was hoping that was not the word."

"They say it does spring eternal. Maybe that can be your comfort. Until it doesn't work anymore."

There was a long pause.

"Is she going to spend that money only on herself?"

"Don't expect her to be a bad daughter."

"But she promised..." Michael began to say.

Drake interrupted, "Do you *really* think that two months of romance could trump two thousand years of culture. Don't think less of her, and don't be cruel."

Michael gave a short, desperate laugh. "Where were you when I needed you?"

"Right beside you." Drake put his hand on Michael's shoulder, never having done so before.

The final negotiation yielded the resolution that Michael and Drake would open a Jim Thompson franchise that only operated in New York and San Francisco. This was assuming that Michael finalized his arrangement with what had still only been described to the Jim Thompson representatives as, "a very upscale store chain." If all was profitable in the first year, and met the mutually agreed upon revenue and profit targets in the second year, then the terms Michael had proposed would become the basis for an expanded deal where the contract and the franchise would go national at a rate deemed optimal by Michael. Essentially, Drake and Michael had negotiated what they had targeted.

The next day Michael departed for home. Malee rode in the taxi with him to the airport, and while she tried to smile, the mood was somber. She had a bracelet of flowers, the same kind of flowers as in the necklace on Samui before. She put the flowers around his wrist. "This for safe journey. Monk bless flowers."

They arrived early at the airport and as they sat together, she held his hand. When the time arrived for him to go through passport control, he could barely look at her. He just squeezed her hand tighter. It suddenly hit him that the only link between them during the upcoming months would be the email addresses that they had exchanged, including Joy's just to make sure that they could stay in touch.

"I wait you."

"I promise I will come."

He wanted to add, "Then we can talk about that other thing," but he let that thought go unspoken, the knot in his stomach preventing him from uttering the words. He looked at the clock. "I have to go now."

She walked with him to the point where only ticketed passengers could proceed. He kissed her quickly on the lips. And then he was gone.

The customs official smiled, "We hope you enjoyed your visit. We wish you a pleasant flight." Michael's passport was stamped with a singular exit notation.

PART 2

Tailspin

First class, aisle seat: a plus. His companion: a minus. His shirt, potbelly and drawl, accompanied by the, "Harold's the name, Hoppy's what they call me," line told Michael all he needed to know. They were held at the gate for half an hour. Hoppy started off by complaining to the stewardess that his screwdriver was short on ice. A minute later, "Where's that damn stewardess?" He turned to see if she was coming back with his ice and, in the process, his elbow brushed against Michael's orange juice knocking it into his lap. A flurry of napkins, paper towels, and apologies—Hoppy thought part of apologizing was talking a lot.

"Some place, that Bangkok, eh?"

"Yeah."

"Ah, so you were there on pleasure, too."

"Business."

"Well, my business was Nana." He leaned in closer. "My idea is to fuck'em real hard, you know, till they can't stand it no more. I love to make'em beg even though I can't understand a fucking word they're saying. Know what I mean?" He gave a chuckle. "What d'ya say your business was?"

"Confidential. Hey, I'm real tired."

"Sorry about that drink again."

"Forget it."

"Wouldn't have happened except for that Goddamned stewardess. Know what I mean?"

Michael sighed, effectively ending the conversation.

The plane was far from full in first class. Michael sought

out the stewardess. "I apologize for Fatso back there. Do me a favor and spill one on him. No ice in the drink." She smiled as he kept talking, "Look. I can't sit next to that slob this whole trip. Okay if I take one of the empty aisle seats?"

She nodded. "I see you wear good luck."

"Yes." Michael's eyes lingered on Malee's last gift.

He was unaware that they had taken off until the pilot's announcement that they had leveled off at 35,000 feet.

"Do you need something?" It was the same stewardess.

"No. Thank you."

"A tissue, perhaps." She brought him several.

"What is your name?" he asked.

"Sarah."

"I mean your real name."

She gave a short laugh, "Americans can't pronounce it."

"I can."

"It is Malivalaya.

He repeated it perfectly.

"Di ma.'"

"Copin ca."

"You speak Thai."

"Very little."

"I will bring you herb tea. Help you sleep."

The tea did help. But sitting up brought only a fitful rest, the kind where near-waking dreams flourish.

Her upset stomach had brought them together. Embarrassed smile when he cleaned the vomit out of her hair. Then, a real smile when she won—Connect Four, then they became connect two. Warm and soft and modest at first. Not modest as an artifice. Modest until there was no need for modesty. "Worried, oh so worried that you let me down."

The captain's announcement to fasten seat belts because of turbulence brought him back to 35,000 feet. Michael's neck was sore. The flower bracelet had browned, and some of the petals had fallen off. On the way to the lavatory, he saw Hoppy engrossed in a movie with three miniature unopened vodka bottles lined up on the middle armrest.

Michael asked Malivalaya for an extra blanket. After the turbulence subsided, the first meal was served, beautifully presented just the way Malee would have done it. He picked at some of the vegetables and the salad and left the rest. A glass of water with no ice, was his drink as well as his desert. He had no appetite. He rubbed his forehead against his palm. Seventeen hours left. Seventeen hours of regret. Something in his heart told him that he should have done things differently with Malee. Maybe should have listened to Drake about the money. Maybe he shouldn't have left. Hoppy was snoring, loudly. When Malivalaya passed by, Michael stopped her. "Here," he said handing her his clean napkin, "stuff this in his mouth. Make everybody happy. Happy with Hoppy."

She laughed. "It's against regulations."

"Then just shoot him."

Some hours must have passed because another meal was being served. It was more substantial than the first. Michael ate it.

Time passed slowly and Michael found that his neck was stiffening. It hurt in every direction. He tried talking with Malivalaya again, but the other stewardesses were up and about so that was out. He had a book, but would read three or four pages and realize he had no idea of what was going on in the narrative. He took a sleeping pill.

It sat glistening blue and white in the Ford Showroom for like forever. He couldn't remember how long. It was used, but you would never know it—a little old lady's who only drove it to church. Michael negotiated with Bill Blake

over and over, but the dealer would not accept Michael's
price. Some days he lingered, just standing outside in
front of the showroom window imagining himself in it.
Michael knew Blake was keen on "moving" the Ford 500
Fairlane hardtop convertible, the kind of car you could
reign in. Michael's persistence and adolescent enthusiasm
wore Blake down, and they finally agreed upon a price,
but Michael's parents nixed the deal. He pleaded every
night when his father came home. And on the day that
they finally relented, Michael ran all the way to the deal-
ership. The car had sold the previous morning! And as if
to pour salt into an already gaping wound, for less than
the price they had agreed upon. "Sorry kid, we just weren't
sure." He stared at the empty space. The slight indent that
the tires had made in the floor from resting in one place for
so long was all that was left to him of his car.

Their emails began. He had originally told her it might
be as long as six months, but the franchise operation had
exceeded initial expectations. That compressed things to four
months at which time he and Drake would meet in Bangkok
to implement the second phase of the Agreement.

During these four months, Malee and Michael exchanged
thirty-eight emails. She told him that she was staying in Koh
Samui with Joy, and had planned two visits to see her parents
in Ubon. He told her that he thought about her every night,
that he looked at her two photos every day and that he could
not bear to wait six months, that he was coming back much
sooner. Excited, he gave her his itinerary. She would meet
him at the hotel or maybe the airport. He said he thought it
would be easier for her to meet at the hotel, but the airport
was okay, too. If anything went amiss, they would hook up by
email.

One day, expecting news from Malee about arrangements
for meeting up in Bangkok, Michael was stunned to find that

he had received an email from Helen, the first contact since she had left him. He read it slowly, still in disbelief:

Michael,

I didn't know how to leave you except by the way I did. I expect this hurt you deeply, but this was not my intention. I had reached the conclusion that my life was stuck in cruise control and that if I stayed in that mode I would simply wither. None of this was your fault. You cared for me very well, and you were always kind. If blame must be assigned, then it belongs to me. I am living in a commune now, happily, and have become very fond of one of the men (I know how you think and, no, it is not Bob). I read in The Times that the company went out of business thanks to Ridley. I never did trust him. Sometimes I wonder what you are doing now, but I am not asking you to tell me, because I would like to ask that you do not respond to this email. I need to continue my journey. I will undoubtedly write you again sometime, but not in response to an email. I hope you are doing well, Helen.

Michael simply closed his browser window forgetting to sign off. He sat there, alone, in silence.

Michael ordered an expensive wine with dinner, "We have to celebrate this. The new Contraco Headquarters Building. Wow what a coup!"

"Yeah, and I beat out SOM—kind of unheard of—for the centerpiece sculpture *and* the design of the plaza to complement it. Here's a schematic." He unrolled an onionskin rendering. They went over it together, Jay leading Michael step-by-step through the objectives of the project.

"Man, I'm impressed. I love it! This is really going to put you on the map."

Over dinner, Michael told Jay about Malee, the plans about going back, her desire for a new baby, and then he showed him the email from Helen.

"Well…" Jay started.

"Well, what?" Michael interrupted.

"Well, you hear that after the break-up of a marriage people are sometimes vulnerable to rebounding into a new relationship."

"I know. I've heard people say that. But this is… I'm certain this is not the case with her."

"Well, you're the one who has to decide, and I'm not saying this is the case. But keep in mind that what you just said is what people in your situation usually say."

"What do you think about Helen?"

"I've never quite been able to figure her out. But I…" he cut off, "Well, you still love her, right?"

"Yes, I do. But not as much as Malee now. You've got to understand, I'm completely enamored of Malee. I long for her. I think about her all the time."

Jay listened and then measured his words, "To me, Helen's a bit of an enigma. She's bright, attractive, and I think caring of you, but sometimes there's a little bit of… I don't know, what? Flakiness or something in her? Sometimes I have this impression that she is looking for something so elusive that she doesn't know where or how to begin the search. I think there is a good chance she is going to want to come back. Who knows, maybe your relationship would be even stronger then. But with Malee around, I would say the longer she stays away, the bigger the risk that she will have lost you completely. Regardless, if she does come back, well, here's what I think. She loves you. And it's obvious that Malee has her hooks planted deep. And then dear brother *you* will have the enviable position, as well as the possibly disagreeable situation, of being wanted by two women, both of whom you love."

Six weeks before his scheduled departure for Thailand, Jay asked him to join in on a two-week rafting trip down the Salmon River in Idaho's backcountry. Michael liked the white water where it was challenging and where the river abandoned civilization. The two of them comprised the entire group, just the two of them and a guide. It felt like a luxury to spend so much time with Jay, especially knowing he was heading back to Asia after the excursion.

The time with Jay on the river was just what he needed. The challenge of the rapids, the heat of the sun and the chill of the river, the exhaustion each evening were all a tonic for the body not to mention the soul. "It changes your focus to the here and now," Michael said to Jay, patting him on the back.

He checked email upon his return. There was one from Malee:

Dear Khun Michael,

Please call. i need talk with you. Very important.

Love, Malee

The email was dated twelve days ago and Michael saw that there was a telephone number at the bottom of the email. He called it immediately. The phone had been disconnected. He sent her an email telling her that he had tried to call, and to email him as soon as she got his note letting him know how to contact her. He checked his email two, three, six times a day for some word from her. Week after week—nothing.

It was now two days before the flight and still no word from her. Illness, accident, death in the family, something else then? He vacillated between being sick with worry and being angry that she sent no message.

He barely ate on the flight and did not recall sleeping. The plane settled on the runway, pillow-like. Another plane at their gate had not pulled out, so they had to wait an extra ten minutes, a terrible ten minutes that he counted down with a kind of dread. Outside customs, there were hundreds of greeters massed in a semi-circle. He searched for her face but did not find it. He was furious with himself that they had not settled upon a definite plan. Low-grade anxiety began to settle in. What if traffic had delayed her on her way to the airport? He searched, had her paged and he waited an hour. She must be at the hotel and wondering where he was.

"Tollway quicker," the cabbie said. "You want toll way?"

"Yes."

"40 Baht more."

He didn't care how much more it cost him if he could just get to her now.

Upon reaching the hotel Michael had the concierge hold his bags. He searched the lobby, the in-hotel shops, and the coffee bar on the lower level. Maybe she had been in the rest room. He checked the lobby again.

"Is there a message for me?" he asked the desk clerk. She looked at the name on his passport and leafed through the message box.

"Look under Smithson."

The clerk looked at the name in the passport again.

"I know, but it might be addressed to a Michael Smithson." At the outset of the first visit, Drake had insisted he use a fake last name. Drake had been doing the same with Dawn. He gave no reason, and Michael had complied. Subsequently, he had asked Drake about giving Malee his real name. "No. If you do, she'll tell Dawn, and then Dawn'll ask me. You could get me killed."

"Look under Michael," he said to the clerk. "It might just say Michael."

"No last name?"

"No."

Empty again.

"Please check one more time. It's a very important message."

There was nothing.

"If someone calls for a Mr. Michael Smithson, please put it through to my room."

"I'm sorry sir. We can't do that. We can only connect phone calls to guests who are registered under that name."

"But I am a registered guest. It's just that the call may come though as a Mr. Smithson."

"I'm sorry sir. It's for security, you know. But let me check." She asked the senior clerk.

"I wish we could help you sir, but this is a security policy. I hope you can understand."

"Yes, I understand. But someone may call for me, but with the name Smithson, not my real name. You can't put that through?"

The senior clerk gave him a wan smile. "I wish I could."

"Could I please talk to the manager?"

"Of course, sir."

The manager was equally gracious, but the answer was the same. Jet lag coupled with concern then anger, then fretting, left Michael nearly beside himself. His heart was sinking into his stomach then back to his throat. He paced back and forth in his room, the same room she and he had shared. It was maddening.

Every hour, he took the elevator to the lobby and looked for her. Then he stopped at a pay-by-the-hour Internet shop where he checked his email. He sent her another, confirming the hotel name and telling her his room number. He alternated between being furious with her and becoming irate with himself for being furious with her. There had to be an explanation.

Drake arrived the next day.

"You look like shit."

Michael explained. "What do you think?"

Drake shrugged, "How about Nana tonight?"

"No, no, I can't. She'll show up tonight."

She did not.

The next morning, over breakfast, Michael asked, "What should I do?"

"I think we're going to Samui."

Michael nodded.

"I got us the same two bungalows."

"What? You," Michael nearly stuttered, "you already took care of everything?"

"Here's your plane ticket. Dawn and I will meet you in the lobby tomorrow at nine o'clock so we can spend the day there. Get some sleep. Or come to Nana. And then get some sleep."

By four o'clock the next afternoon they were already checked in at Bann Mann. Michael's room was back to the original configuration, two single beds with the nightstand in between. They met on the veranda for dinner as they had so many times during the previous trip. Michael had no appetite, but forced himself to eat realizing that he hadn't touched much in the way of sustenance since he left the United States. "Think I'll head over to O'Neill's."

"Little early."

"Just in case."

"We'll see you there at eight."

O'Neill's looked smaller, in a way, insignificant. The same crew was there, plus one new girl who didn't look like she presented much competition. The old-timers all remembered him. He spotted them all to a drink and ordered bottled water for himself.

"Joy still come here?"

"Think she come eight."

One of the girls took out Connect Four. He played a few rounds.

Drake and Dawn arrived a little after eight o'clock and were talking to Michael when Joy walked in. By the look on their faces, Michael knew she was approaching from behind him, but he hoped against hope that it was Malee. He turned, and Joy stopped mid-stride. Then he knew, and he wished he had not eaten. He arose. They greeted each other, and he gestured for Joy to sit at a table off to one side. She was dressed for business, but knew instantly that her night was going to be a 180-degree turn from what she had expected. There was a long silence while they looked at each other, not sure what to say. Finally, Michael cut the tension, "You know why I came."

Joy looked down and nodded.

"She's gone?" Michael could barely articulate the words.

Another nod. "She gone Germany."

"What?"

"With man. I tell her you coming."

"She knew I was coming!" He blurted out barely able to contain himself, but did.

"She tell me, not sure. She tell you call she. You no call."

His throat had gone dry, and he could feel the blood draining from his face.

"I sent her emails. I told her."

"I sorry. I very, very sorry. She go with bad man. Him smoke. Drink. No have money. Many debts—she pronounced the "b". I tell her no. I angry her. I call her now, yes?"

"Yes."

Joy got out her cell phone and called. She got Malee on the first try. Michael nearly went limp, but held himself firm. Joy spoke in Thai at first, then English for Michael's benefit. "Yes. You come back see Khun Michael. He come see you. Good man. You man no good. I know. I see." There was a long pause while Malee was talking. Then Joy spoke in a mix of Thai and English. "Mama she cry. Every day. You bad daughter make Mama cry. Khun Michael, you talk." She handed Michael the phone. He walked some steps away for privacy.

"Malee." She was crying. "I don't understand. You knew I was coming back. Coming back to see you."

"I no sure you come. I tell you call. You no call."

"I did call. The phone didn't work. I sent emails. Many emails."

"I not sure." She was holding back the convulsive sobs that were beginning to reach up from her chest.

"Please, you come back now."

"I no can now."

"Why not?"

"I sorry, Khun Michael. You good man. I make you sad." The intensity of her crying increased.

"Just come back. I'll wait. Do you need plane ticket?"

"No can, Khun Michael."

Crestfallen he simply handed the phone back to Joy and slumped into the closest chair.

There was a heated exchange between sisters in Thai. Joy was speaking loudly, almost shouting. Then there was a long pause. "No!" Tears were streaming down her cheeks. "You no can do." She turned to Michael, crying. "She say she marry."

He staggered, inside.

"She marry bad man. Bad sister. Bad daughter."

Michael took the phone.

"You marry this man?"

"I sorry Khun Michael." It was hard to understand her English mixed with her weeping. "I live Germany now."

Joy took the phone. "I call you tomorrow. You think. I love you. I say what good for you." She hung up.

For the first time, Dawn was not smiling. Michael was in a barroom full of people, yet felt totally alone. "I think I'll take a look at the art gallery." Halfway there, Drake caught him up and was walking beside him.

"Tough break."

"I," He paused looking for the words. "God," another pause, shaking his head from left to right "nightmares do come true."

They were at the art gallery.

"I didn't know you were a man of the arts," Michael said to Drake with a short, desperate laugh.

"Always have been."

"Which one do you like the best?"

Drake scanned the offerings. "That one," pointing.

"Same one she picked," he sighed.

"At least she has good taste in art."

Michael looked up, entreating, "I don't know what to do."

Drake stood stone-faced. Then a smile curled on his lips, and he gave one silent nose-laugh.

"What?"

"Fuck her sister." He said this as matter-of-factly as if making a passing comment about the weather. Michael looked at Drake with a mix of disbelief and incredulity.

When they returned to O'Neill's, Joy offered to buy Michael a drink. "No. Thanks anyway. That's very kind. I'm just going to go back to my place."

"Khun Michael, you not be alone now. I come with you. We sit. Talk more."

They walked in silence back to his bungalow. He helped her in the places on the path where the burned-out lighting had still not been repaired. He turned one light on in the bungalow, the air on low, and each sat on a separate bed.

"We just talk," he said.

"Yes, just talk. I very sad. For you."

And then it came. He was both ashamed and didn't care, and it made no difference anyway because he had no control over it. Joy burst into tears, too. For several minutes, they cried.

The only movement was of him handing her a fistful of tissues while keeping some close by for himself.

"I just can't understand. How could she not tell me that she wouldn't be here? How could she let me fly here knowing that?"

"I call her tomorrow."

"She's not coming back. I know that." He got up slowly and fetched a small package from his briefcase. He opened it up for Joy. "I brought her this." It was a beautiful tanzanite ring accented with diamonds. Joy put in on and admired it.

"I never see so pretty ring."

"Please, give it to Malee when you see her."

"Yes." She sat next to him.

He had no recollection of the chain of events that unfolded, but thought about it afterwards, many times. It astounded him with each attempt that he could not remember how they had ended up in bed together. It was as if he had been stone drunk and was trying to recall what had happened the night before, as if Drake's suggestion had taken on a life of its own and Michael was powerless to stop it. He remembered that it was torrid, her mouth passionate, that neither one showered first. His body recalled her nails digging into his back—he could still feel the sting when he woke up the next morning. They slept together in one of the single beds. But how was it possible not to recollect how it had begun, what had happened after she sat next to him with the ring on her finger? If someone had told him this story, he would not have believed it.

They went for breakfast at the same time as Drake and Dawn emerged from their bungalow. The four ate as if everything were normal. Dawn was her smiley self, chatting with Joy in Thai. Drake was deadpan. Afterwards, when Joy went to fetch a change of clothing and her things, Drake and Michael were alone.

"Don't even ask," Michael said.

"Ask what?"

"Well, just don't."

"I'm impressed."

"I don't even know how it happened."

Drake looked askance. "Just tell me, who pounced first."

"It wasn't like that."

"Mid-air collision?"

"You have no idea how... how... I don't know."

"She was bad?"

"No!" defensively, "and you know that."

"So, she's going to stay with you."

"I don't know."

"What do you mean you *don't know*. She's getting her things."

"Then I guess so."

"You're a quick mover."

"Just shut up, will you?"

"Do a guy a favor, and *this* is what you get."

"Just don't make light of it, okay?" Michael snapped earnestly.

Drake backed off, "Okay."

"I'm sorry, but..." Michael shook his head slowly, unable to finish the thought. He sighed deeply as he rested his chin in his hand looking away, not completing the thought.

"How about a swim?" Drake suggested.

"Why not?"

"You can wash the ocean with your tears."

"You always hit a guy when he's down?"

"Best way to get him up."

Joy went off to see, as she put it, "a friend." She said she would be back by six o'clock that evening. In the mid-afternoon Michael strolled along the beach to where he and Malee had sat the first night they were together. He listened to the slosh of the waves. He counted them. One for every day he estimated that she had left for Germany without telling him. He lost track of how many times he counted the number and started over.

On the walk back, as Michael approached his bungalow, he passed one of the maids. She bowed slightly and smiled, a friendly but puzzling smile. Michael unlocked his door. He stood motionless. The room had been changed—the beds together, nightstand on the other wall, as it had been with Malee. He was aware of his breathing. He felt tingling in his face and arms, particularly his fingers. This was her room, and she was not here.

He closed the door behind him, sat on the bed, his hands folded across his stomach as he slouched forward with his head hanging down. It all replayed, like watching a movie a second time. Michael had not moved from the bed by the time Joy showed up around seven. Joy was pleasantly surprised by the new arrangement. She was still wearing the ring.

The four ate dinner on the beach, an all too familiar custom that haunted Michael throughout the meal. After dinner, Michael and Joy returned to his bungalow. She called Malee again. Her reprimands and anger still could not sway Malee. They had only made her cry again. Michael did not understand it, did not ask to speak to Malee. He was too hurt and desolated, and he did not want to make her feel worse.

Michael and Joy had sex again that night. This time he remembered. She did not hurry him in any way. Afterwards, she told him one more thing about her call to Malee.

"She say she happy you make love me, not strange woman. She know I make you happy. She say that make her happy. She say she happy sister have good man be with."

Joy stayed with him five days—with breaks each day to see her so-called friend. She called Malee every day. The marriage plans were moving ahead with the ceremony planned for two weeks out, and this is what perplexed Michael all the more—if she was not yet attached why not leave this bad man in Germany and come back to him, here in Samui? This he could not reconcile.

The fifth day Joy did not return until nine. She told him that a friend had asked her to come back to Bangkok with him, and she would have to leave the next day. That night, afterwards, Joy cried. He wiped the mascara marked tears from her cheekbones. They would exchange emails. She would tell him about Malee if he wanted to know. As they parted he handed her a 'petit cadeau' discretely placed within in a sealed envelope. She kissed him, thanked him without opening the envelope. It contained 15,000 Baht. Michael noted that she was still wearing Malee's ring.

Drake and Michael walked along the shore.

"I can't understand it. How could she have gone off like that? And with such a lout."

"These girls have no good choices. They have to make the least worst choice. A hundred guys promise they'll come back. Ninety-nine don't."

"But she knew I was coming back. She *had* to know."

Drake shrugged, arching his eyebrows.

"80 then, 80 now instead of the whole 160 would have been better," Michael said.

Drake shrugged again.

"She let me fly all the way to Thailand, halfway around the globe. And she wasn't even here! How could she do that?"

"One thing about the Thai," Drake said in a tone that made it sound like he was a guy who had learned it the hard way, "they *never* give you bad news. They think they're doing you a favor by saying nothing. Took me a while to understand that. Crazy, but that's *them*."

"But how could she have chosen him?"

"Just wish her luck."

"And me?"

"Move on."

"I don't see how."

"Fucking romantic," he said, rolling his eyes and looking away.

That evening Drake took Michael to the small bar next to the art gallery. They had drinks.

"By the way, where's Dawn?"

"I don't know. She'll join us in a bit."

"What do you mean, *'you don't know?'*"

Drake waved off the question as he ordered a second round. Dawn arrived before the second round and was accompanied by an attractive, young woman who was carrying a little cloth bag over her shoulder.

"Dawn's your good friend," he said through a beaming smile aimed at Michael.

Michael ordered two more drinks. The young woman's name was Suchin. She was medium height with a well-proportioned, pleasant face and an eager to please look. Her hair was black and long, but not a long as Malee's had been last time he saw her. Suchin's English was above average.

"Have nice lady for Khun Michael." Dawn smiled at her handiwork. "She be with you."

After a third round for the guys and the second for Dawn and Suchin, they all left. Suchin went with Michael. Money was not discussed.

Suchin was appropriately modest and showered first. If her objective was to please him in bed, she cleared the bar with legroom to spare, and while Michael's heart was not in it, his body certainly was.

There was a new foursome at breakfast. The second night Suchin expressed her concern about their bungalow. Both Drake's and Michael's bungalows were along side the main path to the beach. She was embarrassed to be so close to strolling couples at night. That was fine with Michael. The bungalow carried too many memories anyway. He moved them to an interior bungalow. It was smaller, but the hot water ran at full tap.

"Now, at least I can get some sleep," Drake said. "I don't know how you can make it last so long."

"Well, Dawn's got the opposite complaint," Michael rejoined, feeling a little lighter, the first time since arriving in Thailand and not finding Malee there.

Drake threw a short punch to Michael's closest bicep.

"Got under the armor plate that time, I guess," Michael said with a familiar but fleeting gleam in his eye.

"Not just a fucking romantic. A fucking romantic *prick*."

Suchin became attached quickly. He had brought four packs of dental floss for Malee, so Suchin was introduced to the routine. One day, she said she had to go to the market for a couple of hours—a Joy "friend" kind of thing, he assumed, but he was wrong. She returned in a little more than one hour carrying a large assortment of food. At her request, Michael obtained a brazier from the establishment along with fuel. She cooked him a traditional-style meal on the path in front of their porch. She was an excellent cook. He drank wine for the first time during this second visit. Together they finished an entire bottle.

Over the course of the days they were together, they developed a routine. In the heat of the day, while Michael read the International Tribune and then his latest book, Suchin knit, read comic books, and snuggled up next to him. As it would begin to cool, they would head to the beach.

Unlike Malee, Suchin knew how to swim and was not afraid of the great yellow enemy. Of course, she lathered up with SPF 200 or something before venturing out. Sometimes they swam out more than half a mile. Even then, it was not over Michael's head. It was over hers however, but she had her own private lifeguard.

On the surface, it was a pleasant life, but his thoughts rarely strayed from Malee. He kept this hidden from Suchin knowing that while it should not hurt her feelings, it would. A few days later she presented him with her finished knit scarf. It was in the colors of the Thai flag.

"For me?"

"For cold where you live. Then you remember me."

He thought about Malee far more than he acknowledged to Drake as well, but Drake had that annoying ability of seeing what was going on behind the eyes.

"Is Suchin going to be a replay?" Drake asked.

"I don't think so."

"Only 'don't think so'?" he laughed. "You are a slow learner."

"I wasn't going to ask her."

"You get a B-."

"Why such a low a grade?"

"Because you thought about it."

"Actually, I didn't," Michael countered with more of a bite to the words than he expected.

Suchin saw him off at the airport. Dawn and Drake said their goodbyes to her. Leaving Michael and Suchin to themselves. She comported herself with dignity. She knew the inevitable all too well, and accepted it. Her acknowledging the inescapable with such grace added a new feeling that attached itself to Michael's gnawing sadness. Pity? Guilt? Resignation? He could not place it, and found himself treating Suchin with extra generosity.

As the plane took off, he looked down on Samui and picked out Bann Mann, but the whole island disappeared in the clouds before he could locate their bungalows.

After they had collected their luggage, or rather Michael's

as the other two traveled with only carry-on's, Michael hesitantly turned to Drake and Dawn, "I think I need a couple of
days just to be alone."

Drake scribbled a number on a piece of paper. "Here's
Dawn's number. You call when you're ready."

Michael nodded.

"Not too many days," Drake said. "We have to finalize
things."

"Okay."

For the first three days, the only person Michael saw was the
man pushing in the room service cart and, Prang, the maid
who had introduced herself on his first visit. He sat in his
room's easy chair while Prang cleaned the room. Her English
was excellent and soon Michael found out that she had helped
her husband in a clothing business. They had sold to tourists before he had died in a car accident. When their clothing
business had been doing well, she had taken intensive English
lessons. After her husband's death, she accumulated sufficient
capital to relocate her suk to a better section of town to sell
to an upscale line of clothing. One night, her suk and several
others caught on fire. The suk was salvaged, but she lost her
entire inventory to smoke damage. She still owned the suk
and had repaired the damage, but had no reserves to replace
the inventory. She was forced out of business. An aunt was
paying the carrying costs at present to keep the empty suk for
her, but did not have the extra money necessary for restock-
ing the high-end line. Prang estimated that she needed about
300,000 Baht to replace the ruined merchandise before she
could reopen her business. The only job she could find was the
one at the hotel, and while she was scraping by on her wages,
she had not lost hope about reopening her store.

Prang dressed in the standard maid's uniform and went
about her work, nothing else. By hotel policy, the door was left
open when she was in a guest's room, occupied or not. She was

attractive but hardly stunning. She was in her late 20's. But it was the way she moved. She had a feline grace. It was natural, not suggestive. To his surprise, Michael found her increasingly attractive. Each day while she went tidying his room, he sat in the chair and they talked, each day yielding more intimate knowledge about the life of the other.

Getting a bit restless by the fourth night of being alone, Michael decided that he needed to get out and stretch his legs. He passed by the location where Jin had worked in the foot massage suk. The shop was gone. So were all the other suks—foot massage, tailors, Internet rooms, and bars. In their place, a luxury apartment building was under construction.

Later that evening, Michael found that his feet had directed him down the familiar streets towards Cowboy. He decided to pop into Sunshine Delight. Among the greeters outside, he saw Cindy.

"Hello," he said.

"Hello."

"You remember me?"

"Yes."

"You're still keeping your promise to Mama?"

"Yes."

He raised his eyebrows with an upward nod and pushed through the plastic blinds as Cindy made way. It was active inside but would become more so later in the evening. He looked for Wan but did not see her. He took a seat. A hostess approached to take his drink order. He held up his hand to wave her off, but as she turned to tend to other customers, Michael caught her attention asking, "You know Wan?"

She shook her head no.

"She's a hostess like you."

The hostess shrugged.

At the other side of the stage, he spotted Somo. He signaled her over. She either did not see it or pretended not to.

"Please tell Somo to come see me," he asked the hostess.

Somo acknowledged his hand signal, but she hesitated. Finally, she came over.

They exchanged greetings. Somo was uncomfortable. Her arms were crossed in front of her and she keep looking around, never directly at Michael.

"I was looking for Wan."

"She no longer here."

"Do you know where she is?"

She shrugged and shifted her stance.

"How long ago did she leave?"

"Long time."

"You don't know where she is? Another bar?"

"She *gone*."

"Went back to her family?

"No."

Well, what then? You must know something. She's your friend."

"Her hang self."

There was silence.

She nodded.

"What?!"

She nodded.

"Why? What happened?" He realized that he had raised his voice.

Somo looked down and shifted her feet again. "She no happy me think."

"When? When did this happen?" His mouth had gone dry.

"Long time."

"Like when? How many months ago?"

"Me think."

"What was the date? The month?"

"Me no understand."

"Did she ever speak to you about me?"

Somo did not reply, and he could not read her expression. "Now I go work."

"No! I have to know. Wait here." He found a manager who spoke English fairly well, and she served as a translator.

"It was how many months ago?"

"She thinks maybe three or four. Maybe five. She's not sure. Maybe more. I wasn't here back then. I never knew her," the manager added.

Michael thought for a second. If Somo were correct, then it could have been three or four months after he had left for Samui. "Did Wan ever speak about me to Somo?"

"She doesn't remember."

"How can she not remember?"

The translator asked Somo another question. "Sir, she doesn't. I have to get back to work now. And so does Somo. So, if you'll excuse us."

He left Sunshine Delight. Cindy wished him goodbye as he exited. He barely acknowledged it. On the walk back to his hotel, the hawkers and the hookers disappeared from his view.

"Hey, fella. Watch where you're going," the man said shoving Michael off of the female companion Michael had just bumped into.

"Sorry," Michael said, absently.

He walked three blocks past his hotel before realizing it.

On his way to Sunshine Delight Michael had bought a bottle of Johnny Walker Black to give to Wan as a present. Now it was staring at him from the table in his room. In movies, people often turned to a stiff drink or drinks in times of emotional distress, but Michael had never been tempted that way. That night, however, he did open Wan's bottle, and took one very stiff drink. It didn't do much one way or the other. He never took another drink from that bottle—not that night, not ever again. He spent the night alone. *What a waste* is all that went through his mind, over and over again. *What a waste. What a waste. What a waste.* He felt his thoughts closing in on him. He had no idea when he went to sleep. He awoke with his clothes on. It was noon.

Apart from two days with Drake revising the contract with the Jim Thompson Company based on the success of the stores in New York and San Francisco, Michael had little recollection of how the days had passed.

He got into the habit of falling asleep early, and would wake up sometime after midnight. He knew he would not fall back asleep. One night he showered, shaved and walked out into the night. The streets were quiet.

Michael remembered that Drake had pointed out The Emporium to him on their way to Cowboy. "When the bars shut down, that's where the unlucky hookers go. See if their luck might change. Order a drink and sit down. See what floats by. Or just pick your own." That night The Emporium seemed to fit his mood. Michael walked down the double flight of stairs into a cavernous room with cheap tables and chairs everywhere except in the center where a large four-sided bar was set up. Michael made a perimeter stroll. At one table, four young girls were chatting. Except for their outfits, they might have been mistaken for a "ladies night out". They were all attractive, one particularly so. She was also the one who dressed least in a "For Sale" outfit. Michael said hello to her. She looked up for a second and then ignored him.

Michael ordered a Singh at the bar. As the bartender leveled off the foam, Michael asked, "What's with Miss Emporium over there." He nodded in the direction of the four girls.

The bartender chuckled. "Oh she? She different. You buy her drink. I talk to her. If she like you, she comes see you."

"How does she know who bought it?"

"I take care that."

"All right, a drink."

"She like whisky."

Michael nodded okay.

"Only good whisky."

"Oh, *that's* how it works," Michael said with a touch of humor.

"No understand."

"*Right.* So, what's the lady's drink."

"Johnny Walker Black. On rocks."

Michael paid the tab for the beer and scotch.

"What table you like?"

He glanced around. "How about number nine?"

The bartender wrote "9" on a paper napkin and sent it over with the drink.

Michael sat and surveyed the scene. It was a mix of prowl, tipsy, boredom, and laughter depending on the table. After a few minutes, a girl approached. "You buy me a drink?"

"Sure. What'll it be?"

"Whisky."

"Ice?"

"No thank you."

She was hardly Miss Emporium, but she was nicely slender, had an engaging smile, and spoke English far beyond the requisite name, age, and price. A variation of name, rank and serial number ran through his mind. Her name was Talap. She worked in a travel agency by day and picked up extra money now and again to support herself and her infant daughter. She was vague about the father except to say that he was no longer around.

She came to The Emporium directly from her apartment, that is, after she had taken her daughter over to her sister's place.

They had been talking for a few minutes when Miss Emporium made her appearance.

"I sit?"

Michael nodded.

Talap shifted in her chair. Her eyes asked Michael if

she should leave. He quickly said "No. Stay." He caught the bartender's eye and signaled for another round. When the bartender arrived with his tray, Michael responded to the apparent deficit, "No, two Johnny Walker Blacks, one straight up."

Miss Emporium's name was Porntip—*would she ever have a hard time in the States*, Michael thought. Hers was the more typical broken English to which he had become accustomed to navigating. That, plus the other obvious reason, put a damper on their conversation. Michael paid the tab when the bartender returned with the revised order. After Talap had finished as much of her second drink as she wanted, Michael took her hand as a non-verbal invitation for her to come with him. Feeling a little reckless and quite unlike himself, Michael was not worried about saving face with Porntip. He bid a polite farewell to her and escorted Talap out.

The street was uncharacteristically deserted except for two young, loud drunks, who were clearly on the hunt.

"You didn't mention anything about price," he said.

"I don't like to talk about price," she said and then looked at Michael. "You know, right?"

"Long time okay?"

"Okay."

She showered first, then Michael. They lay in bed side-by-side. She took a condom out from under her pillow. "Should I open this now?"

"No. Not now. Let me just rest here next to you.

As they got more comfortable with one another Talap opened up to Michael's questions. She talked about a number of things: how she learned English, but not well enough to obviate the need for occasional visits to The Emporium, the circumstances of her marriage and why she divorced, what prompted her to sit at his table, what was going through her mind when Porntip joined them. When he explained the meaning of Porntip's name in English they both had a good laugh.

The condom lay unopened near the edge of the bed. She looked at the clock on the night table. "I probably should be going soon," she whispered hesitantly but with the underlying quality of a mother's worry.

"I'd like you to stay. I mean for the whole night. For double."

She thought for a moment.

"Your daughter?"

"Yes."

"Won't she be okay with your sister?"

"All right." She called on her cell phone. It was a long conversation, during which Michael concluded that he had never witnessed a short one between two Thai women. "My sister says okay."

He held her hand in his, fingers intertwined.

"I think you're very sad," she said.

He gave one nod.

"A girlfriend?"

He nodded once more.

"What happened, if I may ask?"

"She's gone."

"I'm sorry. How?"

"Accident. A misunderstanding. Just really bad timing."

When she fell asleep, he draped his arm over her, and they slept that way. He ordered early morning room service, and they ate breakfast together. The condom was still unopened on the bed.

"How about you stay here a couple of nights?"

"I have to go to work."

"I mean when you finish."

"I have to check with my sister."

"And if that's okay, see you at... ?" he paused waiting for her to fill in the rest.

"Six."

"Call here, ask for Michael and this room number, and let me know when you know."

Talap stayed two more nights. They ate dinner together each night with Michael and then read books in English as they lounged in bed. He became her dictionary. It was a small action that somehow made him feel like he was helping her, happy to hear her gain another word. When he tired of reading, he just held her close.

"This okay?"

"If this is what you'd like," she said.

"This is what I'd like."

The third night, they talked about more intimate subjects, and she initiated some hand exploration.

"We can if you like, you know," she said.

"Probably better for you if not, right?"

"It's been a long time."

She showered first, and then he did likewise. She sat on the edge of the bed, facing away, and his fingertips ran down the exposed part of her back. Then she went to lay back, the towel still knotted under her arm. It was a quiet intimacy.

"Glad to see you've reemerged," Drake greeted him. "What was her name?"

"Talap, but it's not what you think."

"How come it's never what I think?"

"Because I know what you think," a light ribbing edged its way into the remark making Michael realize that his humor was better than in had been in days.

"What'll be tonight? Nana or Cowboy?"

"I don't know. Not sure I'm really up to it."

"Cowboy?"

Michael paused, finally acquiescing, "Alright…"

"Ah-haa," Drake held the phrase longer to make his point.

"So..." he hesitated, waiting for Michael to make a protest. None came. "Now *this* is what I like to *HEAR*."

The conversation shifted from the evening plans to their business dealings and was a welcome diversion as far as Michael was concerned. There was one more phase of negotiations with the Jim Thompson people given the success with which the franchise had taken off. Plus Michael and Drake had initiated discussion of a new business—exporting to Europe since Michael had connections with an upscale department chain in England. There was a lot to consider, and the loose details were hammered out that morning leaving Michael feeling more like his old self, certainly more than he had since getting to Thailand. He was again on familiar territory where he knew the parameters, the advantages and the gains.

Thinking about doing successful business in Thailand as a foreigner Michael's mind began to wander and started latching on to all that had happened these last couple of weeks—no Malee, his time with Joy, Suchin's face at the airport, hearing of Wan's suicide, talking to Talap about supplementing her income to support her daughter because her "good job" just didn't quite cover the bills, his own desire to teach Malee and Talap English so they might escape a future filled with drudgery. Michael made a decision not to see Talap again—he knew the score, and so did she. It was a business transaction, and he just couldn't risk her getting attached, not expecting but still wanting more than what it was they had negotiated.

Having decided on this plan of action to protect himself Michael headed out with Drake and Dawn that evening to make a point, mostly to himself. Pretty Paradise was bustling and with the couple looking cozy on the other side of the table Michael started feeling like the odd man out. His resolve began wavering and when they ordered drinks—two beers and one bottled-water—Drake shot Michael a look as if a dare had been issued. Their hostess, Tum, was gorgeous. She was very young and unusually tall for a Thai and her face had almost perfect Caucasian features. She wore flats. At Drake's nudging, Dawn began negotiations without clueing Michael in. She had not gotten far when another hostess, older, intervened. "She my sister. She too young to go with man." Then she and Dawn entered into a long discussion.

"What's she saying?" Michael asked Drake.

"She's telling lies. Says you're a nice man."

The negotiations concluded resulting in the agreement that if Michael was willing to pay double the bar fine, Tum would go with him for 3000 Bhat. Michael shrugged okay, paid and took Tum back to his hotel.

Tum was nervous. She showered for twenty minutes and emerged with two towels wrapped around her. She sat on the easy chair and kneaded her hands.

"Look, don't stay if you don't want to. Here's 1000. Just leave if you want." Tum did not understand. He put the bill in her hand, fetched her clothes and handed them to her. "It's okay. You want to go? You go. No problem." She was undecided, or at least she said nothing for a long time. She smiled, sort of. One foot was jiggling up and down rapidly.

Michael went to shower. Tum was still in the chair when he came out. She was biting the side of a finger.

"I think you want to go."

"I stay," she said with more assuredness. She put the bill on the table next to the chair.

Well, this would be interesting if nothing else Michael mused to himself as he approached Tum, gently taking her hand and escorting her to the bed.

She wanted the lights off. Michael shook his head no. Realizing then that she was a true "eighteen plus one day" he took things slowly. He waiting for her to become comfortable or to remain uncomfortable in which case, as far as he was concerned, it was all over. Gradually she relaxed. He stopped two more times, but they were only pauses. He gave her 4000 plus the 500. The next evening, her sister was friendly toward him. He saw Tum two more times in two more days, and then she had some days off.

Drake had arranged a trip to Hua Hin, a resort town on the southwestern coast.

"Figured you need a change of venue. It's a little sleepy, but okay. Dawn's never been there."

The train had three classes: first was soft seats and air conditioning. Second class was all hard seats and an overhead fan. Third class was hard seats, no fan, and small farm animals. Drake bought seats in second class. He was a big spender with most things, but on train rides economy was the watchword.

"What's the matter with first?" Michael asked.

"I hate air conditioning."

"I hate sweating like a pig."

"Then sweat like some other animal."

The fan was on lazy low, and it was beastly hot in the carriage. On top of it all, with a coal-burner as your engine, you did not open windows. The air soon became stifling. Drake did not mind. Dawn used a hand fan. Michael was miserable. The train pulled out of Bangkok at the slowest speed imaginable—literally moving slower than a person could walk for the first half hour. Finally, it picked up speed. That is to say, perhaps 25 miles per hour except when it slowed up for a station. It stopped at so many stations that Michael lost count. They arrived six long hours later.

The hotel was modest, clean, air conditioned, and it overlooked a pristine bleached-white beach.

At night, they explored the bar scene. The town was dead. The bars were of the outdoor variety, like O'Neill's, but most had no patrons and none had bargirls. On one street they finally found a bar with a bargirl, Noom. She was twenty-three years old, but looked younger. Dawn talked with her briefly. She was inexpensive by Bangkok standards.

"Me think good. Khun Michael take."

"Looks like you got the catch of the day," Drake offered, "or should I say, *today's* catch."

They all had a drink and then walked back to the hotel.

Noom brought some interesting qualities. She was super eager to please, but her English was close to non-existent. Michael soon discovered that even working through her limited verbal capability in anything other than Thai she still exuded unavoidable dullness accompanied by an overt pageant of limited intelligence. Michael tried to be polite, but had scant interest. After she had showered, Michael declined with the universal hand gesture of yawning, suggesting that he was exhausted. They slept together, meaning in the same bed.

The second night was a repeat. Noom was puzzled but pressed for nothing further. Michael's thoughts drifted to, and focused on Wan. He did think of Malee, but Wan held center stage that night, creating in him a sadness that would not go away. His mind kept coming back to Drake's haunting words, "the least worst choice," and that thought drifted into nightmare as Michael started to doze off.

He bolted up in bed, drenched in sweat. His explosive movement awakened Noom. She interpreted this as a sudden sexual desire and was more than willing to accede. But all he could do was sit there motionless, cold sweat beading on his face.

They scheduled their return to Bangkok sooner than originally planned. Noom saw them off. She put the traditional flower bracelet on Michael's wrist and cried as the train pulled out. Michael felt stupidly guilty that he had hurt Noom's feelings. Already a little raw with irritation, Michael had traded in his second-class ticket for first class. *Discomfort be damned*

Michael decided, not caring that his already-purchased second-class ticket had no trade in value. He just gave it to the woman in line behind him who was surprised and delighted. He had offered to buy a first-class seat for Dawn as well, but she was afraid of angering Drake and politely declined.

Michael spent a few more nights at the hotel. He looked forward to Prang's daily cleaning ministrations. If he put out a "Make Up Room Now" sign out, she would show at ten-thirty in the morning, on the dot. He always showered and shaved before her arrival, and they always conversed. Each time she was in his room they became more and more friendly with one another.

"You know, I really like you." It had just come out without his thinking about it.

Prang blushed. "Sir," she said meaningfully, "I am embarrassed."

"Sorry. I don't mean to make you uncomfortable."

She dusted with more single-minded purpose.

"But I do. I'd like to take you to dinner."

"Sir, it is against hotel policy."

"We'll go someplace where no one will know. You pick the place."

"I don't know."

"I take that as a yes."

"Well…" she hesitated, then whispered, "just give the address and the time, and I will be there. It can be a chance meeting. At a nice place."

They met that same night at eight o'clock. Over wine and dinner they shared stories about her growing up and then his life as a young man. They talked about her English. Michael learned that the intrepid Prang had read a fair number of books, novels mainly, and always had a dictionary close by so she could look up every word she did not understand. She had brought a list of idiomatic expressions to dinner, phrases to which she could not discover the meanings. It was two-pages long, making Michael smile at her eagerness and command of the English language. They went through the list, and he explained each to her, delighted when he could see that she had mastered the phrase. There was only one exception: "At night, all cats are gray." Michael professed that he was unclear as to its meaning. She found that amusing. In truth, he was embarrassed to explain it.

When they left the restaurant, Prang was ill at ease. Michael hailed a cab, and when it pulled up, he opened the door for her, pressing a small note into her hand for the fare. He thanked her for the evening as he closed the door and watched while the cab drove away, her lingering smile of thanks still indelible.

The next morning she arrived at ten-thirty as always. There were a few awkward moments and then they both laughed. "I really enjoyed last night," she said softly so no one could hear should they walk by the open room.

"So did I. I wanted to do this before I left."

She looked at him puzzled.

"I am flying back to The States tomorrow."

"Oh," she said half surprised and half as a question that she knew she had no right to ask. She caught herself, "Well, I wish you a safe journey."

"I'll stay here at this hotel again if I return. I hope you'll be here."

"I probably will be." There was resignation in her voice. Then she brightened. "Then maybe you can tell me about the cats at night."

"I'll look it up."

After checking out of the hotel, Michael gave the nearly full bottle of Johnny Walker Black to Simon, the concierge with whom Michael had learned to trust implicitly and had come to like quite a bit. The bottle was discretely packaged. Simon nodded sincere thanks.

Drake and Dawn saw Michael off at the airport, Dawn putting the traditional flower bracelet on him. Her smile was as warm as he had ever seen it.

"Me worry Khun Michael."

He replied in Thai, "Thank you," holding up his wrist, "I'm okay. It was good to see you again."

"Next time, me find better girl you. Next time she wait." She didn't mean it to, but it stung. Dawn leaned forward and kissed him on the cheek.

Drake took him aside.

"I'm taking care of all the costs."

"No."

"Yes, this one's on me."

"Drake, don't make it worse than it is, okay?"

"I'm trying to make it better."

"Look, I really appreciate it. I do. It's a very kind gesture. But it's not going to make it better. Only worse. Email me the amount when you've got it figured out. I'll wire it same as last time. Okay?"

"Okay."

"And no shitting with the numbers."

"Okay, you prick."

"What?"

"For a second there, I thought maybe you were reading my mind."

"Two-way street, huh?"

"God, I hope not."

They shook hands with a quick shake. Drake was not for drawn out affairs, and he was not the hugging type—only with the opposite sex and then with a specific intention.

Jay met Michael at the airport, same as after the first trip. There was a big hug between the brothers.

"Jesus, you lost weight!"

"Ah, a little." His belt was notched on a hole formerly unused.

"And you told me the food was so good over there."

"It is."

"Well, you're no walking advertisement," he laughed. "You all right? I mean, everything okay?"

Michael gave him the story.

"Yeah, that can be really, really rough. You know that I know that."

Michael smiled. "I'll tell you what, it's really good to see you. I mean really good."

"Likewise. You know, you're my favorite brother."

Michael laughed. "Nothing to do with being the only brother, is it?" It was his first real laugh in a long time.

Jay was a gentle soul housed in an athletic body and was exceptionally strong. He carried himself with an air of nonchalance and modesty at the same time. He was at ease with men. Experienced with women—his initiation in high school with the head cheerleader almost got him expelled. Being quarterback of an about-to-be undefeated team is probably what saved him. He later told Michael that he and the cheerleader learned to be more discreet after that.

The brothers had both been on the tennis team, Jay two rungs up from Michael. The year after Jay graduated, Michael worked his way to becoming the top ranked player. Jay had married while in college, and two years later went through a messy divorce. Fortunately, there were no children. Michael helped Jay by being there for him, staying with him in those nights of his darkest moments. Perhaps more importantly, Michael helped with stratagems to counter the maliciousness of his wife who, with her female attorney and cadre of divorced friends, tried first one tactic, then another. They were all vindictive attempts to make Jay's life miserable and more practically to peel away as much of the joint assets as she could

finagle. Jay adhered to the truth despite the fact that sometimes his interests would have been better served by shading it
a little. He ended up in therapy for a year, during which time
he could only sleep with the aid of prescription pills. On those
nights when the pills failed to do their magic, Michael was
there with him, listening, far into the night.

Michael slowly adjusted to the time zone, but there were other
things he was not adjusting to. His appetite still had not come
back. On the scale, he was below his high school weight and
decided to make an armistice with food. If eating did not insist
on presenting itself as an enjoyable experience, he would eat
enough to keep from losing more weight, or at least not much
more. The lack of sleep he blamed on the time zone change,
but that became less valid as the days rolled by. If he could *only*
focus on the joy of being with Malee on his first visit, which
sometimes he could, sleep would come. But mostly it was the
second visit to Thailand that would settle into his mind and
sleep remained elusive.

Getting up was worse. All Michael wanted was to stay
in bed and wait for his headache to go away, which it never
would until he finally dragged himself up to start the day. One
Saturday, he awoke early and played *their* song, "Worried, oh
so worried that you let me down," over and over again on an
automatic-repeat mode. On some play-throughs, Michael listened to pick out and identify each instrument and the occasional muted vocal accompanists backing up Shakin' Stevens
voice. He fixated on the base as it walked down the scale on
the key phrase. The song ran for three minutes and fifty-four
seconds. He did not get out of bed until just before noon.

He tried emailing her, but now all he received was a
non-deliverable notice. He emailed Joy. She responded that
Malee was unhappy and no longer had email. He sent Joy a
second email asking for Malee's phone number, not that he
planned to call her, but he needed to have some way to contact

her just in case. Just in case of what? He had no idea. Joy never responded.

Saturday, Jay was to pick up Michael for dinner and then a musical—they would be going along with Jay's girlfriend and a blind date that Jay's girlfriend had selected for Michael. Michael called at noon.

"Look, uh, I'm going to bow out for tonight."

"What're you talking about?"

"Look, you know, whatever tab is mine, I'll take care of it."

"That's not what I'm talking about. Why're you bowing out?"

"I… I think that's… just better for me today."

"I'm coming over."

"No, no, don't, please."

"See you in fifteen."

"No!" But Jay had already hung up.

"Jesus H. Christ! What the fuck happened?" The garage door was bowed out, and the wood had cracked apart.

Michael tried to dismiss it, "Just a stupid accident."

Inside the garage, the car bumper was tangled with the garage door hardware.

"Hey, come on, we're family."

"I forgot to open the garage door."

Jay turned and stared at him. Michael looked away. "Hey, you got to see someone."

Michael said nothing.

"Do you hear me? You have *GOT* to see someone."

Michael nodded.

"So you're going to?"

Michael pursed his lips.

"You are going to? Right?" Jay inquired with a force that implied it was no longer a question.

"All right."

"You're not just putting me off, are you?"

"No."

Jay put an arm around him and laughed. "Hey, how the hell are you going to get that fucking car out of there?"

"Got a garage guy coming over."

"Boy, is he in for a surprise."

"I can't believe I did this."

"Hey, you're coming tonight, okay?"

"I'm just going to ruin it for everyone."

"You're going to ruin it for me if you don't come. All right?"

"All right."

The couch days were evidently a thing of the past. Michael sat in a stuffed chair facing Dr. Bach. Michael lowered his head. "I'm so ashamed to be here."

"Why?"

"I should just be strong enough." He sniffed in, "It's such a sign of weakness."

"No. It's a sign of courage to admit that you need to be helped."

Dr. Bach waited the half-minute before Michael began to talk. At the end of the session, Dr. Bach summed it up, "Michael, you have the classical symptoms of acute depression. It's a disease, and it's treatable. The pharmacology is well established." He wrote out a prescription for two drugs. "I want to see you again next week, sooner if you think necessary."

Michael held the two white slips in his hand. "I hate taking medicine. How long for these?"

"We'll see. It could be quite a while, but some of that depends on you. It'll take two to three months for these to have any noticeable effect, so let's not rush it. You're still functioning well enough that I'm putting you on a gradual build up. It's a lot better that way, if there's time. And in your case, I believe there may be. But if things get worse, you let me know right away."

Two months later, Michael was starting to feel better. Dr. Bach was cautious about when to consider tapering down. "And even then, we need to talk about a maintenance regime."

"You mean like forever?"

"It would be prudent for a while."

"Christ."

Another email arrived from Helen. It was only the second time she had contacted him since she had left, and it was so out of the blue that it took Michael aback completely.

Michael,

I just got back from three weeks in the Canadian Rockies. I am tanned, stronger, feel like I am breathing deeply on every breath and just happy to be deliciously resting right now. Nothing like 9000 feet to get you in shape quickly. I even rappelled down two cliffs. The first time I was scared because I did not know what to expect. The second time I was petrified because I knew precisely what to expect. One guy broke his ankle and had to be evacuated. Bears in the camp two nights spooked me, but everyone else seemed to take it in stride. Other than that, it was a great escape. Life in the commune seems a bit of a letdown in comparison. I am not even sure why I am writing all this to you. I wanted to tell someone about my little adventure, and it turned out I thought of writing you.

I heard that you were in Thailand on some business venture. There isn't a woman in the world who isn't afraid of Bangkok. I think they picked that name just to torment us all the more. If you partook, I guess I should be

neither surprised nor jealous. But I am a little of the one
without any right to be.

I thought about deleting this email, but obviously I
didn't. Please do not email. I hope you are well, Helen

Jay put down the copy that Michael had printed out.

"I don't know what to make of it. She's beginning to miss you. I'll conclude that. But the clarity of the mountain air is certainly not mirrored in her thought processes. That's for sure."

"I wonder if I should email her back anyway."

"Absolutely not. And guess what? She's probably hoping you do."

"You think so?"

"Look, I know her very well."

"You're pretty wise, you know that. For a man, that is."

"*They* count on us being stupid."

Michael had taken the lead in planning another rafting trip with Jay. This time they would head down the Grand Canyon. Twelve days and the ideal time of year—it was a perfect chance for Michael to clear his head. They flew to Las Vegas and then to Paige. The next day they put in just below the Glen Canyon dam on a 30-foot pontoon raft with open floorboards and a 35 HP outboard for power with four emergency paddles lashed to the side. There was one other outfitter gearing up for a put-in the same day. Fourteen passengers were huddling about waiting for the signal to board that raft. Fourteen plus two crew—that was the legal limit.

"Where are the others on our raft?" Jay asked looking around.

"There are no others," a little giddiness was in the response.

"What do you mean?"

"It's a charter. Just us and the two crew."

"Christ, this must be costing a bloody fortune."

Michael shrugged.

"Well, I'm paying half anyway."

"No way. This is on me."

"No way. No way!" Jay shook his head adamantly.

"Well, then fly back to Vegas. It's just me then."

"Last time I let you plan a vacation."

"Sorry that I *sucked* you in." He smiled wanly. "Actually, I didn't. I really needed you to be along."

Jay laughed. "Damn it. Sometimes I wish I didn't love you."

Michael and Jay loaded up their gear. Each had brought a day sack and waterproof duffel. Both of the crew seemed capable. Daniel, in his twenties, was tall and angular of body, very strong and had been rafting the Colorado long enough to know most of what there was to know about it. He was also deaf which Michael did not realize when he first talked with him.

"That's going to make communicating a little tricky, isn't it?" Jay asked. "Like in the rapids?"

"Look at it this way," Michael said. "Just be sure you're facing him. He'll always be able to hear you. Even over the roar of the rapids."

Daniel's assistant, Marty was a stocky redhead, who, in his late teens, he had been an Australian lifeguard. Now in his early-twenties he was making his tenth trip down the Colorado. They loved the river and the canyon, respecting both deeply.

"It seems we may be three passengers," Jay observed as he was watching his brother who seemed uncharacteristically absent. Michael looked questioningly at him. "The two of us and the one in your head. Forgive and forget," Jay continued.

"I could never *not* forgive, and I can never forget."

"There's no percentage in that."

"It's not a calculation."

"What then?"

Michael shrugged.

"Well, we'll see where the river takes you."

The water was moving swiftly and had a clean scent. The water was very cold. Even small rapids made the water wash in, slosh through the open floorboards and splash over the top of the raft. "48 degrees coming out of the dam," Daniel yelled forward. Within a couple of minutes, their feet went numb. There was no way to keep them dry.

Michael marveled at Daniel's navigating skills. In the bends of the river, he approached with the bow toward the inside of the bend and as the raft went into the bend, he straightened it out and then took it through. For the rapids, he positioned the raft broadside, maneuvering to the center of the smooth glassy flow of the tongue just before the white water and then headed the raft straight into the rapids.

At noon, Daniel brought the raft to shore and walked on ahead to scout the large rapid around the bend. The rapid had been formed by the outwash of a side stream and every Spring the high waters washed out new boulders and changed the character of the rapids. Experienced captains knew this all too well and took caution, with good reason. "Those rocks in the center of the rapids are new." Daniel pointed down the canyon. The big humps of white water cascading over them indicated they were near the surface. Immediately downstream of these rocks were clusters of exposed boulders, the ones toward the far bank were smoother and in deeper water. Further downstream was a large churning hole with a curler that was bigger than any they had seen up to that point.

Jay tapped Daniel on the shoulder. "How are we going to navigate around all of this?"

"We're not," Daniel said like some wizened naturalist-sage. "You see, the river is sort of like life with its bumps along the way. Some of them you hit. You pick your path, put

in, and go. And pray you have the skill to follow that path."
He went quiet then, almost reverent, then added, "That's what
I love about this river. It's alive. Most people don't have a clue.
Strange, isn't it, because it is such a living, moving force."

They ran the rapids the way Daniel planned. They hit the
rocks he said they would and they stayed clear of the large
hole. They came through drenched, and Jay lost his hat.

There was a decision to make. From the second day on, Marty's tooth had been bothering him, and now he was running
a high fever.

"Abscess," Daniel said. "Upper tooth. After Phantom
Ranch it is seven days of total isolation. I don't know. Not a
good idea. Either of you got rafting experience?"

"I've done a half dozen or so," Jay said. "Tame ones, but
still..."

"It'd be like having no co-pilot," Daniel finished Jay's
thought. "That's not a safe scenario."

Michael and Jay looked at each other, nodded in agreement. "We think the pilot will do fine all by himself," Michael
said speaking for both.

"The Park Rangers don't agree with you. I could lose my
license for this."

"It won't be because of anything *we* say," Jay responded
enthusiastically.

Daniel looked at the canyon wall.

"Can't very well port it out, can you," Jay said as he looked
up at the sheer-rock face.

Daniel exhaled a long sigh. "All right, then, but this is a
state secret."

"Eyes only!" Jay emphasized. Michael made a "Scout's
Honor" hand gesture, as both brother's smiled wide grins.

They found a mule to take Marty to the top, and it was not
long before the three were on the river running rapids. During

a quiet patch, Michael turned to Daniel. "I want to swim one of the rapids. A big one."

Daniel pursed his lips. "The river's very fast now, you know. And the water's very cold."

Michael nodded that he was well aware.

"That means you have to get out quickly afterwards."

"I understand."

"You want to do it, truly?"

"Yes."

"All right. I'll let you know when."

Up ahead, Michael could hear the faint roar of an approaching rapid. He waved to Daniel. "Is this a good one?"

"No."

"Why not"?

"It's a seven."

"What's good, then?"

"A five. Five is still big."

The rapids on the Colorado were categorized one through ten, with ten being the biggest. There was one ten at Lava Falls, one nine called Chrystal Falls, a few eight's, a few more seven's, and then the rest. There were occasional fatalities at Lava Falls and even on Chrystal, and almost never on an eight.

Daniel pulled the raft ashore and climbed high enough to see almost the entirety of the rapid. He shook his head. "This is worse now."

Michael tapped him. "How so?"

"Water's faster." He pointed to a set of curlers churning over two huge submerged boulders way up ahead on the far bank. "Those were not there on the last run. Must have tumbled in during that rain we had. They're dangerous. Look," he said putting his arm around Michael's shoulder and pointing, "if you went into this you would have to jump in toward the far bank and enter the rapids on that side to avoid those rocks."

He pointed to smaller, barely exposed rocks off the near bank. "When you passed those rocks, you would still have to stay with the far bank, fighting the bend to avoid that curler in the center channel. When you past the curler, then you would have to work your way toward the near bank very quickly to avoid that big hole." He pointed again to the two new boulders, and Michael saw the white water rushing over and dropping like a waterfall. "You would not want to get stuck in that hole. It could be lethal. You would have to maneuver quickly and with all of your strength to avoid it. And when you got through the rapid, you would have to stay clear of whirlpools. Now do you see why not?"

Michael nodded.

They walked back and pushed off. Daniel brought the raft to the center of the river and pointed downstream. They now could hear the building roar of the rapid, and as the rumble intensified the tips of the white water became visible.

Suddenly Michael stood up. Jay showed alarm and got up too, but within seconds Michael had bounded onto the pontoon and jumped.

"No!" Jay yelled.

Michael hit the water and went down, and down, and it seemed forever before he came up. When his head broke the surface, he was entering the smooth glassy tongue marking the entrance to the rapid where the water started to increase in speed. He had no sensation of water temperature. And then he was in it. He went under the first white wave. He gasped for air when he came out and went under another a split second later. He was going through so fast that he could barely get any air before he was submerged under the next wave. By taking very short gasps, he managed to grab a little air. All he heard was his own gasping, the roar of the river having faded into background static, second to what was going on in his head. Was he past the curlers? He had no idea where he was in the rapid or where the danger was. Panic should have attacked, but there was no time. He was focused with nothing else in his mind. All he could see was the next rush of water the instant before he went through it. *I must be past it by now* he thought as he started maneuvering toward the other bank, forcing his attention to his main worry about staying clear of the hole. He pulled hard, but it had little effect in the rush of the torrent. He strained with all his strength but to no effect, suddenly he was flipping over forward and falling, and with a jarring thud his chest hit against something hard knocking the remaining air out of his lungs. He was being churned over and over, and there was no air, and he tried to haul himself upward as he started losing strength in his arms. Finally, he broke free, gasping in a resuscitative breath.

They pulled him on board, and the raft was left to float towards a quieter stretch of river. Michael was panting. Daniel just shook his head, in amazement and relief. "You were lucky. That hole spit you right out."

"Michael, that was crazy! Just plain crazy!" Jay blurted out, nearly hysterical.

Michael had a look of distant wonder, and then all came coursing back to the present, "Oh." He pressed his palms against his temples. "Every second!" His hands flew out in front of him, shaking with tension, fingers spread in rigid pose. "Alive! So alive. God, I was so alive! Thank God I'm alive. Oh, just to be so alive!"

Both Jay and Daniel looked at each other with concern. Slowly as Michael recovered himself, their anxiousness turned to disbelief, then to relief, and then to therapeutic mirth as they all began laughing out their stress as each retold Michael's adventure from his own vantage point.

To cool down, and to finish shaking off their nerves, all three took a dip in the shallow eddy that was upstream of where the raft was moored. The current was gentle, but they could not make headway against it. The water was numbingly cold—even wearing their blue jeans, T-shirts and life vests—

making their movement's all the more pronounced. Their exposed arms ached, but it felt good for all of them to relax a bit together after the stress of the day's events.

The next day was quiet by comparison and Daniel pulled in early. There was a small, tufted-grass hill behind them, and Michael and Jay climbed up it to take a good look at the surrounding majesty. The river was four hundred feet below, and they could follow the white and tan ribbon up and downstream to the big bends. "Looks tame from up here." Jay lay back, stretching out, with his eyes closed. Michael remained sitting, picking up small rocks and tossing them out to see how far they would tumble down the slope. Finally, Jay stirred and sat up. "Ah, that felt good. Well," he yawned, "think I'll head back. See if I can help Daniel."

"I'll be down in a while."

Michael watched Jay descend, choosing his footing carefully as he made his way. On the far slope, Michael could make out mountain sheep grazing. The breeze had slackened, and it was quiet. Then it was more than quiet, becoming perfectly still. He lay back on the grass, his eyes overwhelmed by the blue of a pre-evening sky. In his mind he imagined the sound of a soprano saxophone scaling skyward, its tone pure, "Worried, oh so worried that you'll let me down." It was a sound that, despite its words, promised that she would be warm under the covers next to him. He rose, beckoned by that sound. His arms lifted upward, and he began turning round and round. The turning became a dance, a movement of slow spirals. His arms stretched out, reaching for her still—the sun glistening in her hair, her warmth pressing against him, her smile an invitation, her laugh resonating, her eyes offering.

And then his face sagged. An overwhelming sadness gave way and the tears began to flow from floodgates that would not close. He kept on dancing. Yes, dancing for all that might have been but now would never be. His tears fell openly on the mountaintop as the sun set slowly on a distant horizon, its light fading more and more, until, at last, it was gone.

She would have liked it here Michael thought to himself, *especially the shooting stars. Catch a falling star, put it in your pocket, save it for a rainy day. No point saving them now, though.* The weight of loss sat heavily. "Every time a star falls, that means a new star is born," is what his cousin Marilyn had told him when they were young. Memories of her still haunted him.

Marilyn had been Michael's favorite cousin. She was a few years older, but they still visited each other in the summer. They would take baths together, back at a time when their different anatomies were still only a passing curiosity.

From a very early age, Marilyn had demonstrated her passion for acting. She would dress up in some of the old clothes from the attic, and then Michael and she would climb up into the tree fort in the big maple outside the kitchen. There she would make up a character, usually a heroine, and act her out. One time she was a princess who had lost her prince. She raised a stub of wood that served as her goblet and drank a poison from it that would end her love-lost life. She collapsed to the floor, and the goblet rolled from her hand, off the platform, falling to the ground. It was her favorite performance, and she did it many times. Sometimes she would even act out the man's role, complete with male garb, making her voice sound husky to complete the illusion.

Then, one year Michael's family moved far away, and he did not see Marilyn again until he was in his late-teens. By then she had become stunning. When he saw her again, he couldn't help but think that she would always be the first woman he had seen naked.

Everyone said she had a promising acting career ahead of her. But something terrible must have happened, because a few months later she took her life. Her parents discovered her when they came down for breakfast. She was hanging from that maple where she and Michael had played together in the tree-fort when they were young. He went with his family to the funeral. Her parents suddenly looked like very old people and he would never forget the pain on their faces. After the service they all went back to her house. The tree had been cut down. Michael looked at the stump understanding that it was a reasonable response to their pain, but to him it seemed pointless to destroy such a magnificent tree. Michael thought that it would have been better to leave the tree standing. Cutting it down seemed to cut her away as well. It seemed a double tragedy to lose her and the place where she had been so much herself, so wonderful and so full of life.

It broke his heart anew to think about Marilyn as he looked at the stars that she had reached for so many years ago. That coupled with the loss of Malee left him feeling utterly empty as he thought about the amount of pain his heart had endured. He sat there until the moon started to rise and then made his way down the hill.

They were on the river shortly after daybreak and were moving fast in the current. Mid morning, Daniel brought the raft ashore. It scraped against the sandy bottom coming in, and Daniel jumped out and tied the bow rope to a bush. "Come with me," he said to both Michael and Jay "I want to show you both this one." They headed downstream. The faint roar of the rapid grew louder and in five minutes they were standing along side a huge rapid.

"Chrystal Rapids," Daniel said looking out over the torrents. The water rushed with a relentless ferocity over and around submerged boulders and rocks. A large branch went through. Michael had never realized how fast objects moved in the turbulence of a truly raging river. Daniel studied the water for a minute or two and then all headed back towards the anchored craft.

"Hold on tight." They cinched up with an extra pull and Daniel took the raft out to the main channel. Within what felt like seconds they approached the tongue, Jay and Daniel were looking at the rapids, and in one startling motion Michael let go of the raft, stood up, hopped onto the pontoon and jumped. Jay shouted simultaneously reaching out, "Michael!" but it was too late. By the time Michael crested the surface he was back in it. The river tossed him like a cork, churning him, flipping him. It was a white chaos, void of air. Michael disappeared from view before he smashed onto and off of a boulder in what felt like one movement. He fought for breath, but the whitewater gave him no time. He felt the thud of his head hitting something unyielding. And then nothing.

At first, he was coughing. It hurt so much. A voice was coming from the far end of a tunnel, and he could not tell whose it was. Then he saw Jay leaning over him, water dripping from his life jacket onto Michael's face, and Daniel right next to him.

"Michael." Entreating worry was capitalized in each syllable, "Michael."

He blinked a few times and suddenly could not stop coughing. He tried to move, but groaning is all that came of his efforts. "Don't move," Daniel said. "You are one lucky son of a bitch." He held up Michael's life vest. It was shredded. Jay placed a hand on Michael's forehead and stroked his head. A trail of blood oozed from an open wound. Daniel wrapped a bandage several times tightly around Michael's forehead. Michael coughed more but was too dazed to register fully the burning in his lungs.

Daniel and Jay made an area in the center of the raft using duffels so that Michael could lie down. By the next morning Michael was feeling better despite the fact that he still had a splitting headache and was stiff and sore from his bruises, especially his right hipbone. "Lava Falls is not too far up ahead.

We'll put in here and take it tomorrow. Give Michael another day rest," Daniel said to Jay, "We'll make up the time later."

The placid waters gave no hint of the most imposing rapid on the river, now only a mile up ahead. As they approached, Daniel pulled ashore, and they all hiked downstream to look, Jay paying extra attention to Michael, who was limping as he went. The roar and white fury made Chrystal Rapids pale in comparison. Daniel shook his head. "I've never seen it this ferocious."

Back at the raft, Daniel checked the ropes, securing the gear, pulling every rope extra taut. He slipped on his life preserver, fastened the snaps on his life vest and yanked the waist belt snug, his indication that it was time to go.

"Hey, what're you doing?" Michael asked Jay. Jay was putting on Michael's tattered life preserver.

"Oh," Jay said, playfully, pretending that he had not noticed. "Oh, well, what's the difference," continuing to fasten it up.

"No! That's mine. I messed it up, so I wear it."

"If you insist," Jay said as he handed it back dismissing the matter.

Michael put it on immediately as to end the discussion.

"Look," Daniel said straight-faced but with an edge, "this is serious. You go in here, chances are you won't come out. All right, let me explain how we are going to do this." You could hear the worry enter in his delivery. "Sit up front, hold on to the two ropes, the bow rope and the side rope. That way, you're only really vulnerable to being flipped out over the bow. Lean back and hold on tight. If you feel the raft is flipping, try to counterweight it. If it flips, let go and stay clear of it. Don't get caught under it, and lead with you feet."

They pushed off and headed for the roar. It was a clear day with only a few white puffy clouds drifted along overhead, indifferent to the unfolding saga below. The raft dipped into the river's tongue, and the ferocity of the torrent let loose. The engine conked out from water, and Daniel lost steerage control. The raft dropped into a hole, and the crest of the wave cleared the tops of Michael and Jay's heads engulfing the entire raft. The ropes cut into their hands. Daniel yelled something, and the raft dropped into another hole and hit broadside against a half-submerged boulder. The whole craft started to tip and fill with water. Michael and Jay shifted their weight against the tip. Everything was happening too fast. The raft twisted off the boulder, came back to upright and then floated to stern and into more white water violence. Another wave hit with such magnitude they lost sight of Daniel for a moment. Jay's side rope snapped, and he grasped the bow rope with both hands just as they slammed into the fiercest wave of them all. And then, as suddenly as they were in it, they were out of it. The water was churning but no longer could be called a rapid. Daniel was not on board.

"My God!" Jay exclaimed.

"Daniel! Daniel!" Michael yelled looking around frantically.

"Over there!" Jay shouted. "Over there. There he is," pointing.

Daniel was floating about fifty yards away.

"You okay?" Michael yelled. There was no answer. Michael waved his arm. Daniel waved back. With the motor being flooded Michael and Jay unlashed two paddles and maneuvered toward Daniel. It took them a couple of minutes to come alongside him. They pulled Daniel aboard.

"You all right?"

"I'm good." He was shivering.

"What happened?"

"We hit that first boulder. I was trying to keep us from flipping. When the raft slipped off, it threw me out. Better me than one of you."

It took several hours before they were back on the river. They realized that they had lost so much time that that they would not reach the Lake Meade take-out spot on schedule, especially now that they were out of the gorge with the river wide and the current slower. They decided to float with the river's flow.

In a brisk upstream wind, the raft made slow headway. "This is what it's like the rest of the trip," Daniel said. In the open, flatter landscape, the river had lost its canyon majesty.

For the first time in ten days, reality began to show its face. Daniel decided that they should all sleep on the raft and let it drift all night to make up lost time. It was starting to dawn on Michael just how thoughtless he had been of his companions. He could see deep concern in Jay's eyes. And Daniel... he had been putting this man's river license in jeopardy, his livelihood. That, and he owed Daniel his life, a life he was beginning to think he could start to live again. The slow night's journey gave Michael time to reflect privately on so many things.

By mid-morning, the three of them had reached Lake Meade. Michael had substantially recovered although he felt like he had gone a few rounds and was paying the price for it. He didn't say anything about it though, putting on a brave face while he and Jay helped Daniel dismantle the raft. When all the gear was finally put away, Michael took Daniel aside and settled up with him, tipping him a tidy sum for all that he had done. They said their genuine farewells, and not long after the last handshake Michael and Jay landed back in the hustle of Las Vegas.

When Michael returned home, he checked his email. There were hundreds, but nothing from Malee. It was clear that she *was* gone. He resisted the urge to email her again that first day. More than that, he resolved never to email her again. His resolve was strong, lasting almost one month. Finally giving in to temptation, he sent a short note, and this time, it was *not* a non-deliverable message. It went through. Michael could barely contain himself. He checked his email every day— more than once, ten times at least. He imagined, or decided to imagine, that she probably checked her emails infrequently, and she had no reason to expect to hear from him. A week later, she emailed him.

Dear Khun Michael,

Ei so happy no you forget me. i think you forget when I no come. i so happy you no forget. you go Thailand more? You tell me what.

Kisses, Khun Malee

He emailed back that he was returning to Thailand in two months. That by then he would have completed laying out the stateside groundwork on the new business he and Drake were launching. He informed Drake of this latest development and received the following email from Singapore.

Dear Deceased,

I would dive in to save a drowning friend, but why bother with one who's already gone. We'll hold a wake for you when we meet up in Thailand.

    With heartfelt condolences,

Drake

And then the following note from Malee when he emailed her his itinerary.

Dear Khun Michael,

Thank you email. i no happy anymore. Husband bad man. him drink too much and when bring ladie back mit him,

*i no can sleep in bed. i sleep flor. i cry. Hie no give money.
To see Mama, i must job. no good job here. no have money
see Mama. i want divorce. i no want live him. i sorry i
no wait you. Now make me cry. Joy say you cry. Make me
cry more. You buy me plane tiket then i stay with you. You
tell me you Thailand, i go to if you can by tiket. you good
man. i want be mit you. If you no can tiket, that Okay.
I try find money be mit you. You tell mie what best to do.*

Love and kisses, Malee

He was happy to buy her a ticket. Cost was not the issue,
not the monetary cost anyway. He hesitated writing, but finally
carefully drafted an email to her pouring out his heart, each
sentence tearing at his pain.

Dear Malee,

Please have a friend who knows English read this to you.
    *Let me start by saying that if you are unhappy, then
that makes me unhappy. As you know, I always pray for
your happiness. I have very mixed feelings. It has taken a
long time to bury you and my memories of you into a deep,
hidden place in my heart that I try to keep tightly locked.
I have felt such pain because of things that have happened
between us that it is easier for me if you become a memory
that fades more and more into the past. I know that in
your culture it is better to say nothing rather than to tell
bad news, but in my culture it is the opposite.*
    *I cannot put into words the pain that I felt when you
did not wait for me, especially after I had made sure that
you did not need to go back to your terrible job. There are
no words for that kind of pain. When I learned that you
had left the country and had married a bad man, and that
you let me travel all the way to your country thinking I*

would see you again knowing that that fact would not be true, I cried. Your sister can tell you about that.

The words were rushing out across the computer screen, streaming through the rising pain.

You did what you felt was best for you, and that is what you should do. So that is okay, but to tell me nothing, to leave me wondering if you had maybe died. That was terrible. So now when you write, when you come back into my life, it makes it impossible for me to keep you hidden away, to keep my memory of you locked away. And I fear that I will have great pain again. And I have had so much pain I do not want anymore. The feeling is too awful. You must feel the same kind of pain not ever being able to see your first-born child. Maybe that pain is much worse.

Before we arrange to meet, please search your heart and tell me the thoughts in your mind. Remember, I would rather have bad news than no news. No news is the worst thing that you could do to me, and I pray that you do not do it again.

It may be a mistake for me to write this letter because now I will wait anxiously for your reply, now that you have rekindled yourself in my heart. I fear it would have been better for me if you had not written me again. Better to have let my memory of you slowly fade further and further into that hidden place, although I don't know if that could ever happen. You will always be part of me no matter how hard I try to hide you away.

But maybe someday I could make it all become just a marvelous dream. It would be so much easier for me now if that were the case. Deep down in my heart, I think that I will never hear back from you. You will find it easier to

give me no news rather than to tell me something that you
think may hurt me.
    I am afraid to end this letter. I am afraid to send it.

Michael agonized for three days whether to send this email, and never did. It had helped to write it but to send it would have felt like he was just unloading on her, and that was something he could not countenance.

Instead, he sent her a short email explaining that he would pay for her ticket. Wary, he had checked with Lufthansa and discovered that he could purchase a refundable, prepaid round-trip ticket. There would be a small service fee for refunding, but that was all. For the dates she wanted, exactly three months in Thailand, he purchased the prepaid ticket in her name and sent her the locator number. All she had to do was show up at the airport with her passport on the day of departure, give the locator number, and the airline would issue her a ticket. It took four emails before she finally understood the procedure.

As Michael had it planned out Malee was scheduled to arrive three weeks before him, this would give her time to make the obligatory family visits before he got there. He sent her his itinerary, and, learning from his previous trip and all of the pain that had ensued, he created a foolproof plan in which she was to meet him at the airport. Michael was planning to stay for one month. Drake would arrive a couple of days before him. Michael was praying that it would be like the first time.

Nervous, Michael called her two times before her departure. Broken English, now mixed with German, on the phone, proved less satisfactory than email. The latter was easier to understand. Plus email was private, and he was never sure who was within earshot of the phone calls. He did, however, love to hear her slightly husky voice with her joy at his call. The calls all ended with, "Ya, you call me again, no?"

He couldn't believe it when an email came in from Helen, right in the middle of his making plans with Malee. *How was it that she knew when he was at his at his most vulnerable?* He opened it. The letter began without greeting:

> *The commune's dining hall burned to the ground four nights ago. One person died, and two are in the hospital with smoke inhalation. We are all in a state of shock. I never imagined how fast a fire could become an inferno. We are determined to rebuild the dining hall as soon as possible. We will use our own labor, but we need money for the demolition and the building materials. No one has much money. We estimate it will cost about $75,000 total. Would you please be so kind to wire this amount to me as I have very little of the money I left with. The wire instructions are attached. I appreciate it very much, Helen.*

He wired the money the next day, and although this was the first email from Helen without a request that he not write, he decided it was best not to open that door, especially when she had asked to keep it closed up until now. *Better to leave well enough alone on that front,* he thought realizing that her disappearance was a wound that had not yet fully healed.

Before he left for Thailand, Michael confirmed with Lufthansa that her prepaid ticket had been used. His flight was twenty hours of contradiction—he was sure that she would meet him at the airport *and* he was sick with worry that she would not. He tried to prepare for the eventuality that he would never see her again. He convinced himself that this would be okay, that he could deal with it, but he had a terrifying fear, deep down, that he would not know how to handle it.

The flight was interminable and yet he almost dreaded its arrival. He steeled himself with the notion that it would be better just to assume that, for whatever reason, they would never meet again. If they did, well, what a delightful surprise, but certainly nothing to count on. He hung on to that notion as tight as he could, but he knew that it would not take much of a pull for that to slip from his grip. He let himself dream of how it would be when they met, and how he could not wait to hold her again. But, God, what if she were not there? The steel was more molten than solid, but he had to try and prepare to face the worst case, telling himself he could handle it. If only he could assume disappointment and be true to that expectation. He could and he could not, depending on the moment. The long flight was a torment where minutes ticked away as if each were an agonizing day.

The plane touched down with a light bounce. The taxiing seemed to take an eternity. His stomach was aflutter, and this crazy thought flitted through his mind that they had landed at the wrong airport and were going by ground to Bangkok. Finally, the plane stopped. The door opened. Then he remembered that of course he had to go through immigration and customs before entering the terminal where a semicircle-sea of faces would be waiting to greet passengers. He counted eighteen immigration booths. Only two were open. It was maddening, taking over an hour. He was getting enraged when finally he was to the agent. The process was quick and then he entered the terminal. She saw him before he saw her, but then, holding his breath, he spotted her waving hand, saw her smile. A tremendous weight evaporated as he exhaled for the first time in months.

PART 3

Many Happy Returns

He drank in her features—seeing her for the first time again—her face, the smile and slightly husky voice, shapely figure, a little fleshier that he remembered. She took his hand and led him to the airport taxi service. On the way in to town, he wondered whether to tell her about his doubts. The answer was obvious. Even wondering about it was muddled thinking. He could call it jet lag, but decided to let it go.

Reservations had been made for the same hotel, same room on the same floor. He wanted everything to be the same so that it would seem like it was just the next day, like some time continuum that allowed for the sadness and the cultural miscues to melt away, so they could start where they had left off.

She sat of the edge of the bed.

"Your hair is longer, a lot longer."

"Yes."

"About five inches."

She did not understand.

"About twelve centimeters."

"Yes."

Your husband likes it long?"

"No, him say cut short. Him no happy long hair."

He stroked her hair. "Truly a wonder. I hope you always leave it long. Let me comb it."

She retrieved a brush. There were no snarls, and the brush glided through. After every few brush stokes, he lifted her hair high from the bottom and let it cascade through his open fingers.

"You know, I liked to dream about your hair. And in my dreams, it was longer, just like this."

They showered, and she lay in bed wrapped in the towel.

"Me shy." His fingers ran down her far cheek, then the near one. The touch calmed her face. "Me still shy."

"That's okay. You stay shy. I'll just look. Just touch." Her warmth permeated the towel. The flight had taken its toll, and his eyes half closed.

She shifted to a kneeling position, face to the headboard and hands together.

"You pray?"

"I pray Buddha."

He watched for the few seconds it took.

"What did Buddha say?"

"Buddha no say. Buddha only listen."

She lay back down and removed the towel. And it was Samui again. Except this time the closeness and touching lasted a long time, until the shyness was gone and he was touching her in a different way. Her abdomen contracted. She suppressed the sound, and when the intensity became too much she twisted and turned and her thighs squeezed tight. "Now. Me want now. Go me now." But he held back and she went wilder still and her sounds were no longer suppressed. Afterward, she lay limp by his side. His tiredness had vanished the minute they had gotten into bed, but it began to resurface as Malee turned and snuggled into his side, peaceful and content from the night's exertions.

When Michael awoke early the next morning, Malee was asleep with her arm resting across his chest. He had to urinate, but the slow heave of her chest and her draped arm—he wanted that to never change, so he did not move, savoring the moment, letting his growing need wait rather then lose the moment.

There was a knock on the door. Malee awoke. Michael slipped on a bathrobe and opened the door.

"Prang!" he said softly.

"Khun Michael. Oh, I did not know." She smiled her happily surprised welcome. She saw the pair of heels on the floor, looked at him, then puzzled at the expression on his face, a look derived from the fact that he could hold back no longer, not even ten seconds.

"You come back later, afternoon, okay?" It came out as one sentence. She nodded and he closed the door as she turned to leave. Michael shuffled to the bathroom as quickly as he could go. It was so bad that it did not all come out the first time. He used the bathroom three more times before he was empty. Malee was concerned. "You eat bad food on plane?"

"No." He said as he came back to bed.

"So, let me see."

She gave him a toothy smile. Great choppers.

"All right, show me how you use it." She had become adept. It was German dental floss.

"I brought you five new containers. Better than that stuff. Here, try it. No, no, not so fast. Slowly. Really clean." It had become part of the ritual they shared that he wanted to maintain. She gave a proud smile when she had finished. "Now you won't lose them."

That day they had lunch with Drake and Dawn. Michael's head started drooping as the soup was being served.

"What, you a rock star of something?" Drake asked.

"What?"

"Elvis was drowning in his soup, too, until someone pulled him out. Stick to solids."

"No, the soup looks good." Malee fed him.

Drake dropped his napkin on the table. "Christ, this is turning into a fucking nursing home."

"I think I'm going to go lie down now."

"How about dinner?" Drake asked.

"Yeah, dinner's better."

They quickly got the check and headed out.

Once Malee and Michael got back to the hotel, they had a chance just to sit with one another, drinking in the other's physicality. Some of the jet lag had abated with lunch, and as they, talked Michael began playing with Malee's fingers.

"You're not wearing the ring I brought you."

"Very pretty ring."

"Yes. I thought you would like it. I designed it."

She did not understand. He explained how he had worked with a jeweler to create it. It was the deep purple of a high-grade tanzanite, 2.3 carats emerald cut, surrounded by diamond baguettes in 18-karat. The diamonds were VVS-1. Of course, this was all over her head.

"Joy, she like too."

"I'm glad."

"Joy wear ring."

"What do you mean? I gave it to her to give to you."

"Joy love ring."

"You gave it to Joy?"

"She keep. Make her happy."

Michael laughed. "She kept it?"

"Me love Joy. Me want Joy be happy."

Michael laughed again. "You are a good sister."

"Joy good sister, too."

"I give up. I'm glad she likes it."

"Joy afraid see you now. Think you be angry."

"No. If it makes you happy to give it to her, it makes me happy too."

"You good man. I tell Joy you no angry."

"I no angry."

Malee touched his cheek playfully. "I think you very, very handsome man. All girls chase you. You still handsome man. How old you?"

"How old do you think?"

"Maybe forty less."

"Yes. Forty less."

"Still handsome man. You have picture young man?"

"No."

"I like see you young man. Must be so handsome."

"Not as handsome as you are beautiful."

"Face too round."

"No, face not too round. Perfect round."

She frowned. She put her hands to her face as if to hide it. He took one of the hands. "Make your hands dance again." Her hands undulated close to his face, and he watched, mesmerized.

The next day Michael asked her to teach him some specific expressions in Thai. It was laborious, especially with the double-checking that he had spelled phonetically the correct pronunciation. "Why you learn Thai? You not like firang. Firang learn 'How much short time.' No want learn more."

"Why? Because I want you to be my teacher, too."

That same afternoon, while Malee absorbed herself in Thai soaps, Michael asked Simon, the concierge, for a confidential recommendation. After making a call, he gave Michael directions on how to get to this unusual contact.

It was not an elaborate storefront in one of the high-overhead districts; rather it was a small shop on a side street with no display window. The open door led to a locked metal door with a small window in the center. Through a speaker system, Michael identified himself as the American Simon had sent.

A buzzer released the lock allowing Michael access to another small entry that confronted another locked door. The door behind him closed and locked. The second door opened. An old man who was bent over at the waist, with little hair left on his head and deep-set wrinkles on his aged face, greeted him with a hand gesture.

"Simon told me to come to you. My name is Michael," he said in Thai.

"That okay. I speak English. Enough. I Trisan. Mother make up name. She like sound."

Trisan made jewelry for the finest stores in Bangkok, even for stores that made most of their own jewelry in their own factories. Michael explained what he wanted. Trisan led him to a long wooden table on which he placed six folded white paper packets. He opened each carefully, lovingly, one by one. Each packet contained about fifty loose rubies. In this dingy little shop, Michael was staring at what would end up in the display windows of the highest-end retailers in all of Bangkok.

"You see," Trisan said. "Matched color. Each about 1.5 carat. About. Make necklace, all look same. He picked up a ruby from one of the packets and rested it, hand closed, between the third and fourth fingers of his left hand. It caught the shaft of the overhead light. "Diamonds. Quality easy to know. All formula. Not so, ruby. Ruby, quality know by eye. Okay, little bit formula. But the eye know. Eye no lie." He put the ruby back in the packet from which it had come. Trisan leaned back from the table. "Okay. Now you tell me," he said gesturing to the six packets. "Which number one, number two, all six? You put in order. Number one first."

Michael examined the stones in the packets. He picked up two or three from each packet and studied them.

"Listen to eyes," Trisan said. "Only eyes. They tell you."

"These are the best quality," Michael said pointing to the second packet from the left. He moved it over to the first position. He went on to position the remaining five.

Trisan looked up at him but said nothing. He folded his hands together, resting them under his chin, elbows on the table. Then he smiled—his eyes, his mouth, his whole face, "You six for six."

Michael shrugged outwardly while he sighed inside.

"You see. Eyes know. Now you tell me what quality you want. Number one very expensive. But give you good price."

"I want one ruby from number one." Michael opened the envelope and laid out the rubies, going through them carefully and finally settling on the most exquisitely colored ruby that Michael had ever seen. It was the stone he wanted. They discussed the design. Michael wanted two VVS-1 diamonds on either side, diamonds of an appropriate size. And he wanted the ring to be platinum. They went over every detail—the cut of the diamonds, the way their settings would nestle together, the width of the band and whether there would be an engraving or not.

They settled on a price.

"You in hurry? Yes, I see."

Michael nodded.

Trisan smiled again. "For you, two days. Because you six for six. If no six for six, then longer."

Michael took out his wallet to leave a deposit.

"No. If from Simon, no need."

The ring was ready two days later.

After his second trip to see Trisan, Michael returned late in the afternoon to find Malee, as was typical, engrossed in a Thai soap.

"This is for you," he sat down next to her, handing her the small gift box.

She opened it, and what was inside took her breath away.

"For me?"

"Not for Joy," he said.

"So beautiful. I no know what to say."

"Say nothing. Just wear it. That's all."

He had sized it perfectly to fit her right ring finger.

"I never have so beautiful."

That evening, Michael could no longer contain his need to know, a need to know that he knew was mixed with jealousy. "What is your husband's name?"

"Gerhard."

"How did you meet him?"

"O'Neill's."

"Like me?"

"Yes."

"You saw him after me?"

"Yes."

"How long after?"

"No know. Many month.

"You went with him."

"Yes."

"Why?"

"Me need money."

"But I gave you so much Baht. What happened?"

At first she made no reply. She went quiet and looked across the room as if something had caught her eye.

"You give it to Mama and Papa?" He had gotten her attention.

"Me good daughter."

"You gave it all to them?"

"No all. Keep some."

"But not enough, I guess."

"Me good daughter. Never can give money Mama and Papa. Joy give all time. Me no good daughter. Want be good daughter."

"So you went back to Samui. And went with Gerhard. For how long?"

"Ten day I think."

"How many were there after me?"

"Two."

"Gerhard and…" he pressed, His heart had started racing.

"One more."

"I thought that you would just be visiting Joy."

"Me visit Joy. Meet you. You good man. So good me. Job Bangkok no good. Lose job. Joy tell me come back Samui."

"You go with every man who asked you?"

"No. Other men I say no."

"What about the two after me?"

"Joy say okay. Both she be with before, but she no like Gerhard. I need money. Her say okay."

"How long did you stay with these…" Michael's tongue stumbled over the words, "these two men?"

"No one night. I no go one night. One week, two week, more, okay."

"How much did you ask for?"

"I no ask money. Firang give what he want."

"Which was like, how much? How much did Gerhard give you?"

"He give 20,000."

"For how long?"

"I say. Me think ten."

"And the other man?"

"Other give 25,000. One week me think."

"Good time in bed with them?"

"I no like question."

"So, um, good then?"

She said nothing. She became agitated. An explosion was building.

"So, it *was* good."

She burst into tears. "Mai dee! Mia dee! No! No!" Tears started streamed down her cheeks and her body was heaving. "No good. Only good mit you. Lak Khun Michael. No like be mit other firang."

"Not even Gerhard?"

"No…" She almost couldn't get the words out. No, later him send me 25,000 Germany and plane ticket. Tell me come."

"Why did you go? Smoker, drinker, bad man. *Why?*" he demanded.

The tears flowed faster. She kneaded her hands. "I no know. I dream Europe. I want see. Me think maybe him marry. I no think you come." She was trying to answer while weeping. He wiped her tears with his hands but more fell from her cheek. "I no know so bad. I no know so unhappy. I no know! I so unhappy." She put her hands over her face and rocked back and forth.

"Did he make you do funny things?"

"I no understand."

"Funny things in bed?"

"I no do funny thing in bed." She was sobbing in heaves. "Now I cry more you ask."

Michael stopped asking, but she was wrecked, and so was the night. They ended up staying in. He ordered room service, but neither of them had much of an appetite. After Malee fell asleep Michael took a spare blanket from the closet and sat in the stuffed chair in the living room with the blanket wrapped tight. He felt ashamed because, had the situation been reversed, he would never have been so open. But she answered with no hesitations, no dissembling, just truth. None of what she had said made him angry. Michael realized that she had made the best choice—her least worst. She did what she thought she had to do. She wanted him only; that he knew. He began to feel guilty. *He had made her go with these other men.* The thought repeated in his head, but even seeing the illogic of it assuaged no guilt. Maybe she thought he would abandon her even still. He let the blanket slide to the floor and walked back into the bedroom and turned on the dim light. She was asleep. He climbed into bed. She stirred and woke. "I want to be with you. No matter what," he whispered to her. She took his hand in hers and squeezed it, drawing him closer to her.

Two days later, Michael and Drake were having drinks before lunch on the veranda of Michael's hotel. The girls were off shopping.

"Shoes," Drake said shaking his head.

"What?"

"I mean, how much can shoes cost?"

"I don't follow."

"I keep thinking about what's going to happen to Dawn when I'm gone? You know my cholesterol problem and all, right?"

"Yeah."

"I mean, theoretically, I could go any minute."

"Pshhh. You'll outlive us all."

"I'm serious. I don't know what she does with her time. Her English lessons are hopeless. She gets worse every year instead of better. She has no real skills. No ambition. No way to earn money. And she just smiles as if it's no problem. If I talk to her about it, I just get more smiles and she hugs me. Christ, I've done what I promised myself I'd never do. I have to take care of her. And she's much younger than I am. So guess what. Come on, think!" He was really on a rant now. "You know what I did last year? I opened up a bank account for her, just in her name, and I deposited 500,000 Baht. And I checked it with her last week, and there's only like 200,000 Baht left. I figure rent and food, and some clothes, and utilities. I mean that's less than 100,000 Baht for the whole year. And she can't spend that much on shoes. I see the new shoes. There're not that many. And there's no room for them anyway. You know what I mean. You tripped all over them. 'So where's the money?' I ask her. She has no idea. She has no idea about money. It drives me crazy. She's has no family. None! I mean literally, *none*! She's *all* alone. So it's not disappearing that way. So where is it going? I don't have a clue. And neither does she. And I believe her." Michael held up a finger, trying to interject, but Drake kept going. "And what if I croak now, she has nothing to live on. I can't leave her like that. I won't leave her like that. And I'm not going to let her do the other thing. And she couldn't do it anyway! What a joke that would be. And it's not going to happen. No way. I'm putting in 500,000 Baht again. And this time, it's going to be a joint account. Only one signatory needed. But I'm going to check it every week. This way, I'll see when the money's coming out, and I'll ask her then, what's going on."

"What if she left you?" Michael finally got in a word.

The question caught Drake so off-guard that he made no response. The tirade was subsiding.

"Yes, left you," Michael repeated.

Still he made no response.

"I see. I guess I got under the armor plate on that one, didn't I?"

"She never would."

"But what if…" Michael's question was cut off by Drake who shook his head so fast and so slightly that it was like a shiver. "I'd be lost. Yeah, that would finish me. I couldn't take that. She has to be there when I need her."

"500,000 Baht."

Drake stared off to the side.

Michael couldn't resist prodding his friend, "You know, sometimes I think you're a closet romantic."

Drake recovered, "I've killed for insults less than that."

"But not for the truth."

Drake got up.

"Where're you going?" Michael asked.

"Get a Herald Tribune."

Michael slapped his hand against the newspaper. "You're reading it!"

Drake walked off.

At Dawn's urging, Drake made reservations for four at a pricey restaurant.

"Maybe this is where it all goes when I'm not around."

"Check to see if the maitre d' recognizes her."

"Ah, getting smarter in your old age. What's that smile for?"

"Just a smile," Michael beamed with a Cheshire grin.

"Shut up then."

Dinner was lavish. One hostess was assigned as their exclusive attendant. Drake ordered far more than they could eat. They went through two bottles of red wine—that is, Michael had one glass and Malee none. Dawn's smile was bigger than ever. Drake showed no signs of wear and tear. Malee was quieter than usual. Mostly she was her usual attentiveness to Michael, but then, at times, she would lapse into pensiveness sadness.

"You all right?" Michael whispered.

"Okay." But he had never seen that look in her eyes.

As the meal was ending, a troop of four waiters marched smartly towards the two couple's table with a large cake with ten lit candles in the center. In barbershop quartet fashion, they sang "Happy Birthday" to Drake. Dawn clapped. Drake hated ceremony, and he hated sweet desserts, and he was being served both.

"Make a wish," Michael said, almost as if it were a quip.

"I wish they'd go away and take the fucking thing with them."

"Then blow out the candles."

Drake blew them out and made a gesture to take the whole thing away. Michael made a counter gesture and prevailed. Drake declined a serving. Dawn and Malee each had a small serving, Michael a normal serving. The ten candles were still in the center.

"That was very clever of them," Michael said.

"What?"

"Well look, they put your age in dog-years."

"Son of a bitch."

"I think that under the circumstances, that designation belongs to you."

"You know how to ruin a fine dinner."

"Like I knew it was your birthday?"

Dawn was beaming. She had also failed to understand Drake's comments.

"I would like papaya and mango," Drake said to the waiter.

On the taxi ride back to the hotel, Malee was silent.

"Something wrong?"

"No feel good."

"Getting sick?"

"No feel good. Tell taxi stop."

She got out and threw up. Across the street, a 7-11 Store was open. Michael bought two bottles of water for her to use. The hotel was two blocks away.

"We walk now."

"Really? Isn't the taxi better?"

"No. Walk."

He supported her, holding her up from under her shoulder. She stumbled twice. As soon as they got back to the room she took a bath. Eventually she emerged in one of the white terrycloth hotel robes. She made her way across the room then sat gently on the bed. Her hands were folded and her knuckles were white.

"I go sleep now."

"Sure."

She pulled the sheet all the way to her chin, but instead of falling right to sleep she stared wistfully at the ceiling.

"Would you like me to rub your back?"

She shook her head.

"How about comb you hair?" It was glistening from her bath.

"No," she said softly, and with uncharacteristic brevity.

"Something's wrong. What is it?"

"I sleep now. No talk."

Michael gave in and stopped asking questions.

In the morning, Malee gave Michael a look that he had never seen before. He did not know how to translate it.

"You want to see a doctor?"

"No. Very headache. I okay later."

"You know I go with Drake today."

"I know."

"I'll be back before supper. You need anything before I go?"

She shook her head.

"When I come back, you tell me what is wrong."

She turned her face away and nodded.

Just after lunchtime, Drake and Michael were meeting with a few well-connected Thai investors. They were working to set up another export business, this one specializing in unique Thai products such as the stingray wallets and purses, the kind that Michael had been drawn to on his first trip. It proved to be a day of tough negotiations.

Michael returned to the hotel around six o'clock that evening and was surprised that he did not hear the muffled sound of the TV. As he slid the plastic card into the lock and then opened the door he froze. His heart pounded, and the hair on the back of his head tingled. The tingling spread to his forearms, then to his hands and fingers. It was that same sensation he had experienced when, on his second trip to Samui, he turned and first saw Joy's face as she approached on that awful night at O'Neill's. A chair had been moved so it would be directly in front of the door as you walked into the room. There was a folded note on the chair. Michael closed the door and leaned against it. He looked around the room. Everything looked normal. His black cashmere sweater, the one that he had given to Malee, and the white windbreaker he had bought for her were draped over the sofa. He walked into the bedroom. Her clothes, or at least most of the few that she had, were hanging in the closet. Her make-up kit was all there next to the sink in the bathroom. *So everything must be all right* he thought, reassuring himself. But the suite had a terrible feeling of emptiness. He dropped the key on the bed. The very prominence of the note was a bad sign. He was afraid to read it. He was afraid to touch it. He stood over it and stared. Then he snatched it up. The note had been written on the hotel's stationary.

> *Dear Khun Michael,*
>
> *i can no long be with you. No can do love. i sorry I make you not happy I cry when I think you read this. I cry now. You good man. I no want you be not happy. Please think me good person.*
>
> *Love,*
>
> *Malee*

He sat down heavily. He reread the note. And reread it again. He dropped the note onto the bed as he frantically sprang up from the chair rushing to the window. Maybe she had just left a moment before, and he would see her on the street. She was not there. He grabbed the note and turned it to the other side. It was blank.

But there was the obvious—all her things were still in the room, everything except, as far as he could tell, her pocketbook. *So she would come back* he though. *She would have to.* And then another wave hit him, harder than when he had first read the note. All her things, all her things left here, that meant something very different. That meant she would never come back. No, he was not thinking clearly. Of course she would be back. It must have been as devastating for her to write the note as it was for him to read it. She would come to her senses and return—at least to collect her things. He sat again. His mouth was like cotton and made a sticking sound when he opened it. Restless, he got up again and started pacing the room, telling himself, like it was a mantra, *all right, be calm, and just think clearly.* He opened the door to the room and looked up and down the hall to see if she was there. No. Maybe she was in the lobby, sobbing in some corner chair. It was a definite possibility. The door clicked closed as he ran to the bank of elevators. Suddenly he hesitated. What if she were on her way up while he was taking the elevator down. He could not risk that. There were four elevators. He pressed the up button. When the first elevator arrived, he reached in and pressed the top floor. He did the same for the next two. When the fourth arrived, the other three were still above his floor.

She was not in the lobby. Keeping an eye on the elevators to see who was taking them up, he walked over to Simon, trying to contain his frantic state.

"Simon, have you seen, you know, Khun Malee, the person I was with?"

"Yes sir, about an hour ago."

"Was she leaving?"

"Yes, sir."

"How...how did she look?"

"Very sad, sir."

"Oh," he was crestfallen.

"I am sorry, sir."

He had to contact her. Her cell phone! He had never written down the number. He had only called her once and now he could not recall it. It was 8-6 something, something, something, something...he buried his head in his hands trying to remember. If he just calmed down, maybe he could recall the rest. 86...3-...or was it 864-. It was useless.

He returned to his room. The door had locked when it closed, and he had left the key on the bed. He thought he heard the phone ring. He tried to force the door.

He took the elevator to the lobby again using the same

procedure as before. Simon's shift had ended. He did not know the new concierge. Did he have his passport? No, it was in a hotel lock-box, and that key was in the room as well. Papers signed, and fifteen minutes later they unlocked his room door.

There were papers and things in the wastebasket. He dumped the contents on the floor—five facial tissues, two still moist, a few papers, one a first draft of the note. The rest was nothing useful. He was numb.

He would wait. She had to come back. She would never just leave her things. He opened the room door again and looked down the hall. No, not yet. As he closed the door, he noticed the reflection of something on the carpet next to the chair. It was the second plastic room key, the one he had given her. His breathing became shallow and then turned to panting. Nearly hyperventilating he was getting tunnel vision. He had to sit down and compose himself, but this lasted maybe a minute before the force of his anxiety moved him to action once again.

He went through all her things. What? He couldn't believe it. Her cell phone was in the pocket of her white windbreaker. God, this must have been so terrible for her. But maybe he had a way to contact her now. He figured out how to use it and scrolled down the numbers called. One number repeated many times. Joy, of course, it had to be. He wrote down the number in case Malee's battery went dead. He wrote down all the other numbers as well, even the ones that appeared only once. He called the number he assumed to be Joy's. He let it ring until the message came on. It was in Thai. He did not understand it but it sounded like Joy, at least he thought it did. Every ten minutes he called. It was always the recorded message.

He went through all of Malee's clothes and make up kit again. In one of her pockets he found a wrinkled scrape with a phone number, different from the one he had been calling. Maybe this was Joy's. But Malee would know that number by heart. He called it anyway. No message came on. He let it ring fifty times. Every ten minutes he called that number again, too.

Obsessing, needing to try and make sense of what was happening, he searched through her clothes again. Finding nothing new he desperately rummaged through the waste papers on the floor hoping for a clue, some answer, some direction. Nothing. He opened every drawer. One had two pairs of undergarments. He closed it quickly. Another wave swept through him, worse than before. He was spiraling.

He remembered Dr. Bach's words, "If things start to go bad, you can increase the dose by fifty percent. In a crisis, you can double up. But at that level, not for long. Two days at the most." He increased the dose by fifty percent.

He lay down with a pillow over his eyes, but within seconds sprung up and opened the door to see if she were walking down the hall. He looked out the window. He searched her clothes yet another time. He called the numbers again. He was very thirsty. He poured a glass of Evian and drank a sip. And then he saw it. How could he have not noticed before? It was a sealed, hotel envelope, with a bulge in the center, resting on the mantel over the faux fireplace.

He could not bring himself to open it. He collapsed on the bed.

He was alone, more desolate than he had ever been before— more crushed than when she first left, then when Helen left. Michael never imagined he could feel so empty. Anger mixing with grief, feeling, if only for that singular moment, like he had been duped, and that he had walked into a trap. He refused to believe it. His heart sank into despair, wrenched from his chest. He was exhausted.

Michael slowly took out his iPod and headphones and scrolled to Sibelius' 2nd Symphony. After it had played, he scrolled to the fourth movement and put the iPod on repeat.

He was cold. He pulled up the blankets and bedspread then curled up into a fetal position as he slipped into a black mood.

He awoke. He must have slept—everything was still foggy. He was fully clothed. The glass of Evian was empty. The iPod had run down. He needed to use the toilet, but he did not want to move. His head hurt so much, and he was nauseous. *The medicine, the fucking medicine*, he thought through the throbbing in his temples. He forced himself to get up but after he used the toilet, he went back to bed, yanking his shoes off, untied, before pulling the covers up again. He reached out for the phone and called the two numbers three more times each. There was no answer.

At ten-thirty the following morning there was a knock on the door. Michael bolted upright, hearing the key unlock the door. It was Prang. Surprised to find Michael there, she made a quick scan of the shambled room. "She's gone?" she asked.

He nodded.

"Do you need some food?"

He shook his head.

"I can call room service."

He shook his head no.

She filled his glass with Evian.

"Should I clean the room?"

He shook his head, again, no.

"All right." She left quietly.

Other than calling the numbers every few minutes, drinking the Evian, and using the toilet, he stayed covered up in bed. At one o'clock that afternoon, the phone rang. Michael lunged at the receiver, "Hey, I thought we were having lunch." It was Drake.

"Sorry. Must have forgotten." He said it so distantly that all unintentional meaning was conveyed.

"Oh, shit. I knew she was going to do this."

"How'd you know?"

"You didn't see it, huh?"

"See it?"

"Yeah, that she was…oh well, what's the difference."

"I didn't see it. I mean, well, she was acting a little strange. I guess I should have seen it."

"The brain-dead rarely do."

"I don't know," Michael said trying to dismiss the whole conversation. His heart just couldn't take it.

"I'll bet she had a headache last night, too."

"Yeah. How'd you know?"

"You're hopeless."

"She threw up, too."

"Well, okay, I'll give her a point for that. How about joining me for Cowboy tonight?"

"No. No. NO," Michael ended up almost shouting. "I need time. Or something."

"You always need time. Or something. Christ, you are *really* hard to deal with."

"I need to be alone right now, okay? I feel like…I don't know. I don't *KNOW.*"

"You sound like shit. That fucking bitch!"

"No! No, she's not that. No. Please don't say that."

"Look, let me tell you something. Not that it'll do you any good. You got it backwards. She's fucking with your brains. And you're supposed to be fucking with hers. That's the way it's supposed to go. It's all a *fucking game,* and you got it all fucked up. How many times does she have to fuck you over before you get it?"

"She gave back the ruby ring, you know."

"Okay, I'll give her another point. I'll even give her two for that. She's a nice girl. End of story. Come on. I'll bring Dawn with us to Cowboy. Let her do her thing again. She's pretty good at choosing you know."

"Drake, I can't. Not now."

"When?"

"I don't know."

"All right. Well, give me a call. Two days, that's all. Or I'm coming over. Kick your Goddamn door in."

Around eight o'clock, there was a knock on his door. He bolted upright. She did not have a key. Maybe she was coming back for her things after all. *No*, he thought, *don't get your hopes up. Worst thing you can do. Oh, it must be Drake. Good ole Drake. He sure as Hell didn't wait two days, that's for sure.* He opened the door to a woman in a full black chador with only the eyes showing. She was carrying a large bag. He was stunned and searched for words.

"Excuse me?" he asked.

She gestured that she wished to enter.

"I…I think you have the wrong room or something."

She gestured again to enter.

"I," he paused, "I'm the only one in this room."

She was insistent, and he let her enter. She closed the door behind her, and then took off her headpiece.

"Prang! I mean…" He didn't know what to say.

"You frightened me this morning. I didn't think you should be alone."

He was at a loss for words.

"For a minute I didn't think you were going to let me in."

"Well, you can understand why, right?"

"Yes, I understand why," she grinned.

"Where'd you get that outfit?" he asked laughing.

"We have a few guests dressed like this right now."

"So how'd you get one?"

"It was thrown out. I guess because it's torn here." She showed him the tear with a makeshift repair.

"There're some of them here now, dressed like that, at the hotel?"

"Yes."

"Talk about incongruity." He had to explain the meaning. "Wait, I'm worried about you. You could lose your job. You told me."

"Not in this, I won't." She started to remove it.

"No, no. Just stay in that...that tent."

"It's too hot." She removed it. She was dressed the same as when he had taken her to dinner. She opened the bag. "I brought you some food. And Evian. You need it."

He laughed. "It is incredibly stupid to have to be reminded by someone else that you're famished." She looked at him quizzically on that last word. "Oh, means the same thing as 'very hungry'." He spelled it out.

She went to the closet, lifted off the two pillows, and took out the plates and utensils underneath.

He laughed again. "So you knew they were there."

She nodded.

"I was just putting them there for safe keeping."

"Yes, of course."

"I was only borrowing them," he added, feeling a little guilty.

"I know," she returned with a warm smile.

Using a clean towel for a tablecloth, she spread out a cooked dinner. He sat on the bed, she on a chair pulled up next to the table. The food smelled good. "A little spicy, but not too. I wasn't sure how you liked it."

He filled two glasses with Evian, and then dug into his dinner, his stomach suddenly remembering how hungry he truly was. After they had finished, he leaned back, "Hey, that was delicious." He sat up. "Wait a minute, how much do I owe you for all this?"

"Nothing."

"No. I mean, right here, right now. Just imagine that I am taking you to dinner again. It's just a different sort of restaurant here, that's all."

"You owe me nothing."

"That's not fair."

"You owe me *nothing*," she was emphatic on this point and followed with, "for this, or for anything else."

"Well, now you make me upset. I have to do something. Maybe I can give you, like an English lesson or something, at least."

She got up and retrieved an English idiomatic expressions book. "You come prepared. I'll say that." Michael said a little more cheerfully than he expected. "All right, the lesson's for as long as you want."

"First, I want to shower. It was very hot under that thing."

After she showered, she emerged in one of the white terry cloth bathrobes supplied by the hotel. She handed Michael a fresh towel and ushered him into the bathroom. He emerged similarly attired. They climbed into bed together under the sheet, and she opened the book.

They went through a long list of idioms: "taken for a ride", "double entendre", "fat chance", "a sorry lot", "hell in a hand basket", "jump through hoops", "to pull a fast one", "about face", "double talk", "tied up for lunch", "pay through the nose", as well as a couple more. Then he tested her. She pronounced each one correctly, recited its meaning, and used it in an appropriate sentence. "If only I could learn Thai that fast."

"What about, '*at night, all cats are gray*?' I didn't find that in the book."

"You looked?"

"First thing."

"Well…"

"You know, but you won't tell me," she said, understanding his hesitation.

"Well, for a Thai, isn't it better to give no comment rather than say something crude?"

"But you're not Thai."

He explained it to her.

"Am I just a gray cat?" she asked.

"No. No, you are certainly *not* a gray cat."

She was good in bed. When he had reached for a condom, she had put out a restraining hand.

"What?"

"Don't."

"Isn't it safer this way?"

"You think you need it with me?"

"No. No, I don't think I do. But what about you? Both ways, I mean."

"Both ways safe I think."

She showered afterwards and came back into the bed.

"What?" she asked.

"I don't know..."

"Well, I do know. I know already. And it's all right."

"What?"

"That if she comes back, you go back to her."

"It makes me feel... not real good about what we did."

"It is *very* all right with me."

"Let me take you to dinner tomorrow. To a decent place."

"I like this restaurant."

He shook his head. "No. No you're definitely not... you're not gray. You're a rainbow."

"Tomorrow at eight o'clock?"

He laughed. "I mean, what if she comes back? Like at nine o'clock or something?"

"Well, she will be, what?" Prang searched for the phrase, "in surprise. I know how Thai women think. She'll not be back tomorrow. I know you still try to find her. That's okay."

"I don't know whether this is all a dream or that I'm just going crazy."

"I better leave soon. I can't come to work from elevator. Or wearing tent."

"I know what you said, but can't I...

"No." she interrupted. "We said okay. Don't make me gray."

He helped her into the tent, kissed her goodnight and pulled down the veil.

The next day, Michael left his room for several hours in the morning. He sat at a bar where he was unlikely to encounter Drake. When he returned, the room was made up. He tried the two telephone numbers at least twenty times. There was never an answer. Prang arrived at eight o'clock. Around midnight, as she was readying herself to leave, she said, "The tents are all checking out tomorrow."

"The last supper then," Michael responded heavily. This was the best restaurant."

"Please. You must promise me one thing."

"What?"

"That you are... that you don't feel bad about," she paused furtively, "about us. For different reason, that I no say more about, this good for me. So you promise?"

"I promise."

"This is a real promise?"

"A real promise."

The next morning Michael continued the fifty percent increased dosage of medicine. It was a simple tradeoff. A splitting headache was preferable to panic. He called the first number again. Joy answered.

"Hello, Joy?"

"Khun Michael. You find my number."

"Yes. Is Malee with you?" The line went quiet. He faintly heard a man's voice in the background.

"Is there a man there? With Malee?" The questions were daggers in his heart.

"He my husband," Joy said flatly. "Me married now."

"I want to speak with Malee."

"She cry."

"Let me speak with her."

There was a long pause.

"Khun Michael?" Malee's voice was hoarse from crying.

"Khun Malee. Can we talk?"

"I sorry. Khun Michael. I no good for you."

"If only you knew."

"I no understand what you say."

"Come back and we will talk."

"No good come back. I cry all night. Joy tell you."

"Come back. We only talk. Please. Please, come back."

There was another pause. His heart was beating very fast.

"Okay. I come back."

"When?"

"Three hour. Maybe four."

"I'll wait for you."

Michael showered and shaved and put on clean clothes. An hour later Prang knocked on the door to clean the room.

"It's all right," she said.

"How do you know?"

"It is easy for a woman to know."

Michael could not look while she made up the bed fresh. He heard the sounds as she pulled the sheets and blankets tight and the thumping sound as the pillows exited their cases, then the slap of her hand to make them lie smooth and flat in their clean linens. He heard her in the bathroom cleaning it. After she had finished, he looked up at her, finally making eye contact. "No," she said. "You said it was a real promise." "It was. I am sorry I made it seem otherwise. I am very grateful to you." She touched his hand for a moment and then was gone.

Michael speculated how things would go with Malee. He took the final extra fifty percent of Dr. Bach's medicine, the amount he had been cautioned to take for no more than two days.

Their reunion was uneventful. There was no rush to embrace. No tears. No gush of words. They stood looking at each other with no emotion on either of their faces. *Perhaps*, Michael thought, *they had, temporarily at least, drained themselves of their emotional reservoirs.* It was true in his case.

She sat on the bed. He lay down on the other side. Then she lay down on her side, too. He moved close to her, but did not touch her.

"Why?" he implored but did not press. She put her hand to her forehead.

"I can't understand if you say nothing."

"No can do anymore. Love in bed."

He waited for her to say more.

"I pray Buddha."

"Yes, every night your prayers were longer."

"Me married woman now."

"You were a married woman when you returned to me."

"No can explain. Too hard. No can do no more."

"I pray to Buddha, too."

"You no know Buddha."

"I read a book. Buddhism is a good religion."

"What Buddha tell you?"

"You know. He listens. No answer."

He handed her back the ring.

"No. No can have."

"I want you to have it. I had it made for you."

She began crying.

"Yes. You take it. You wear it."

"I no can longer be woman for you. I bad to keep ring."

"I want you to keep it."

"You no see? I no can do love. I no honest keep ring. You honest man. I love Khun Michael. You best man ever for me. But you need woman. I…oh," she paused as she rubbed her hand against her forehead and turned away, crying. "I so headache. I cry all night. Joy husband mad. He no can sleep."

He put his arms around her. "Please do not cry."

"I no can not."

He reached over and handed her a few tissues.

After a while, she stopped crying. She turned toward him.

"I stay. I find woman for you."

"What?" Michael couldn't believe what he had heard.

"We go bar. I find good woman. I wait downstairs. Short time, long time, okay. I want you be happy."

"No!"

"I want you be happy."

"But I want *you*."

"I no can."

"You do not like me anymore?"

"I say already. I love Khun Michael."

"Having a different woman. A new woman. This is no good for me."

"You try. I pick good woman. Maybe you like she better me."

"No. Not possible."

"But you try. I find you one. Okay if you no love her."

"No, I won't be happy then. Not ever happy."

"But I want…"

"Here." He gently put the ring on her finger.

"Okay, but then I take you bar."

They went to two clubs in Nana. Malee selected Yung. "She good. Speak English better me. I tell her long time. Okay?"

"But I don't want you just sitting in the lobby." Michael was torn and didn't know what else to say. He felt pressured by her. It was all too much for him, too foreign, but he went along with it because strangely, he felt that he was doing it for her.

"No. Me okay. You try," Malee said urging him on.

Michael and Yung walked to the elevator.

"She no come with us?" Yung asked looking between Malee and Michael.

"No."

"She no watch?"

"No."

"I no understand."

"It's a long story."

"Like *long time*?"

"Yes, like *long time*. Long time ago."

"I no understand you."

They were at the door to his room. He held the plastic key card in his hand. He just stood there staring down at the handle to the door, undecided as to whether he could go through with it.

Finally, she asked, "We go in?"

"Yes," he replied as he slowly opened the door.

She put her purse on the dresser.

"Where did you learn English?"

"America boyfriend."

"Where is he?"

"He leave."

"Did he promise to come back?"

"Yes. He no come back."

"Does he help you, I mean, with money?"

"No know where he is."

"You are very pretty."

"I take shower now."

"No. Just sit here." He patted the bed next to where he was sitting.

"We make shower first."

"Maybe. Just sit here now."

She complied. After a minute or so of silence, she asked, "What we do?"

"You want something to drink? I have red wine and some beer, too."

"Red wine good."

He opened a bottle. They each had a glass and talked a little.

"You strange firang. What your friend she do downstairs?"

"She waits."

"Wait what?"

"Waits until I come back down."

"Oh. We take shower now."

"No. We go downstairs now." He paid her for long time. Malee greeted him with a smile. "It okay?"

He shrugged.

"You like she better me?"

"No."

"Why no long time?"

"Just short time."

"I find new lady tomorrow? Maybe better next time."

"No. No more ladies. Only you." He paused. "Yes, I know." Nothing else needed to be said.

From then on, he slept only with Malee. They were playful in bed and slept in embrace, but that was it.

With the new arrangement between himself and Malee, Michael found himself turning more and more to his music. Until now, Michael had used it only once in Thailand but music was a familiar salve, one he often used after Helen was gone. He had brought a splitter to Thailand this trip so they each could have headphones and he could share the music he so loved with Malee. They could listen to Sibelius together. He wanted to share this part of himself with her, but Malee was always engrossed with her soaps. "Hey, come here," he finally said, one afternoon. "Listen to this." She held up her hand silently signaling that he would have to wait a few minutes. "I have see how story end. Very sad. She lose she man."

He acquiesced. Finally when she joined him, he showed her how to insert the headphones and began playing Sibelius' 2nd Symphony. Malee listened for a minute or two. She took out the headphones. "I no like this music," she said dismissively. He switched to Finlandia. The same result. Even the

Eroica Symphony did not interest her. Malee returned to her soaps, and he continued listening to the end of the Eroica, alone.

"Tell me, when you left, what were you going to do about all your things?"

She shook her head. "I no know."

"You were going to leave them?"

She looked at him pained. "Please no talk. I no thinking then. I think how much make you sad. And you good man to me."

Michael went shopping with Malee. He insisted she buy something for herself. They took the Sky Train to the new Superstore that had recently opened. After descending to the sidewalk, Malee had to ask three different people to figure out how to enter the complex. Everything was glass, chrome, and overpriced. The price on the first item that Malee took off the rack was staggering. It made Neiman Marcus look like a factory outlet store by comparison.

"Oh, too expensive!" Malee said. "No like this store. We go better place."

The better place was a seven story nondescript building with hundreds of small suks selling just about anything, although the emphasis was clearly on women's clothing and shoes. It was definitely a "buyer beware" atmosphere, a fact punctuated for both Michael and Malee when they discovered that some of the items she liked had stains, tears, and seams coming undone, all of which escaped a casual first glance. There were good deals to be had, however if you were willing to paw through the racks. Malee found some of the same items that she had wanted but put back because of one flaw or another in perfect condition in a different pile. Malee, that is Michael, bought five items that together cost one-quarter of the price of the one item at the Superstore. She beamed with the success of her expedition.

As they were heading out, purchases in hand, Michael and Malee passed the camera enclave. Michael kept walking but Malee pulled him back and inside amongst all the electronics. She quickly decided that she wanted a digital camera, and the salesperson was all smiles and help after seeing Michael with her. The choice was quickly reduced to two models by the same manufacturer—the more expensive was half again as much and was loaded with features that Michael knew Malee would never use, let alone understand. But this was the one she wanted. He reasoned with her that the less expensive model would do all the same basics, and that was no need for all the extra bells and whistles. They purchased the less expensive model.

On the way out, Malee turned to sullen-poutiness.

"What's the matter?"

"Me want other camera. You make me have this."

"I didn't make you have it. I told you it's the same camera."

"Me wanted other."

"All right, we'll go back."

The clerk was more than happy to exchange for the upgraded model. Malee went from sullen to happy in the time it took for the upgrade to be placed in a bag. Rather than annoying him, her transition amused him.

They had dinner with Drake and Dawn almost every night. When Drake learned of the new arrangement, his only utterance to Michael was that he was 'certifiable' and then assured Michael that he would not visit him at 'the Home'. The first night that the couples were back together, Drake talked with Malee in Thai. Dawn listened and at one point giggled. As soon as the Thai conversation ended, Michael inquired of Drake. The English they spoke was complex enough that they could talk freely without the girls understanding what was being said.

"They were two healthy ones."

"What are you talking about?" Michael asked.

"The two water buffalo she bought her parents."

"Well, I certainly appreciate your continuing interest in my certifiability. Makes me wonder about your 50-50 split all over again."

"Half a loaf would have made her interested in the other half. Who knows? She might have waited. Playing the bad odds."

"You have such a nice way of putting things."

"I hope not. I have an image to protect. Besides, I have no interest in putting things nicely to you—only clearly. And that's challenge enough."

"All right, so I'm crazy. I admit it. When in Rome…" he shook his head thinking that it was not the first time since he had been in Thailand where that phrase had crossed his mind.

That afternoon, Malee went to visit Joy whose first baby was about due. Malee returned that evening, and the following morning she snuggled over to Michael.

"Khun Michael, you so good to me. I have problem. I no like ask you, but I don't what to do. Problem brother. Him no work. Him lazy. Drink in bar. Him fight bar. Now teeth broken." She indicated the top front teeth. "Him sad. No smile now. Teeth ugly. I see. Doctor say must have 8500 Baht make teeth good. Brother have no money. Mama, Papa have no much money. What to do? I no know."

"I thought you didn't like your brother," Michael commented, remembering a previous conversation.

"Him lazy. Live Mama, Papa. No help. Him boy so him king. Mama give everything. Even no money, she give. Bad he no help Mama, Papa. Make me, make Joy sad."

"So why do you want to help him?"

She looked surprised by the question. "But him brother. Must help."

Michael already knew what he was going to do. He figured Malee also knew.

"Where is brother now?"

"Him with Joy. He no go out. Him mouth bad."

"Tell him to come to the hotel this afternoon. We will talk."

"You good man."

The three met at the hotel's café. Malee's brother Trong held his right hand over his mouth. He made a quick shift to shake hands and then his right hand assumed its defensive position. He managed to drink his tea with his concealing hand in place.

Trong was embarrassed, if not mortified, to be there. He was asking money of Malee's firang, and of course he knew what Malee did if she stayed with a firang.

"Can you ask him to show me his teeth?"

Malee translated. He looked around to make sure no one else was near. He took his hand away from his mouth. His lips were pressed tight. Finally, with downcast eyes, he opened his mouth. It looked awful. His four top front teeth were broken off in a straight diagonal from left to right. The lowest of the four on the left was almost missing in its entirety. He re-covered his mouth, ashamed.

"Tell your brother I will give him 8500 Baht for his teeth. I do not want him to suffer for the rest of life." Malee translated what Michael assumed was the essence of the message. Michael opened his wallet and produced what had been promised. Trong bowed as he accepted the money. His eyes remained focused on the ground. "I hope the doctor makes teeth good and strong." Malee translated again. The tea was over. Trong bowed, mumbled "thank you" in Thai through his protective hand, and made a quick switch to shake hands farewell.

The next morning Michael announced, "We are going to Chiang Mai. Drake told me where to stay—a hotel next to the Great Market. He says it is a nice hotel. I have tickets for tomorrow." Malee was delighted. Other than Ubon, Bangkok, and Samui, she had seen no other parts of Thailand. Chiang Mai, they discovered, was a scaled down, tamer version of Bangkok. Its only saving grace was less air pollution. The Great Market was a great disappointment—amusement park quality food and endless suks with hustlers hawking fake antiquities and even cheaper imitations of the fakes for gullible firangs. The suks were doing a brisk business, but Michael and Malee were not impressed. By the third morning, Michael decided to cut the trip short.

Killing time the morning before they were going to leave, Michael and Malee were walking back from the market when a woman approached them as they were standing in front of their hotel. She spoke fluent English and was bubbly. Her name was Nan.

"I will take you to all the nice places in the hill country. Very beautiful. All day—she pointed to her black sedan—3000 Baht. Everything. Except for spa if you want. It's the best spa in Thailand. You should not miss it. But with or without the spa, you will have a very good time. If not, you don't pay me. Michael looked at Malee, whose eyes had brightened with the possibility of getting out of the main part of town. He turned to Nan and said, "Why not?" They were off within fifteen minutes.

The car had air-conditioning—a surprise to find in Thailand most of the time—though once they climbed high into the hills toward Laos, it became unnecessary. The first stop was the spa, in the strict sense of the word. It was immaculate with white tile flooring throughout. Full treatment was 1000 Baht each, with separate facilities for men and women.

First Michael had a shower, then a full mudpack except where the towel was wrapped. The attendant was pleasant and efficient. After the mud had dried to the point where it cracked if he moved or smiled, Michael was ushered back to the shower followed by a hot springs mineral bath. The bath, done in light blue tiles, was twice the size of a normal swimming pool. It was waist deep with ledges around the perimeter on which to sit. There was only one other person in the men's facility. This uninterested stranger sat on the ledge reading a Thai newspaper, ignoring Michael completely, which was just fine with him. The water was not too hot but hot enough that the room was filled with steam. There was no time limit on one's stay in the mineral bath. Michael lingered. Finally, there was a Thai massage, not of the bone crunching variety that Jin had given him during his first days in Thailand, but rather a soothing massage. Michael fell asleep. He and Malee exited at about the same time. She was ecstatic. Being pampered had not been her lot in life.

Nan took them to the Queen's Summer Palace where, for 20 Baht each, Michael and Malee rode around the manicured grounds in an open-air electric cart while Nan waited with the car. This brush with royalty was a first for both Michael and Malee, and Malee was in awe. In her enthusiasm she peppered the driver with something that sounded more like an interrogation than simple curiosity. The question and answer session was all in Thai, but Michael did not much care—he simply enjoyed the landscaping and spending time with Malee. Later, outside the grounds, the three had lunch at a roadside stand, enjoying the scenic countryside.

As they drove into the higher hills, the road started to wind and gradually became little more than a wide dirt path. Malee suddenly requested that Nan stop. She got out and tried to hide behind some kind of shack. She did not make it and threw up. Nan was distressed as if it were all her fault. Michael explained that Malee sometimes became carsick, which made Nan feel a little better as she found some water and a towel that Malee used to clean herself up.

Finally, the three of them came to a quaint village at the peak of one of the last hills that edged Thailand, beyond which one descended into Laos. They stopped, and Malee threw up again. Nan was clearly worried, but Michael waved her off as if to tell her that it was okay. He took Malee for a short walk to breathe in some of the fresh air.

While in this pastoral setting, Nan arranged for Malee to be dressed in a traditional wedding outfit covered in fine embroidery of every color imaginable. It came with a hat of similar design and color. Malee looked the exquisite bride. She wanted Michael to wear a wedding outfit, too. A tan front zippered Mao jacket and pants were found from somewhere. The pants were much too short so Nan had a tailor sew on an additional length, and even though the extra fabric was a slightly different color it looked fine. Malee took out her camera and had Nan take pictures of her first and then of her and Michael together in the traditional pose of a newlywed couple. On the way back, Malee threw up one more time. It was retching rather than throwing up since there nothing left. Back at Chiang Mai, Michael paid the fee and tipped Nan 500 Baht.

Michael and Malee decided to stay in Chiang Mai for another night, and as Malee recovered in bed he held her close. It had been a good day, and other than throwing up because of the winding car travel, her appetite had been good—if anything, she was eating more than he recalled from the first time they had met. As Michael was holding her she became somber. "What is it?" Michael asked.

"Me no good woman for you. You need haf woman do love and I no do. You good to me. Me no good you."

"I do not want to make love with you because you do not want to."

"Me no can explain you."

"I didn't ask you to explain."

"Me love Khun Michael."

"Well, pray to Buddha again."

"You know. Buddha no give answer. Me want you do love mit woman. Me still be mit you. Me still want mit you."

"All right, then," Michael said trying to reassure and quiet her.

The next day they returned to Bangkok as planned. The little holiday was over.

Drake and Michael had one more meeting to finalize the terms for the new export company with the Thai investors whom Drake had found through his Royal connections. One of these men was the president of a talent and modeling agency and Michael was seated next to him for the entire meeting. Over the course of the day Michael learned the basics of this man's industry, the main clients in the business, as well as anecdotal do's and don't's. It was enlightening for Michael and the two struck up what was certainly a cordial if not friendly relationship.

The meeting had gone very well and Drake was in a celebratory mood. "We'll stop at the Watering Hole on the way back," Drake said. "Another option if you're looking for something before the bars open. It's cheaper than Julie's, not as elegant, but the girls are more," he smiled, "adventuresome. And you could use some adventure regardless of whatever crazy vows you made or whatever you call them."

"I don't know," Michael said, hesitating.

"You don't know anything when it comes to women. This is what she's been trying to get for you every night. Obviously she doesn't mind. This'll make her happy. You'll be doing her a favor. She won't feel so guilty."

"Look, I don't want…"

"Hold it," Drake interrupted. He pointed a finger at Michael. "I'm taking this fucking horse to the Watering Hole!"

"I don't think…"

Drake interrupted again. "You're damn right. You don't think. All right, I'll wait right here."

"Wait? For what?"

"Wait for you to go back and get a permission slip from, *you know who.*"

It was off Sukhumvit Road and a then few turns on back streets to The Ranch. There was a bar on the ground floor with girls lounging around. As soon as they spotted Drake and Michael approaching, the girls scattered, or more precisely, repaired to the second floor to primp behind the large one-way mirror. There was another, smaller bar on the second floor where Michael and Drake headed first. Both were declining drinks when Mary, the Madame of the establishment who clearly knew Drake, came over. She escorted them to the one-way mirror where a dozen or so scantily clad girls had assembled. Mary spoke English and described the various attributes and proclivities of each girl. Drake recommended No.9 to Michael. Her name was Carol, and it turned out to be a good choice. When Michael returned to the bar, Drake was nowhere to be seen.

"He went long time back," Mary said. "He say you very slow. But maybe good slow, yes? Next time, you choose me. Okay?"

"How much will you pay me?"

She burst into laughter and gave him a friendly shove. "You funny man. I pay you many, many Baht. But first, you pay me more Baht, no?"

"Tell me your number so I remember next time."

She gave him another friendly shove. "I like you. What is your name?"

"Michael."

"You number one, Michael. I remember you next time, too."

The next time turned out to be the next day. Drake was upbeat.

"Finally, the big 4-0." Michael did not understand, and then, quickly recollected a conversation he had had with Drake about the age differentials of the girls.

"She was eighteen! Just off the farm."

"So, Mr. Mathematician, what's your goal?" Michael asked.

"Hopefully, the big 6-0. But clearly I have to be patient," he said with a wink.

Drake chose the same girl again, and the two disappeared through the curtain.

Mary was chattier with Michael the second time seeing him and gave him a big hug making sure that she pressed her breasts and crotch tight against him.

"Oh, darling, I wait for you. I did no sleep last night. I dream of you. You choose me today?" Her eyes were full of humor and mischievousness. "I very cheap. I big boss and only 2000."

"I'll take little boss. Carol again."

"I am hurt." She flashed a vaudevillian look of disappointment. "But Carol, she is good choice. For you, still only 1500. For everything. Except one thing. You must talk with her for that."

Michael handed her 2250 Baht. "This is not for the other thing. You tell her it is for three hours, not two."

Mary raised her eyebrow. "Khun Drake right. You slow. But I think for right reason." She laughed and put her hand, gently, into his crotch. "Oh, you ready Teddy. Next time, you take me three hours. You never forget. I promise. I make you go crazy."

Michael leaned forward and whispered, "You already do. But I want to live longer." He held his hand over his heart.

"You crazy firang. I like you. I like you. Maybe free with me next time."

"Just very big tip, right?"

"You too smart."

Carol had a shapely figure—smooth skin and long hair dyed golden brown. Her skin was a perfect tan, that is, perfect if one did not aspire to the albino look of the soap stars. She spoke good English. She was dressed in a bikini with *plenty of swing*, he noticed, as she walked in front of him. She took him by the hand and pulled him into a different room from the first one they had made good use of the night before. This new room sported a plaque with the name "The Den". With familiarity, she flipped a switch that illuminated a red light over the door.

Apart from the bed the most dominant feature was an over-sized tiled tub with a tiled drying area attached. The ceramic pieces that covered the entire bath were small, multi-colored and laid out like a mosaic in a geometric pattern—it was done by someone who clearly cared how it turned out. In the drying area, there were two sets of new disposable rubber-bottomed slippers and their utility was quickly demonstrated. Like the day before, Carol suggested that he undress while she went out for a few moments.

Michael noted that the room décor was more spruced up than the other room and that it was meant to look opulent and clean, but it was an old building that suffered from the signs of its age. The king-size bed against the far wall was dominated by a bas-relief in gold leaf of a larger than life nude woman sitting with thighs spread. She had flowing hair that curled around, rather than over, her breasts and then flowed back towards her abdomen to cover her crotch. Her face was turned sideways with a beguiling glance.

Carol returned with a plastic carrying case of various shampoos, soaps, and gels. Like the night before the routine was the same, but this time they had double the space, this tub being twice the size of the one from the night before. Carol slipped out of her bikini and filled the tub with warm water. They started to take the traditional bath, then he cut it short, much shorter than the first time where she slithered on top of him, front to front, with plenty of soap to make for a slippery ride using her two breasts as washcloths. Michael was more eager than he expected. "We can dry off now," he said after a minute or so.

They took baby steps in the tiled drying area that was slippery as ice. She showed him a nasty bruise on her hip where she had slipped and fallen before. Wisely, they put on rubber-bottomed slippers because as she was rinsing him off with the flexible shower hose, the gilded old building suddenly came to life in the form of the largest cockroach he had ever seen. Having emerged from somewhere, the creature, larger than an ordinary mouse, scurried about. Carol lurched back in horror with a half scream. The only weapon at hand was the flexible shower hose. Michael put the temperature to hot and directed the jet of steaming water at the cockroach. All *that* did was make the cockroach run frantically this way and that in the drying area trying to escape this rain of terror. No matter how many times Michael hit it dead on the critter only kept trying to flee. Michael shut off the water and tiptoed in his slippers out of the wet tile area seizing the next available weapon: one of Carol's high heels. With one swat he sent the cockroach into two-dimensional heaven, then put the shoe down victoriously. Carol looked at the carnage, reached for her shoe and turned the water back on washing and rewashing the bottom of her shoe to clean off whatever part of the cockroach might still be clinging to the sole. Finally, she set the shoe on the floor, distastefully, as if it had been forever contaminated. As she gave up on her shoe shaking her head, she looked over at Michael who had been standing there watching her, still half amazed at the size of the roach. As they made eye contact they both smiled, then burst into laughter. They finished drying off while keeping a wary eye on the floor, finally making their way to the king-size bed.

"Mama-san…" Carol started to say.

"Mary?" he interrupted, "Yes?"

Said this is for three hours."

"Yes. This way we do not look at the clock."

They talked. She was twenty-six and had been working at The Ranch for six months. She, of course, sent money home to her parents, but she wanted to save enough to open a beauty parlor. She calculated two million Baht for the license, the suk and the equipment. Two years at The Ranch would do it. Less if she did not have too many Indian customers. "They think 200 Baht big tip."

Drake had instructed Michael not to tip more than 500, ever. Drake's words flooded back to Michael's mind, "You're destroying the whole fucking economy single-handedly." Michael had given Carol 1000 Baht the first time. He laughed to himself about what Drake would say *now*.

"You want me give you back rub?" she asked.

"Not right now. I will give you a back rub."

She lay down on her stomach.

"No," he said. "Better to turn over. Different kind of back rub."

"You no want me fake it?"

"No. That would make me very unhappy."

"I should tell you, I don't come."

"That's okay."

As it turned out, she was wrong. Thirty minutes later, she was flying high.

"Oh, my God! Oh, my God!" When her breathing slowed, she murmured, "You ruin me. Now you ruin me. If next customer, I fall asleep."

"You can fall asleep now. We have time."

"Where you learn this?"

His face moved in close, and his eyes opened wide. "In a book."

She laughed with her available energy. "You joke me. Mama-san tell me you funny firang. Now I know."

They bathed again, both on the idiotic lookout for cockroaches. Then it was back to bed. They talked while he gave her a *real* backrub. He told her about himself, the business he was setting up in Thailand, his business background in the States, his separation.

"Me know she still want you."

"How do you know that?"

"Women know things men no know."

"Like what?"

"Like men."

"Maybe she hates me."

"She wait you. Know you return."

"Maybe she's a bad person."

"You no marry bad person. You too smart."

He gave a short laugh.

"Me know she no want divorce."

"Well, you're right. She doesn't."

"See, me know. You need she, too."

He continued the back rub. She purred. "You do this wife."

"Yes."

"But now you find girl Ubon. Yes?"

"Yes."

"You no marry she."

"She's married."

"He bad man. Me know all."

"So it would seem," Michael said playfully.

"You worry she."

He held up his hand for her to stop and nudged her to turn over. She did so while adding, "I never be coming two times. You not get angry?"

"No."

Again, she was wrong. Afterward, they rested together for the balance of the three hours. Neither one said much. She fell asleep during the third hour.

He tipped her 3000 Baht.

"You very kind man. Me hope you do good business."

The remaining few days before Michael's departure were uneventful, especially as far as things went with Malee. She knew he had been somewhere and she seemed genuinely pleased that he was able to find the thing that she could no longer offer. Drake was right. She was happy for him. He saw Carol two more times and liked her better each time. Both times were long times. Both times Malee was spending the night with Joy whose baby had just arrived.

Malee accompanied him to the airport. She gave him the traditional good-luck white and red flower bracelet. She also gave him the two pictures from their trip to the high country north of Chiang Mai. This now made four pictures he had of her. "Look," he said, "here are the Baht I have left. You take it. He gave her the bills from his wallet—16,540 Baht. Write me an email. I will check my email first thing. Okay?" She nodded. He gave her a kiss on the cheek and with a small wave disappeared into customs control. For a split second, he thought of Helen. Inexplicably it felt as if he were returning to her after a long business trip. He shook his head slightly but vigorously as if ridding himself of the thought. As fast as it had come, it disappeared. And he was left with thoughts of Malee.

The flight back was uneventful and endless, and the first day back in the States he sent her an email greeting. A day later, she emailed back telling him how happy she was to hear from him. A week later he sent another email and heard back three days later.

He thought about Malee every day, a random gamut from missing her so much that it ached, to being glad that he was out of her grasp, even though he was not. He daydreamed about the wondrous delight of their love making and shuddered, remembering the pain of being so terribly hurt that she

had left him. Michael marveled at her honesty and appreci-
ated that what could have been perceived as dishonesty was
actually a form of Thai cultural integrity. He worried about
her wellbeing, spending hours in reflection. He would imagine
her eyes and thought about her slightly husky voice, about
how much he loved the way she had held her ground over the
camera, about her desire for his happiness. He would think
about her commitment to her family. About the joy he felt
seeing the ruby ring on her finger. He would grow somber
when remembering his panic after finding it on the mantle.
If he thought about it long enough he could almost feel her
beguiling touch. Then all would come crashing down when
he would think of her having to continually choose the least
worst decision as her lot in life. He would drift off absorbed in
the memory of how her sheer long skirts drove him crazy with
desire. He would smile when thinking about the vomit in her
hair during their introduction, his happiness at imagining her
wearing the clothes he had given her. He daydreamed about
how her broken English could communicate her feelings so
completely, and also about her awakening that night to the
sound of his silent tears, her comforting him. It was an endless kaleidoscope of delicious joys and unbearable pains. He
waited impatiently for her emails, which became fewer and
fewer, as his personal reveries started taking him further into
dreams.

Despite his preoccupation with Malee, Michael re-engaged
professionally when he got back to the States. It was the
one area of his life where he could find certainty and focus.
Michael made a trip to New York to continue to press for better terms for the European initiative from Neimans now that
he had concrete arrangements on the Thailand end. It dragged
on and he ended up staying longer in New York because the
wife of the key executive for Neimans tragically died in an
automobile accident. Having been gone much longer than

he had expected, Michael kept in close contact with Jay who was still worried about him. Knowing that he had time on his hands Michael took two weeks off to hike in the Green Mountains with a college roommate. It was a welcome curative for Michael and eased Jay's mind.

A lot of Michael's time was taken up conferring with his lawyer about the testimony he would be compelled to give as a witness in Ridley's trial. It was testimony that caused him no angst or anxiety since he had known nothing about Ridley's fraud. The truth was an easy thing to remember. If he could not recall certain detailed information about the company's operations, he decided that since he had done nothing wrong it was not cause for worry. Michael filled his remaining hours by visiting old haunts in the city, reconnecting with former company employees and starting to read again.

While he was still in New York another college friend contacted him about becoming a founding investor in a computer-based start-up company. It was an unexpected offer, but Michael was intrigued by the proposition and the possibilities. He invested a million dollars and spent considerable time helping with the launch when he was back home.

It continued this way for months. Michael buried himself in his work and when not working he would fall into a forlorn hopelessness. Malee's emails became more infrequent until finally there were none. Michael couldn't keep his mind from the longing he felt. He emailed her again. No reply. He thought of her every day, every night. Dread set in. He conjured up different reasons—maybe she had been injured in an accident or, God forbid, she had been killed. Then, to his next email, there was a response, "Message Failure—address unknown". So, that was it? She was gone? Again. He could not accept that, but what difference did it make that he could not. He emailed Joy but received no response.

He obsessively checked his email, sometimes five times a day, sometimes more. He didn't admit that to anyone, not even to Dr. Bach who changed the dosage on his meds to a clinical level. Every week he emailed her. Now it was always "Message Failure".

One day Michael took out the four pictures of her: 16 sitting before Buddha, 17 as a model, 29 in village wedding dress with him, and alone in the ceremonial wedding dress. The next day, he took out the pictures again. He stared a long time at the one with Buddha. He tore that one up first, then the other three. He went to his computer and erased the emails he had sent to and received from her. He kept only one, the email that had her birthday noted. Immediately, he was both pleased with his decisiveness and regretted his action.

Michael fell out of touch with almost everyone after Malee's emails stopped. Drake called from Manila.

"No. No, I don't want to go back. Not for a while," Michael said in answer to Drake's frustrated entreaty.

"When did you have in mind going back? Hey, we now have business over there, you know. You still on the phone? Hello?" Drake prodded.

"Yeah."

"So what gives?"

"I still haven't heard back from her.

"I'm well aware."

"Look, can you handle the business stuff this year without me? Everything's now basically done at both ends, just a few things to tie up. I know this is finking out on you, but I just have to think things through."

"So how is *that* news?"

"Drake, I have to stop thinking about Thailand for a while."

There was silence at the other end.

"Hey Drake, please..." he trailed off.

"Michael, you have to ask yourself, is she worth it."

"You don't understand."

"I understand that if she isn't Dawn, it won't work. That is, won't work for you. So who is she? Something's up and you may never know what."

"I'm just going to keep her in the past."

"You should refresh your knowledge of tenses."

"Maybe next trip, okay?"

"No. I'm not going to let our businesses fall apart because she fucked you up. We both need to be there, at least at the outset. Or did you forget that? Besides you sure need that pill now."

"What pill?"

"TWP—Thailand Wonderful Prescription."

There was silence on the other end.

"After you finalized things with Neimans on Europe. That's when we said. Remember?"

"All right," Michael finally conceded.

Five months had passed since Michael had heard from Malee, but she still haunted his thoughts. Two weeks after he returned home from the business trip to New York, Michael emailed Malee again, this time with birthday greetings. It went through! He checked email three, four, five times a day for the next five days. There was no reply. One night, Michael stayed up past midnight writing a poem. He was hardly a poet and had not written a poem since high school, but tonight was different. The words tumbled out of him and onto the page.

TO MALEE

I had my chance to hold you tight,
But I lost you to the stars one night.
Now all I have is memory
Of your face, your smile, your siren-call.
The tide comes in and castles fall.

You're in the wind, you're in the sun,
You're gone, you're gone, and now you're none.

But I'm haunted by your memory.
Please fade away, fade in my mind
So that peace and rest I again may find.

Inside I think I've made you die
So why is it each night I cry.
I can't erase the memory
Of your face, your smile, your siren-call.
The tide comes in and castles fall.

Through a friend of a friend, he had it translated into Thai. He sent her the poem by email in both Thai and English. Two days later, she emailed him:

Dear Khun Michael,

i happy you no forgt birthday. It beautiful poem. i cry my friend cry. No one nevr wrote poem for me before. Make me want be mit you. Me life good an bad now. Me cry life.

Love,

Khun Malee.

Dear Khun Malee,

I was so happy to hear from you. I think of you every day. Tell me why life is both good and bad for you in Germany. I do not understand. Have you been back to Thailand since I last saw you? I am coming back to Thailand. I hope to hear from you soon.

Love,

Khun Michael

Malee responded with the news that she had a daughter, Regina. She gave her birth date—just over five months after they had parted. She attached two photos. The first was of

Regina alone. The second was mother and daughter together. Both pictures were taken too close up so they had moon-like distortions. He noted in the background of the pictures an out-of-focus, drab apartment, sparsely furnished.

He could not help but give a short laugh, "So, Regina. It was Regina," he said to himself as he continued smiling.

He called Drake who was now in Singapore.

"You'll never guess!"

"I already have."

"Yes, I got an email from her. She wants to get together again."

"Surprise," Drake said ironically.

"She has a baby now."

"Must be a few months old by now."

"How did you know?"

"It's called addition."

"You knew?"

"Yeah."

"You did? I mean, when? Did she tell you?"

"Noooo. She doesn't have to tell me how to add. And, come on, Michael, think. She would have told you before she ever told me."

"So when?

"When I saw her."

"Oh, I can't believe this. I mean, you could tell? Then? How?"

"You learn to see things."

"Christ! Is there *any* hope for me?"

"No."

"Why didn't you tell me?"

"Would you have *wanted* me to tell you?"

There was a pause on the line.

"Would it have made any difference?" Drake asked.

Michael said nothing.

"Yeah, I didn't think so."

"You make me feel like a complete idiot."

"Well, good to have an honest picture of yourself."

Michael laughed. "Will I ever get a compliment out of you?"

"Sure, when you deserve one," Drake ribbed in response.

"Look, if I can arrange to meet her back there, what do you say we take a little vacation again? Afterwards. You know, like Samui."

"Last time we spoke, you didn't want to go. Now you're in heat."

"You still with Dawn?"

"Not in Singapore," he said with a laugh.

"I don't mean Singapore."

"Of course I'm still with her. 'En principe.' After all, I have to keep track of my money."

"You had to make another *investment?*"

"No comment."

"I guess they don't give Prada away." Michael hit home.

"All right. Just give me the details."

"Details?"

"Details. Of how it's going to be in Samui. Is it two 'Dawns' or not?"

"What do you mean?"

"Like who's going to Samui."

"Just the four of us."

"After you make the arrangements with her, give me the details."

"Sure. No problem."

Dear Khun Michael,

i think you. so not happy here housband more bad now. him smoke drink much. i headache!!! don,t what do. hie give me no money. i work bad job clean floors clean toilets no much money. him mom take care Regina i work. now i sad all time. Too much headache. me want leave housband. divorce but then how i live??

Sometime housband bring lady home mit him then i sleep on floor next to Regina. him no hit me but i cry all time now. i miss you. so sorry i come Germany i be happy see you again be mit you. You say yes me divorce be mit you

Love,

Khun Malee

Dear Khun Malee,

It makes me so sad that you have a terrible life with a bad husband. I arrive in Thailand May 1. First we go to Samui for one week. But just the two of us. Then Bangkok. Regina can stay with Joy or your mother. I will buy a ticket for you and Regina.

Love,

Khun Michael

Dear Khun Michael,

Wenn you come Thailand, I very happy. I bring Regina mit me. Mama come take care her. Four us, we travl together Samui. This good. We all together and Mama take care Regina. You and me be alone. I can come back Thailand wen you say. You tell me wen.

Lvoe and kisses, Khun Malee

Michael sent the proposed plan to Drake. The reply was the following day.

Dear Michael,

I thought it would be four, too. But I was thinking of a different four. If you are bringing a caravan with you, then you are on your own, and I wish you luck. We'll do the business meetings, but that's all. Then we can get together when common sense returns. Drake

Dear Khun Malee,

I am not happy with what you suggest. I want us to be together, just the two of us, for the month of May. Regina can stay with your mother in Ubon. It is common in my country for a granddaughter to visit with her grandmother for several weeks.

I want it to be like the first time we met. If it cannot be that way, then maybe it is better that we not meet. This would make me sad, very, very sad, but I do not want to meet unless it can be just the two of us alone. I think you understand what I mean. If you do not want this, then please tell me now. You know, I love you deeply, but I also have had great pain because of this love. I do not want more pain. It is too terrible for me. So maybe it is better if we do not meet. You tell me.

Love,

Khun Michael

Dear Khun Michael,

I want be mit you. It be like Samui. You and i. Regina stay Mama ubon. i make you very happy. i no what you mean. i want you be very very happy mit me. i want leave Germany. have problem mit housband long time now i stay his mom mit Regina. i very sad but don't know what

*what can i do. Now I don't have job i take care Regina
him mom take care i and Regina. i cry to much. now i
wait for finish? i don,t hnow i come back to thailand i
look for job. I DON,T KNOW?????????????? Too much
problem. Very headache. I want be mit you.*

love khun Malee i miss you

Michael cleared it with Drake that the month of May
would work out and then informed Drake that it would be
only Malee and himself, that the baby would stay with Malee's
mom in Ubon. Malee wanted to go one week before the beginning of May and stay until one week before the end of July—
three months exactly. He noted with some curiosity that it was
exactly three months. She would meet him at the airport on
May 1. She would meet him alone. Everything was set.

One week later, he received a confusing email from Malee,

Dear Khun Michael,

*i cannot say you. i afraid tell. i lend $2000 from lady.
Her say must pay her money before i Thailand. Her say
if Thailand i no pay she. Friend give me $1000. first say
$2000. Now $1000. i no can ask you $1000. you good
man. give me to much. What do? i cry big headache. I sad
all time. you lend $1000. then i pay you back if Thailand
all okay. If you no send $1000, that okay. You no warry.
But you send money, then better. i no like ask. Make me
cry more. You good man very very.*

Love

Khun Malee. Kisses.

Dear Khun Malee,

*I will send you the $1000. I will wire money to your bank.
You tell the bank that you need an ABA number. The bank*

*understands what this means. They will give you all the
information that you must email me. I am sorry you are
sad. I want to make you happy.*

Love,

Khun Michael

Dear Khun Michael:

*Bad bad thing happen. Friend have no money. i no no
why. Now you only one. Must give she $2000. You no
worry if no have money. Lady tell me give ring then okay.
i tell she no. i die first. Lady bad person. You tell me what.
i pay you back Thailand.*

Love Khun Malee

He called Drake to seek his advice.

"Why do you want my advice?" he asked.

"Because I value it."

"Then you should take it some time."

"Come on, will you give me your advice on this?"

"My advice is that it's useless to give you advice."

"Why do you say that?"

"Because you've already made up your mind. You're going
to send her the money. And if you hadn't already made up your
mind, this would have been my advice anyway. Hell, so you
risk two grand. What's that to you?"

"I couldn't handle it if she doesn't show. Then it wouldn't
just be a tailspin. It would be a crash. I don't know how I could
handle it. If the same thing happens all over again."

"I already gave you the advice on that."

"What was it?"

"Oh, Christ. Look, she's already sent your judgment into
blotto-land. Now she's erased your memory, too? Does 50-50
split ring a bell?"

234 WILLIAM McALLISTER III

"Yeah." He could hear Drake's sigh of exasperation on the other end.

"So make the second $1000 C.O.D."

"What if she can't come then?"

"Trust me. She'll find a way."

dear khun michael

how are you? now i have all together a big problem with money. i must pay for room and for regina passport back and now friend no money hav for me. Lady keep regina passport and no give if no $3000.

can you help me again please !!! now i am trouble veally .i veally need money 3000 dollar when you can come to me in Germany very good!!!. I am sorry to have trouble you again? please last time! I have so much think and very cry. I have nobody when you can help me I never forget your kindness and very good man for me! when all okay

I can come back Thailand with you in May in Thailand!!! I make you so much happy. you can tok with my friend phone number i gave you her tok english

love khun malee regina

Dear Khun Malee:

I want to help you, but you said $2000, and that is all I can send right now. When we meet in Thailand, then I will have the extra $1000. You can wire that back to the woman then. You know I am a man of my word, and you can trust me. You must tell this woman that she has to trust me. That is all I can do. The woman cannot hold Regina's passport. In my country that is illegal. Woman should go to jail.

Love,

Khun Michael

Michael got together with Jay and explained the latest developments. Jay shook his head slowly and pursed his lips pityingly, "Michael, oh, my dear Michael. Don't you see? You must. I know you do. You've dug yourself into a deep hole, and your solution is to dig it deeper." Michael kneaded his hands while Jay continued, "Your chance was when you first met her. To sweep her up, divorce Helen, and make her your wife. But you knew you weren't about to do that." Michael's whole body tightened, but he said nothing. Jay kept talking through Michael's tension, "In some respects, based on what you told me, I think that she would have made the best wife a man could possibly wish for. But she would not have been a complete woman for you. And I know you know this. The whole intellectual, educational, cultural side? There would have been a chasm, forever."

Jay paused and waited for Michael to speak. The silence seemed interminable. Finally Michael blurted out defensively, "I know Drake thinks she's shaking me down now."

Jay responded protectively, "That's a mere tangent. But I'll speak to that, too. Malee is probably the most honorable person you will ever meet in your life."

"What makes you say that?"

"You told me."

"I did?"

"Yes, when you told me about the ruby ring on the mantle. Quite a few years of income I would guess."

Michael nodded slowly, "So what do you suggest?"

"I can't get inside of how deeply you feel, but I know you've risked your heart and that it's genuine because, at the very least, you're being unrealistic if not totally irrational. And I've never seen you irrational before."

"So?"

"I think you have no choice. You have to go back. Not to be cruel. One thing you are *not* is cruel. Rejoice in you time together, I venture to say your last, then provide for her comfort. You will feel good about yourself for the rest of your life if you provide for her. Her whole life has been suffering."

Dear khun michael

Thanks for your trouble ! Don't worry I have the money you send. This money I make everything finish. Tell lady her must trust you. Her say okay. I really happy when everything can finish!!!!!!!! love and miss you !!!!

you are very good man!!!!!!!!!!!! I hope with you in future!!! the money come in the my bank. I 29 years old. I still young. LOVE khun Malee.

He reread those last two sentences. Then he closed the email. Moments later, he re-opened it and reread her closing remarks. He felt so sad for her—the unfairness of it all. He could not pretend that he was not a part of it. That evening, he began feeling bad. He could not pinpoint the reason, but he kept coming back to those last two sentences. They kept resurfacing in his mind—the clock ticking mercilessly on her, her reckoning of that fact. She was much more than that to him. She had to be. He had climbed to exquisite peaks with her, elevations that he never knew existed, and through her he had dropped into chasms that he could never have anticipated, the depths of which he still could not fathom.

Michael thought he would be in high spirits over the soon-to-be reunion, but time began to wear on him. Bad became worse. He felt himself spiraling downward, the beginnings of a panic attack. He had already doubled Dr. Bach's dosage but decided to take the second half of the fifty percent increase. Moments later, Michael realized that with all of his distractions he had mixed up the pills and had taken an extra full dose rather than the intended half.

That night, his mind ran riot with nightmares. Tossing in a fitful half-sleep, he could not remember most of those visions, only phantoms of the final images before he would stir turning over and falling back to sleep. The few he could remember, he did not want to, and to his surprise trying to force himself to forget those few proved successful with all but one or two. When he fully awoke, it was barely light out. Where was he? Nothing seemed familiar. He had difficulty getting out of bed. Stepping into his slippers he instead pushed one of them under his dresser. He retrieved it after crouching and then having to get on all fours. Trying to stand up, he wobbled and rolled onto his back. Finally, he managed to get upright. Something smelled terrible. He staggered out of his bedroom.

"Oh, fuck it," he moaned. The bathroom mirror showed him that he thrown up all over himself. "Gotta clean up…oh, shit."

He took off his clothes. The vomit had not completely dried yet, and the smell made him gag. He washed off his face while he let the tub fill. He rubbed the mirror clear and ran his fingertips down one cheek. Smooth and no hint of wrinkles yet. That struck him as an odd thought. He started to shave. He got startled when suddenly front and center in the mirror was Malee, in all her allure. She was on some kind of platform that inclined upward, and she was being pulled slowly away from him. Her hands reached out toward him. He seized the can of shaving cream and sprayed the mirror. The foam obliterated the image but also splattered back on him, on his face, on his hair. It was now both foam and vomit.

He was no longer outside of the mirror. He was standing before her on the ramp. He grabbed her wrists, trying to pull her back. Her hands clung to him. The power dragging her away was strong. With all his might, he brought the contest to a standstill, but their grip began slipping, just a little, and then more. She looked at him, her eyes filled with terror. He squeezed tighter and held firm. Then, to his right, out of the corner of his eye, he saw something that transfixed him—a very young woman, standing, moving toward him on a conveyor belt. She was barefoot and clad only in a white bra and panties. A large red-ribbon bow was tied around her forehead. One of those plastic numbered disks was attached to her panties. She smiled knowingly. "No!" he cried out. The force of his voice stopped the conveyor, but only for a few seconds before it resumed its delivery. For just a moment he let go of Malee, grabbed his prize fishing rod and rammed it into the conveyor belt gearing, bringing it to a halt. He turned back and reached for Malee, but she was further away now, far enough that they could only grip by locking their fingers. His legs could not move, and the pulling of the conveyor belt pried their fingers open—slowly, inexorably. Finally, only the first knuckles of each finger of their hands joined them together. The outside force was too great. They slipped off. By stretching out with one hand, he made fingertip contact before she was beyond reach. She was crying and reaching out for him. "Malee!" he shouted. He tried climbing after her, but the surface was slippery. He started sliding down the incline. The fishing rod was slowly disappearing under the grinding force of the gear, and the young woman was moving closer, still with a persistent smile, still inviting him while dangling a new pair of shoes from one finger. Behind her, he stared in horror as he saw Malee's face and her outstretched hand fading further and further away until she was gone.

He lunged for the can of shaving cream and sprayed the young woman. The foam covered her, but nowhere near completely. She rubbed it over her body, playing with her contours. Her smile never left his gaze. He sprayed until the foam was all gone. All gone except for a foul smelling black liquid that dripped into one of his slippers from the nozzle of the now emptied can. He slid his foot out in disgust. The smell made him retch, but there was nothing left to vomit out. She stretched her out hand and touched his smooth face, exploring his features. She was wearing Malee's ruby ring. "No!" he cried out. He tried pulling it off her finger, but it would not budge. She laughed as she held up her hand admiring the ring.

He recoiled, staggering back from the mirror. The backs of his knees collided with the side of the tub. He lost balance and fell into the tub, his head hitting the tiled soap holder with a thud, knocking him senseless. He slid down the side of the porcelain. His head was slumped over toward one shoulder. He saw the surface of the water turned red in a swirling abstract. The water level was mid-way up his neck and rising. He heard water gurgling through the overflow hole near the top of the tub. Then everything went black.

He forced his eyes to open as a bright light shone down on him. He turned away from the glare and saw a green curtain instead of a wall. Jay leaned over.

"How you doing?"

Michael tried to move, but couldn't. He was belted to the bed. He tried to nod. It hurt.

"Lucky for you your front door was open. Called 911. Then I got Dr. Bach, and he came right over to the ER. He said they did a blood test. You OD'd. It was an accident, right?"

"Yeah."

"God, you know, there was shaving cream everywhere, and you threw up all over the place. I'll clean it up when I leave here. You don't vomit nice."

Michael managed a short laugh. "Jay, you're...you know. What can I say? Hey, come closer." Jay moved nearer alongside Michael's gurney. Michael whispered, "How about loosening these belts a little? They're starting to dig in."

"Hey, look, the nurse is right here," he whispered back. "And she's going kick me out in a minute. They wouldn't even let me in. No visitors. It's only because I'm your brother."

"Fucking nurse."

"Hey, but it's going to be okay."

"No. No. It won't be okay."

"No, come on, you'll see. Get some sleep now. That's what they say. Then you'll be okay." Jay lightly squeezed Michael's arm as the nurse pulled the curtain aside and nodded to him.

Michael closed his eyes. When he opened them, Malee was wiping off the puffs of shaving foam and vomit still stuck to his hair. Then she cut up his food and fed it to him.

"No, I'll never be okay. Never. Never." He closed his eyes, and tears squeezed out.

The day after he was released an email came in from Helen. Her timing unnerved him.

Michael,

Things did not work out with Charles—that was his name—and I now realize they never would. After a while, we really didn't have much left to say or to share with each other. The relationship was finite, and before I ended things, we were little more than intimate strangers. Yes, I am not going to pretend that things didn't happen. It happened. That's all. I just wanted to let you know. I expect you and I have may have something in common that way.

Helen

Michael had lunch with Jay the day before the flight to Thailand. He filled him in on all the correspondence with Malee.

"I hope things go well. I brought you something that might be of interest." Jay handed the paper to Michael on which was written,

"The never once married wife will give you all her love and make you happy.

The widow without child will give you half her love.

And the widow with young child will give her love to the child and never be truly yours."

"Who wrote that?"

"Rumi"

"Who is he?"

"A wise man."

"That's not what I meant."

"But that's what's important. You can always look him up. He's a Persian poet."

"This relates to me? And her?"

"As I said, it might be of interest. In any event, have a safe and happy journey, my dear brother."

They stood and gave each other a hug.

PART 4

The Long Road

He spotted her as soon as he cleared customs. She waved and smiled and looked smaller than he had remembered. She was alone. They registered at the same hotel as last time. Simon took care of making sure it was the same room and also arranged for them to have Executive Privilege status.

They spent several hours reacquainting, engaging both their minds and bodies. Her English, such as it was, made a comeback, not up to the level of two years of German, but adequate enough to express feelings. Her sentences were now sprinkled with German words that she mistook for English. In bed, she was responsive without the initial shyness he had anticipated. She did not ask that he turn down the lights. Her tongue sought out his with eagerness that stoked a desire that was already wildly alive within him.

Michael had arranged for a lavish breakfast-in-bed with a bouquet of flowers as the centerpiece. She fed him before she would eat, as it had always been. She peeled the fruit, cut it into bit-size morsels, and smiled each time he accepted her offering.

"You're wearing the ring."

"I never take off. Lady, she want me leave it for $1000 come. I say no. Never take off. She angry. I say no. She hold back money. I say no. Then she give money."

In the afternoon, after they went to the bank where Michael cashed $1000 in traveler's checks and wired the money to the ABA number the lady had given her. He took Malee shopping at Robinson. She did not want him to spend much on clothing, but he insisted, so she bought a few items.

After wearing themselves out shopping Michael took Malee for another treat. They ate at a seafood restaurant where, when you ordered a steamed fish, a sous-sous chef would net your order from a fish tank extending half way down one wall. Twenty minutes later the fish arrived at your table perfectly cooked. Malee deboned it and fed Michael and then herself. Noodles and an assortment of Thai vegetables completed the dinner. "Is Regina in Ubon with Grandma?" Michael found himself asking.

"No. Mama and her with Joy in Bangkok."

Michael's engine was running full throttle thinking about later—holding her so close that her heat became his, her eyelashes brushing his cheeks when she blinked, their sexuality fusing so tight that they were joined the way they were meant to be.

Around ten o'clock, Malee turned on the TV.

"What's up?"

"Me watch. Good TV. Happy story."

She sat in the easy chair with her legs crisscrossed and feet tucked under.

"When is it over?"

"It go two hours."

"What? No. No TV for two hours." He clicked off the set. "Time for bed now."

Malee walked into the bedroom and used the bathroom first. Then she slid under the sheets of the familiar king-size bed. Michael was in the bathroom for less than five minutes. When he came out, Malee was resting on her side facing away from the bathroom, on the far edge of the bed. She was so far over that had she been an inch further she might have fallen off. And she was asleep. He stood over her watching her slow, deep breathing. Michael was so primed that he found it impossible to de-prime. He lay in bed, at the far side from Malee, and stewed. The longer he lay there, the more he simmered, making it all the harder to go to sleep. Jet lag should have put him out, but four hours later he was still awake.

In the morning, he was sullen. Malee greeted him while stretching, but he barely uttered a sound. Malee sat up.

"What wrong?"

He did not look at her. "Nothing."

"You no happy."

"*Right.*" He drew out the vowel of it as he turned his back to her.

"Tell me what wrong?"

"Nothing," His clipped intonation was audible in the delivery of two distinct syllables.

She moved over to him and put her hand on his shoulder. "I do something wrong?"

He did not answer.

"You no talk to me?"

"No."

She burst into the tears. "I can no be like this. You no like me, I go. I want be mit you, but you no want. You no talk. I no know what do?"

He turned toward her. "You could stay up two hours for the TV but not five minutes for me."

"I tired."

"But not for TV."

"I no understand."

"Look, if you do not want to be with me, then tell me. Then go with Joy. Go on, be with Joy if you want."

Tears were cascading down Malee's cheeks. "I want be mit Khun Michael. I tired. Go to sleep."

"Forget it. If you want to stay, I want you to stay. If you want to go, then you should go."

She put both arms around him. "I want stay. I want be mit you."

"I did not think so last night."

She put both arms over him, tears still flowing. She melted into him. He relented as his anger and hurt dissipated, "To make you cry is a sin. A person as good as you. I was just very angry last night."

"You angry now?"

"No. Now I am sad that I made you cry."

The next hour went from tentative to tender to forgiving to torrid.

The next day there were numerous calls between Joy and Malee. Even though he did not understand a word, something was amiss. That night they made love, but he could tell that a backstory was present. It may have been slight, and she kept it silent, but it was there, and it related to her calls with Joy. In the morning, he asked her about it. At first she was unusually cagey, but finally opened up, "Joy say Regina cry all time. Regina want me. She no happy mit Mama. Mama can no talk her. Mama no spreken what her say. Joy husband angry. Only two bedroom. He have office one. Joy no can sleep Regina cry. Husband no can work. Apartment too small. Too many. Mama no happy Bangkok. No happy apartment. She want go Ubon. I promise I stay mit you by alone. I no know what do. I go see Regina today. I come back not too later. You angry me I go?"

"No," Michael answered, understanding the situation, but inwardly feeling his growing disappointment.

After Malee left, Michael fell asleep—Jet lag finally exacted its toll. He did not know how long he slept, but when he was awakened by a knock on the door he found himself happily surprised to see Prang come into the room. Michael was not sure that she would be there. He had not seen her since his arrival at the hotel, but if he were honest, upon seeing Prang come through the door he realized that he had been too preoccupied with Malee to think much about her. For a few moments, neither spoke.

WILLIAM MCALLISTER III

"I make up the room now?"

How he hated to hear those words from her. "I...I didn't see you here earlier."

"No. I was visiting my parents. I just returned."

"Oh."

"I make up the room." She decided and started making up the bed. He looked away again. "It's all right. It's my job."

She left without a further exchange of words. Her graciousness and silence gnawed at him. He could not bear the thought of her making up the bed for another woman, feeling, maybe illogically that he had or it demeaned her somehow. He climbed in between the clean sheets. He was tired, but sleep was elusive. *It was funny*, after seeing Prang his thoughts were more of her than of Malee. The idea that kept filtering through his mind was of Prang representing that missing half that Jay had alluded to.

Later Malee called. She could not bear to see Regina cry, to see her so desperate for her mama. She would stay at Joy's tonight and come back in the morning. Michael spent the evening alone. Early the next morning, Malee called again. She could not sleep last night. She wanted to be with Michael, but could she bring Regina back with her? The question offered no choice.

A few minutes after Michael called Simon, a full-size crib arrived, all made up and with cushioning around its four sides. Prang showed up before Malee's return. She looked with puzzlement at the crib.

"You have a baby now?"

He shook his head.

"I don't understand."

"I will be having a baby stay here." He needed to give no further explanation.

"Same lady?"

He nodded.

"Very…" she said, searching for the right word.

He interjected, "Complicated."

"Yes," she said. "Complicated."

"It's good to see you. And bad."

Her eyes asked for elaboration.

"I am really happy to see you. But not in this job."

"But then you would not see me," she rejoined, maybe too quickly.

"Consistency has never been my strong suit." She was lost. He explained the meaning.

"Another idiom?"

"Yes. You know, when you speak to a foreigner who speaks good English, you forget that sometimes you're using idioms."

"I must finish my work. Not take too much time. You understand."

"Yes. No tents staying at the hotel?"

She grinned then finished her work and left.

Malee arrived with Regina. In the photos Malee had sent him, Regina had looked adorable. In person, less so. Given Malee's physical perfection, he was surprised. He blamed it on Gerhard.

Regina was the only youngster in the Executive Privilege lounge. She was reasonably well behaved, sometimes squirmy, but Malee had things under control. The hostesses were agog to have someone so young in their care and doted on her while Malee selected hors d'oeuvres.

There was something not right with Regina. Her tongue periodically protruded and then slid to the right. Every time this happened, Malee pushed Regina's tongue back into her mouth. Malee made it look casual, but Michael saw that she was worried too.

At night, Malee was in bed with Michael the whole night, part of the night or none of the night. Regina was calling the shots. Drake called to check in, and Michael filled him in.

"Well, I'm stuck in Singapore anyway. And I do a little work when I can."

"What about Dawn?"

"When I get to Bangkok, I'll be getting stuck there instead."

"Am I going to see you?"

"I already told you, *not* at nursery school. And from the way you describe it, they just made you the principal."

"You figured this was going to happen, didn't you?"

"Didn't take any figuring."

"I hate the way you're always right."

"I'm not *always* right." Drake stressed the always meaningfully, then added a quick jab, "Except with you."

"Well, the situation's not exactly what I wanted either."

"Please, don't tell me that the baby is sleeping between the two of you."

"No! Of course not!"

"But sometimes she and mom sleep together."

Michael did not respond as he visualized Drake shaking his head as if, with anyone other than Michael, this would be inconceivable.

"Rare."

"We're not talking about how you like your meat cooked," Drake shot back. "Well, I assume you're eating meat every night."

Another telltale pause.

"Christ! You are...fucking hopeless! If word gets around..." Drake paused looking for the words. "I don't know if we can ever be seen in public again. I have to think of myself too, you know."

"Look, it's not ideal. Okay?"

"Other than that, Mrs. Lincoln, how did you enjoy the play? Christ, even I can't believe you. So how many times have you popped her cork?" Drake asked out of exasperation.

There was another pause, but this time for another reason. Michael suddenly realized that he didn't even know the answer to the question. He confessed the same to Drake.

"Well, my only recommendation is to get yourself to an emergency room as fast as possible."

"When are we going to get together?"

"Well, if I can ever get the cork out of the bottle here, I'll try for next week. But I wouldn't do this for anyone else, you know. Coming to a fucking nursery school."

Michael was abashed in the face of Drake's palpable frustration, "I was looking forward to seeing you. Thinking, you know, that maybe you could put me, you know, back on the right track."

"Never been there myself. Anyway, if you ever figure out how to be *just* a couple or *if* you find someone else to couple up with, let me know. That'll motivate me. Besides, we have some businesses to check up on. At least I remember to think about *that* little thing that helps to keep us *both* afloat," Drake remarked wih a meaningful jab. Michael knew he deserved it. Drake kept going, "And I want to see Dawn, so I'll try to be down next week. With the condition you're in, sounds like I'll be taking care of our investments solo."

"I hope not," Michael answered as best he could.

"We'll see. I don't know when I'll be back. Because this one up here, she's a real ocotopussy. Like being in Heaven. Which is a good thing because once I cash it in, I'll never see the place."

One night when Regina was asleep in the sitting room Michael asked Malee about her life in Germany—Frankfurt to be exact.

"I no like Germany. No friend. Only one Thai lady friend. Her help me mit English. Germany people cold. No like American firang. Weather cold. I no like snow, no ice. I bad job. I clean foor and toilet big building. No good money. No good job. Husband mother take care Regina when I work. Her love Regina. Her know husband no much good. Him drive car. Give me bicycle. No good shopping when rain. No good when snow. I cold. Sometime must take Regina mit me. Then I cry when Regina cry. Husband no give money. I want visit Thailand, see Mama and Papa. Him say use my money. Husband work at bar. Him work late. Him drink sometime. All lady like him. Him bring lady home sometime. Tell me sleep mit Regina. I no like. Regina I live mit him mother now.

"Sometime him tell me come back. Me know why. Want sex. One time week. I no like do sex mit him. Me want divorce. Me want to live in Thailand. Don't know what to do."

"Who would keep Regina if divorce?" Michael asked.

"If him keep, I die. I no want live. Regina my life. I can no do no Regina. You understand?"

"Yes."

That night, they made love. Michael found himself counting *for the fourth time, the fifth time, maybe the sixth, no, not the sixth, in how many weeks?* He had not been kidding with Drake. He could not remember how many times. How could he forget something like that? Malee initiated the lovemaking. She clung tight. Afterwards, she did not let go and finally she fell asleep that way.

Regina woke up early that next morning, early enough that at the Executive Privilege lounge breakfast Michael was the only man not sporting a necktie. Malee left Regina sitting at the table while she went to fetch the foods for which Regina had expressed a preference. A hostess came to refill Michael's orange juice.

"Your daughter is so well behaved."

"Thank you," Michael said.

"Does she know both Thai and English?"

"No. Thai and German."

"Oh." The hostess said, reddening a little as she bowed, leaving as soon as she had finished filling his juice.

When Malee was at Joy's, she had called Dawn just to say hello. Over the course of their conversation the two girls caught up and Malee had ended up telling Dawn that Michael was back in Bangkok for business, anticipating Drake's return. Malee also mentioned that her mother was going back to Ubon the next day, and that she was planning on spending the last night with Regina and her mother at Joy's. Dawn chatted about Bangkok and about Drake coming to town to see her.

The next day Malee and Regina left for Joy's in the late afternoon. An hour or so later, Michael decided to go for a walk to clear his head. On his way out of the lobby, Simon beckoned him over. "I have a note for you, sir. I was told to give it to you."

Outwardly, Michael acted composed, but inside, it was turmoil revisited. He stood motionless.

"Sir? The note?" Simon had it in his hand.

"Oh. Yes, sorry."

"Sir, I was told to read it to you."

"What?"

"I know not why, sir."

Michael stood there motionless and silent.

"Should I...open it?" Simon paused awaiting an answer. "Sir?"

Michael finally nodded, "Read it to me."

"Yes, sir." Simon broke the seal with care and unfolded the note. "Ah, yes. Sir, it is in Thai."

"Thai?"

"Yes, sir."

"Simon, come over here." He gestured to a vacant area of the lobby where there was a table and two chairs. "I want this to be private."

"Of course, sir"

They sat.
"Should I begin, sir?"
"All right."
Simon put on his glasses, and read, translating as he went.

Dear Khun Michael,

Malee told me she would be visiting with her mother tonight. You should not eat alone tonight. So I will make you dinner. I hope you can join me. I am cooking for you. I have written out my address for you to give the taxi man. I hope see you at eight o'clock tonight

Dawn

"Sir, are you all right?"
"Yes, Simon," he said shaking his head with relief. "Yes, Simon, I am all right. Very all right. Thank you for reading it."

Michael had misgivings about going to Dawn's where it would be just the two of them. His apprehension increased when he recalled what Malee had told him about her instincts regarding Dawn during Michael's first visit to Bangkok. He no longer had the phone number for Dawn, so Michael could not call with an excuse. And simply not showing up would cause Dawn to lose face. He resigned himself.

At first he thought about bringing her flowers, but flowers would last a few days. The same was true of a box of chocolates. He decided upon wine. Despite Dawn's limited sophistication, she had a discriminating palate when it came to wine. He remembered the red wine she had served when the four of them had dined at her apartment, and he bought a bottle of the same vintage.

The taxi made many turns onto side streets. Michael knew he would need a taxi for his return, so he paid the 140 Baht fare along with a tip of 20 Baht and asked the driver to wait

there for him. Michael offered 200 Baht per hour for waiting, plus the fare when he was driven back. The driver readily
agreed.

Dawn had slimmed down a lot from when he had last
seen her and her dress broadcast rather than hid this fact. Her
smile was the same—omnipresent.

"Oh, Khun Michael...I..." she giggled. "I happy...you
come." Dawn spoke English slowly still hunting for each
word, often with the result that she could not find it.

"Thank you for inviting me." He offered her the bottle of
wine.

"Thank you. I like...bottle."

The apartment looked the same. "Many, many shoes,"
Dawn exploded into a giggle, "You fall...last day." She laughed.
"No fall...be..." she could not find the words so changed tac-
tics. "Many, many. Sorry."

Even though Dawn had a bottle of red wine already
opened this did not stop her from opening Michael's gift
as well. "Last...day...you drink...much, much wine." She
laughed again, thinking back on that night, and to hide her
nervousness.

As they sat down to dinner, Michael remembered that
cooking was not Dawn's strong suit and by the time they were
finishing the main course they were well into the second bottle. Michael was still on his first glass. Dawn glistened with a
light inebriation and smiled at Michael uninhibitedly.

"I happy you come."

"It was very nice of you to invite me."

"You same." There was a very long pause, "Look," she put
her hand over her mouth and tittered, "very handsome."

"You look very nice, too. And thank you for such a good
dinner."

"Dessert? I Bring." Unlike Drake, Dawn had a sweet
tooth and served a pie-sized crème caramel. It was the culi-
nary highlight of the meal.

254   WILLIAM MCALLISTER III

She stood up. "Come. I…tell you apartment."

She led him out to the balcony.

"Very quiet," he noted. Pretty city lights."

She smiled. "I like sit."

Michael began to sit in one of the chairs.

"No…tell you…other room." She led him to the bedroom. She sat on the bed. "I like…sleep. Sleep good." She patted the bed for him to sit down. He sat next to her. She put her hand on his thigh.

Within seconds, he had run through a series of options. He settled on one. "Stomach not so good." He rubbed his stomach to more fully communicate. Dawn was alarmed. "No," he added quickly. "No, not dinner. Dinner very, very good. Dinner delicious. You very good cook. Lunch. You understand? Lunch. Lunch, I ate fish. I think fish no good. Fish?"

"Doctor?"

"No, no. Not too bad. Little bad. You understand?"

"Little okay."

"I think I use bathroom."

"Good. You…wash…first."

Michael closed the bathroom door. "Oh, God," he said softly to himself and rubbed his hand over his face again and again. "Oh, God." He buried his face in both hands. *"Oh, shit. No. Oh, Christ. Oh, this is going to be horrible."* He got down on his knees and opened the toilet cover and leaned over. He started putting his finger down his throat but at the first reflex of gagging he pulled it out. *"Oh, shit. Come on, you fucking coward. Oh, wait, let me think. There's got to be some other way."* If there were, he could not think of it. Once more, he tried putting his finger down his throat, this time further, but the gagging reflex was so powerful he pulled his finger out. He looked at his finger. *"All right, you bastard. This time you're doing it. You hear me?"* Quickly he leaned over again, stuck his finger in way down, and it worked. It was horrible, more horrible than if it had been for bad food. Once it started it had a mind of its own. He could not stop. It was so violent and in such rapid sequence that he could barely breathe. He felt he was suffocating. He must have made a lot of noise because Dawn came rushing into the bathroom.

"Khun Michael!" she exclaimed and was at his side immediately. It had stopped. He turned and looked up at her, his eyes glazed. Michael was aware that vomit or bile or something was dripping out of his mouth, but felt too weak to do much about it. "Lunch," he managed to utter. As he began recovering he realized that his throat was raw. Something that came up burned so badly that it was hard to swallow.

Dawn was an angel. She paid no heed to how revolting he looked. She cared for him in every way she could. She helped him clean up, and didn't even bother when a drop of vomit stained her dress. She brought him water so he could rinse his mouth. She wiped off the top of his shirt with detergent water. He stood up. The wobble was gone.

"Khun Dawn, I think I need to go back to the hotel. I do not feel good."

"Yes, go back. Must…bed…sleep."

"I am so sorry. It was not dinner. Please. It was not dinner. It was lunch. Bad fish."

"I hope…not dinner."

"No! Lunch. I am so sorry. I make terrible mess. And you are so kind. I have taxi. I will go now."

They bid farewell. Michael went right to bed after returning to the hotel, feeling that he had escaped *mostly* unscathed.

The next morning, Michael woke before sunrise, long before Malee would be returning. He found himself to be uncharacteristically moody. In trying to force himself into a brighter disposition, he began reflecting on Malee. *Everything they had agreed upon before his trip had fallen apart. He did not blame her. How could he? She had tried her best to live up to her end of the bargain, but what he had asked of her was impossible.*

And that impossibility was so predictable if had he stopped and given it any thought. Drake, of course, had seen it all coming, "Just tell me the plan." Michael just lay there, resignation making him sigh.

Regina was Malee's life, and if she were crying out and pleading for her mother as any child that age would, Malee had no choice. She was doing the right thing. It would have been better to let her forever live in his dreams and in his poem. *She would have been one trip less to Thailand worse off for it, and he would have been a whole lot better off.* Or at least that is what he thought that he thought.

Malee and Regina arrived mid-morning.

"I don't understand why you won't take English lessons. It's the only way for you to get a good job. If you study hard, you can learn English very well in one year. I'll pay for the rent and the food. I'll pay for the lessons. I don't understand," he realized that he was exasperated with her in a way that he had never been before and that it was coming out in his tone. He backed off and went to hold her hand. She did not respond.

"I no can stay Thailand." She was on the verge of tears.

"What?"

"You no understand?"

"No, I don't." He was genuinely shocked.

Tears began pooling in her eyes. "Regina no have Thai passport."

"Wait, what? I mean she's Thai." Michael almost stuttered the words.

"Her born Germany. She German passport."

"Doesn't she have a Thai one too?"

"No, her no have. Only can stay Thailand three months."

"Ohhh, three months. Now I see," his thoughts trailed off. Well, can't you get her a Thai passport? I mean you're Thai..."

Malee interjected, "Husband must sign paper, too. Him

never sign. Know I want take Regina Thailand live. Him love Regina. I know. Him say never sign."

"Did you ask the Thai Embassy in Germany what you can do?"

"I no understand what tell me. I think no possible."

"It must be," he said reassuringly, "It has to be."

Michael explained the matter to Simon.

"I think Ministry of Interior here, maybe," Simon said.

"Would you call them and find out how to do this. What the procedures are."

"I will try, sir."

The following day Simon had discouraging news, "They tell me they can do nothing here. She must contact the Embassy in Germany. And I think there may be no way without the husband's signature."

Michael told Malee stone-faced, "You are right. You need your husband's signature. I never thought about this."

"You see, must live Germany. Me no like Germany. Me no like husband. Want divorce. But me no job. Divorce no job, must leave Germany. With no Regina. What to do?"

He immediately thought about the tragedy with her first daughter, and he could not imagine what a replay of this would do to her. He feared she would not survive.

That night Regina went to sleep early, sleeping soundly in the crib. Michael and Malee were in bed together. Malee cuddled up to him and made her intent clear. His response was perfunctory.

"You no want?"

"I don't know."

"Why you no know?"

"I'm not even sure."

She smiled. "You do good love."

Her smile ripped into him.

"If you no want, you tell me. That okay."

He got up and went to the bathroom. Not to wash up, but because he did not want her to feel around his eyes.

When he emerged, he dimmed the lights.

"You no wash?"

"No, not yet."

"You very sad."

"I'm okay."

"I wash first?"

"All right."

The next day, Malee asked if she could go to Joy's for dinner and spend the night at her house.

"I thought there was no room."

"Joy say Mama gone, now okay."

"Yes, you go if you want."

"I find you nice lady first?"

"No. No, that's okay."

Michael did not fancy spending the night alone in his suite. Around nine o'clock, he headed off to Pretty Paradise at Cowboy. He was more than pleasantly surprised to find Tum still working there, and still as a hostess. She was more gorgeous than ever. Tum's sister recognized him immediately, came over to him at once, and negotiations were handled with dispatch.

They were in bed together. Michael stopped. "Look, you don't need to act. I'm not into acting. Just be yourself. If I'm just another firang you're going to forget about ten minutes later that's okay. I prefer that to acting." He laughed. "Did you understand anything I said?"

"Yes, I think understood." To his astonishment, she retrieved a dictionary from her purse, tried to pronounce the words "act" and "prefer" and had him look them up in English so she could understand with the Thai translation. Then she said, "I prefer no this job, but maybe with you okay. Other firangs, no. We make love now. I no act. Promise." The atmosphere was relaxed. And then things became intense. Not as intense as when she had been pretending, but it was real, and that was better.

"How about you," he asked. "Good? I want the truth." She turned away in a blush rather than in avoidance. They showered together and then slid back into his bed.

"What are you going to do with your life?"

"No know what can do."

"Then maybe Ping-Pong in fifteen years?" He studied her reaction. Her chin quivered. "You would die first, right?" She nodded. He opened his wallet and paid her. "Here is the bar fine for tomorrow. You come back tomorrow ten o'clock in the morning." She looked puzzled. "Ten AM," he repeated emphasizing the AM. She took the money and nodded. "Very important you come back tomorrow ten o'clock AM. Very, very important." She nodded again. "What size do you wear and can you fit into one size smaller?" She gave him the size and nodded yes on the one-smaller size. He could have guessed it anyway, but wanted confirmation. "Then tomorrow—ten AM. No later. And bring your dictionary. Understood?"

"Yes."

He called Malee on her cell phone. He roused her. "Listen, you stay with Joy one more night, okay?"

"What?" was the groggy response.

He repeated himself.

"You find new girl?"

"No. I just need you to stay away tomorrow. Okay?"

"You find new girl."

"No," he said trying to reassure her. "Just stay away one more day."

"Okay. I no understand."

"Too difficult to explain."

"I no understand what you say English."

"Just go to sleep. Have fun with Joy tomorrow. Then I see you. Day after."

"Okay. But I think you have new girl."

"No!" he said with emphatic gentleness. "You understand when I say 'no'?"

"I understand. But I no understand, too."

Michael found Simon and told him exactly what he wanted. Simon obtained the phone numbers and addresses of the places Michael requested. He said he would have the other item in two hours.

"Chez Elite," Michael paused. "This is a serious establishment?"

"Yes sir."

You know what I mean by serious."

"I know what you mean, sir. It is the best one, sir."

First stop was for the rental of a red silk dress with yellow accents. Then on to Andre's. His shop was chic with the carriage trade. Andre insisted on speaking in French even though most of his clientele could not understand a word he said. Andre was in such high demand that he could get away with it, and those who could not speak French brought along their own interpreters so that everything would come out right. Michael arrived alone.

"The hair, like black diamonds," Michael spoke in French.

"D'accord, monsieur," Andre nodded, appreciative of those who spoke the language.

"Her face white. Whiter. But not too white. In any event not too much make-up," Michael said with his hands pressed lightly against his cheeks.

Andre nodded.

"And the hands," he said holding up his hands, "very soft, very beautiful."

"Mais oui, monsieur."

"And this will be all finished by what time?" Michael asked looking at his watch.

"By three o'clock, s'il vous plait."

"No. That does not work. By two o'clock at the latest."

"But I have many ladies to take care of."

"Two o'clock. How much would that cost me?"

"10,000 Baht, I believe."

"D'accord," Michael said. He handed Andre ten 1000 Baht notes. "All right then, a deux heures. Sans faut."

"Without fail, monsieur."

He handed Andre the red silk dress. "And make sure this goes well with what you do."

"Ah, mais oui, monsieur. This is very pretty. This dress."

Michael took Tum in a taxi to Chez Elite for a three o'clock appointment. On the way, Michael explained. "If you are asked what payment you want right now for signing, you say 100,000 Baht." Tum's eyes widened. "You understand?"

"I understand."

"All right. Let's practice." Michael acted like the agent, "And what amount of payment are you looking for to get things started, Tum?"

"100,000 Baht," she responded in English.

"No. Say it with authority. Gracious authority."

She looked up "gracious" and "authority".

He repeated the question.

"100,000 Baht."

"Better. One more time."

She did better.

"Of course, if you are not asked, do not say anything.

Now listen. Very carefully. After I talk with the man, he will suggest an amount. It will be less than 100,000. You look politely disappointed," she looked up "disappointed". "I will tell you that this is fair and that you should accept it. And then you accept. Okay?"

"I understand."

"Okay, we're going to practice this one, too." She did it very well. "Do it just as well in Thai."

In the first ten seconds, Michael knew that things would go well. He represented himself as Tum's agent—Simon had arranged for a dozen business cards, to make this role more believable.

"I think you'll agree with me," Michael said, "that a woman of this beauty is a rare find. Like a precious ruby."

They negotiated the details of a one-year contract with a guaranteed monthly minimum of 50,000 Baht, and the terms of her additional commission if things went as well as they both expected.

"Can I talk with you privately for a moment?" Michael signaled for Tum to remain seated.

The two men walked to the far corner of the room.

"Look, we both know that she's not your typical model. And she is only 20. We're all going to make a lot of money with her. She told me she wanted 100,000 Baht for, you know, the signing bonus. I told her not to be greedy. I said, 'You're going to do very well with this agency. They are the best, and they are honest. Don't ruin it now.' So I suggest you offer her 75,000. Give it to her in cash. You have my word. I will do whatever it takes to convince her that this is fair and appropriate, and that it is a sign of your appreciation of her qualities and potential."

Tum played her part perfectly. The contract was signed, with Michael making sure that the provisions for her extra commissions were very clear in the contract. Michael and Tum, with 75,000 Baht in hand, left. The modeling agency wanted her to begin in two days.

The day had left Tum bewildered and overwhelmed. "What you want from me?" she finally summoned up the courage to ask.

"Well, I would say, 'return the dress to Andre, then buy some nice clothes, tell Pi-sow that you're no longer working as a hostess, don't drink, don't ever smoke, don't ever take drugs.' Here is the card of a good agent. You will need an agent. Let him work for you." He handed her the name and phone number that Simon had given him. "And email me once in a while to let me how things are going." He handed her his business card with his email address. "Who knows, maybe I'll even see you in America some day."

"Why you do for me? All this?"

Michael paused. "Let's just say that the reason is unimportant."

"I stay with you tonight?"

Michael shook his head. "You don't need to."

"I stay with you tonight."

Michael did not press for favors in bed, but Tum overrode his absence of expectation. That was easy for her. In bed she finally let herself go with Michael. It was like the first time they got together, when she had been acting, but now there were no theatrics. None were needed.

Later, Michael was quiet, thoughtful. Tum worried that something was wrong. She looked at him and asked, "I make you sad?"

"No."

"But you are sad," she asked and answered at the same time.

"Yes."

"Why?"

He half smiled. "I'm okay."

"I think you are sad."

"I am happy for you."

In the morning they had breakfast together, and then Michael saw Tum off. She was speechless with gratitude and just smiled, kissed him on the cheek and got in the cab that he had hailed. Michael returned to his room, a little sad, but satisfied.

Malee returned with Regina in the early afternoon.

"You find girl you like?"

"Yes."

"You see she before?"

"Yes."

"You like she better me?"

"Is that what you would like? For me to like her better?"

The question stopped Malee. She put her hand on her forehead, "Here, yes...I no real woman for you." She put her hand over her heart, "Here, no."

"This is my answer." He placed his hand over her heart.

She smiled. "That good, then."

"I suppose," he said, with a catch in his voice.

"What you say?"

"Nothing." He felt sick to his stomach, like someone had taken a knife to his gut, but he had made his decision. He fetched some documents. "I'll be back soon."

"I be here for you."

Her words were another knife blow.

Michael went over the details with Simon. While Simon was on the phone, Michael sat in one of the lounge chairs—expressionless, emotionless.

"Is there anything I can get you, sir?" a hostess asked.

"No. No thanks. There's nothing."

Simon signaled with his hand. Michael stood up, resigned. All was in order. He returned the modified documents to Michael.

Regina was fussing about something. Malee looked up as he entered.

"Something not good," Malee said.

"I am going back to America tomorrow."

"You no stay month?"

"No."

"Why you no stay?"

"I need to go."

"I know," she said. "You go Samui. Find new girl."

"No. I'm going home."

"I think you joke me."

"No. No joking."

"Why you leave? Only half month?"

"I wanted something different between you and me." He gestured with his hand. "Not possible. I am not angry. I'm never angry with you. Not possible. All I do is love you. And miss you. Maybe you do not understand what I am saying."

"Me know. Me understand Kuhn Michael"

"So."

"I stay with you tonight."

"Only if you want to."

"Want to."

They did not eat at the Executive Privilege lounge. He ordered a room service dinner instead. After Regina was asleep in her crib, he turned off the lights. Malee and Michael lay in bed together, neither one speaking. She put her arm and leg over him. She felt around his face with her hand.

"You no cry."

"I cry inside this time."

"You come back Thailand?"

"I don't know."

"Me sad, too."

He thought about the pictures of her he had torn up. He turned on the nightlight, propped himself up with an elbow and looked down at her face.

"What?"

"I just want to look at you." He bit down on his lower lip. There was something he wanted to tell her. About what he had intended to do, or at least thought he intended to do, when he had come back that second time. But there was no point. It would only make her more miserable. And maybe he wouldn't have done it anyway—that is what Jay thought and what Drake wanted. Michael lay back down. There was another period of silence.

"You will always wear the ring?"

"Always."

"You promise?"

"Me promise."

"Some day, you give to Regina."

"Yes."

"You know the words wholesale and retail?" he asked. She did not, so he found them for her in her Thai-English dictionary. "Do you understand them now?"

"Me understand."

He lifted up her ring hand. "Just so you know, wholesale, this ring is very valuable. Very valuable. Be sure you give to Regina some day. Or have someone keep it for her."

"Why you say that?" He made no reply. "You worried Regina?"

"A little. Like you."

She looked at the ring. "Why you give me? So good ring."

"Because I wanted to."

"I no want leave you."

"You and Regina, you can leave in the morning. I leave after you."

"I no know what say."

"Let's say nothing. Let's just be together."

It was easy for her to pack. She had so little, even with Regina. He found three more packs of dental floss in his suitcase that he had forgotten were there. "Here, you take all of these."

He accompanied her out to the street where he handed her an envelope. "Here is the Bhat I have left." It was 30,000

Baht plus a few small bills. "Enough for travel to Ubon and to live in Bangkok until you go back to Germany."

He hailed a cab. She burst into tears. The taxi stopped, blocking the curbside lane of traffic. The honking was deafening. "And I have given you another gift." The cabbie in the vehicle behind Malee's stuck his arm outside his window and gave Michael the finger with vehement shaking. Michael didn't care, continuing, "I have already deposited it into your bank account. Go see your bank account. You will see." The honking was louder than ever as the lane was backing up with ten or more cars. Another finger from the next car.

"Khun Michael…"

He kissed her cheek to silence her. "Quick, you must get in."

He helped them in.

"Khun Michael…"

"Khun Malee. Khun Malee, goodbye." Michael closed the door and looked away. The taxi pulled out and disappeared in the traffic of Bangkok.

When Malee checked her bank account, she would find that Michael had deposited two million Baht. He smiled as he imagined her expression. He hoped she would not cry. But knew she probably would.

Michael stood on the sidewalk outside of the hotel staring off into the bustle of Bangkok. He focused on nothing while thinking on everything. He stood there awhile before he returned to his room to finish packing.

When he was done, he called Drake in Singapore. "Look, you handle it alone when you get here. I can't stay. I'm hanging on by very little. You know what I mean."

"I figured as much would happen," Drake responded sympathetically. "So the business suffers a little. Better than you a lot. We'll talk again soon."

"Yeah, definitely."

There were just two more things Michael wanted to do, and late that morning he had his chance to complete one of them when a knock came at the door. Prang entered.

"Oh!" She saw his luggage was ready by the door.

"Yes, I'm leaving today. For America."

"And your friend? And baby?"

"Going back to Germany."

"Oh."

"Khun Prang." She looked at him quizzically—this was the first time he had used "Kuhn" when addressing her. "I have something for you, but you must promise me something first. You must promise that you will guard what I give you very carefully and that you will not open it until you finish work today."

She looked at him, still perplexed.

"You promise?"

"I promise."

He handed her a thick, tan, large envelope. "I am going to go for a walk now. So this is goodbye."

She nodded.

She was gone when he returned.

The envelope contained 500,000 Baht in crisp one thousand Baht denomination bills. And a note that simply read,

I hope your suk is a success. No need to thank me, I am the one who thanks you, but sometime let me know how the suk is doing. Michael.

The note had his personal email address.

His flight was at midnight, but the hotel had allowed him to remain in his room until he left for the airport. Michael knew that Simon's shift ended at five o'clock so shortly before the evening shift came on, Michael took the elevator down to the lobby and walked over to the concierge desk.

"Simon, you are the best."

"We are here to help, sir."

Discretely, Michael handed him an envelope. It contained 20,000 Baht.

Just before Michael left for the airport, an email arrived from Helen. It struck him as strange that it felt warmly familiar, seeing her name in his in-box like he was just getting ready to head home from some long trip, even if that disorienting yet calming sensation was fleeting. He let the mouse hover over the blank subject line, but finally opened it.

> *Dear Michael,*
>
> *I stayed awake all last night because I finally realized that this whole journey that I've been on has lead me nowhere. This awareness has hit me like a thunderbolt and I knew that I had to write to you today. You have moved on with your life. A wiser woman has probably found you and given you what you need and deserve. It was 'for better or for worse', you know. I have given you the worse but there was better once. Maybe now I can give you the better again. I can't think of anything I would want more.*
>
> *Please write.*
>
> *Love, Helen*

The flight was delayed five hours. The seat in the waiting area was hard and made him fidgety and restless, which added to his growing anxiety and deepening emptiness. Thoughts began to trickle in, one by one, then a steady stream, then it was a torrent. He got up, paced the floor, and then discovered himself sitting motionless at the far end of the terminal. He bolted up to retrieve the briefcase he had just left behind, fetched it, he then took another seat.

He would never return to Thailand. He knew that. That

would only reawaken the dreams and the demons. He could never have envisioned the joy Malee had brought him and the suffering she had caused him. How could he have ever imagined that? And to have never met Malee? How could he ever imagine wishing he hadn't? If he had lived her dream, there would have been no suffering. Only impossibility.

An elderly Thai woman was gazing at him from her seat opposite, her face wrinkled like soft, worn leather. She was inscrutable. They stared at each other and with no discernible change in her expression sadness crept into her eyes. Michael was sure that, somehow, she knew. She understood that he had lost someone, someone he never truly had.

His eyes dropped. Maybe he could find some place in himself where, when he thought about her, he could also, at the same time, not think about her. Could such a space really exist? But even if it did, he still knew that sometimes it would fail him, that she would be there, and he would relive it all with the same intensity. Perhaps the best he could wish for was that, one day when that happened, she would, at last, finally, come back to him only as a dispassionate memory of a passionate time. There was some comfort in that hope.

He would tell Drake he wasn't coming back. Drake would not understand, or if he did, he wouldn't let on. Either way, it was fine. Everything would be fine. It would just take some time.

As the plane lifted off, sunrise was hinting its arrival in faint pink. For a moment Michael studied the changing colors, then pulled down the window shade and was asleep.